To Terry and Joy. Thank you for your encouragement and support on this long and winding writing road.

Chapter One

Katie Chambers was already late, which she absolutely loathed. It was 7:04 PM, according to her Outback's dashboard.

The last remnants of the September sun peeked through the partly cloudy sky, with minutes to spare before it set. Katie considered it a personal failure to let her fellow members of the South Island Jigsaw Crew down. But as the vice president of product design and development of the Cedar Bay Puzzle Company, or CBP as it was known to the locals, it was her job to make sure every puzzle created by her team produced the most pleasure as was humanly possible. That's why she'd spent the last few hours perfecting a tricky tab that wouldn't lock into place the way their puzzles were renowned for before introducing the puzzle to the crew.

She zipped up her fleece, grabbed her purse and two square boxes from the passenger seat, and opened the car door. Outside, she closed her eyes and drew in a deep breath. Savored the saltwater air. She never imagined how much she'd miss that when she'd first left home. She'd adored going to school in Fort Collins, Colorado, and she'd loved, loved, loved working as the head of product design for a small, independent book publisher in Denver. But she never got used to Denver's traffic and the crowds. Nor did she stop feeling like an outsider, no matter how many other transplants she knew. Now, she wouldn't miss an opportunity to remind herself how blessed she was to be back home, regardless of the reason for her return.

Wearing a satisfied grin, she headed toward the library, though she made it no more than two steps before nearly slipping in a puddle, which almost sent her purse and boxes flying.

Leaning into a gust of wind, she hugged the freshly manufactured jigsaw puzzle prototypes to her chest and carefully crossed the Cedar Bay Public Library rear parking lot. She finally found sanctuary beneath the awning outside the building's basement entrance. Once inside, she was greeted by two puzzlers, neither of whom seemed angry, but were certainly annoyed.

"What's wrong?" she said, unzipping her fleece.

Ken Gorman, a sixtyish Santa Claus of a man, who used to be an attorney but now spent his days volunteering at the Presbyterian Assisted Living Center, reached for the conference room doorknob and twisted. He mournfully shook his head.

"Locked," said Hannah Jackson, the reigning two-time Whidbey Island Jigsaw Puzzle Teen Champion and a dead ringer for the musician Alicia Keys.

"Where's everybody else?"

Hannah gestured upstairs. "Checking out the library's puzzle aisle."

Despite sharing her late mother's passion for puzzles, Katie had been reluctant to restart her mother's old crew, especially so soon after the accident. But Dad had insisted. He thought they missed the group, and the majority of them were library patrons anyway. So naturally, she caved. For Mom. And Dad.

She pulled her phone from her purse and called him.

"You've reached the voice mail of Jim Chambers, head librarian for the Cedar Bay Public Library . . ."

She hung up and texted him.

Dad, the room's locked. Where are you?

"It's not like him to go AWOL like this," Ken said.

"Do you think he's okay?" Hannah said. "I hope they don't find him dead floating in the bay and—"

Katie threw the girl a sharp glare.

"Sorry!" Hannah patted the stack of books in front of her. "I just checked out a few Stephen King novels . . ." She stopped. Dropped her chin. "I'll shut up now."

Katie ignored the comment. "Could you work on gathering the others so we can finish at a reasonable hour? I'll work on getting the door unlocked."

Katie hadn't considered that there might be a real problem with Dad until Hannah planted that unnerving nugget into her head. A tinge of panic grew inside her. She phoned Dad again, only to go to voicemail again.

Upstairs, she found the main desk unoccupied. That was strange. She wormed her way through stacks of books ready to be reshelved and found her way to the main office door. Which was shut.

She knocked.

"Dad? Are you in there?"

No reply.

Another knock.

Her phone vibrated in her purse.

It was Dad.

"Where the heck are you?" she asked.

"Where are you?" her father said. "Everybody's waiting."

She jammed her thumb against the big red button. Always a comedian.

She marched downstairs again. Light leaked out of the Puget Sound Conference Room. She was about to open the door, ready to scold Dad for making the group even later than she had when suddenly it opened . . .

"Surprise!" the room shouted.

She stopped.

Ten people stood around the conference room table. A cake shaped like a double-wing jigsaw puzzle piece sat in the middle, with one large candle sticking out of it.

Without warning, Dad tightly wrapped his arms around her. "Happy anniversary, honey."

"Anniversary?" she said with what little breath she could muster.

Ken Gorman said, "It's been six months since the South Island Jigsaw Crew has been back in business, give or take a few days."

"And it's all thanks to you," Hannah said.

The room erupted in applause.

When her dad let go, Katie set her notebook and pages at the end of the conference room table. "I'm not the one you should be thanking." She cast an admiring eye on Dad. "He's the one who made this all happen."

The group applauded again.

If she didn't know better, she'd swear he blushed. Then again, he wasn't the same man he was when Mom was alive. Back then, he was tough. Strong and assured. Over the past six months, though, his strength had waned since Mom's passing, until Katie came back to become the tough one in their complicated relationship.

While the rest ate cake and drank punch, Katie went to the whiteboard and made a note about the two puzzles they'd be testing for the company.

"What are these about?" Dad asked.

"Same as last week. The Winter Paradise series. The one on the left is a 500-piece artistic watercolor rendition of a gorgeous Crystal Mountain ski lodge near Mount Rainier. The one on the right is a 1,000-piece postmodern pastel snowman. Oh, I see. The three pieces of coal and the carrot in the puddle. Very clever." She eyed Elena Larsson to her right. "I think these are much more interesting than last week's."

Dad smiled. "Sounds fun. You folks have a good time."

She kissed him on the cheek. "We will."

He excused himself from the room.

"Later, Mr. C," Hannah said while the rest took their seats.

Katie distributed a puzzle box to each group and sat down at the end of the table. "Ken, can you monitor the timer?"

Mildred Wilson, who was pushing ninety, muttered, "Oh, brother," a little louder than she probably intended, which produced several snickers.

Ken, on the other hand, grinned, proud as a peacock. He took out his phone, opened the timer app and set the phone on the table. "Let's see if we can set a record for the group."

"We wouldn't expect anything less," Katie said.

Mildred rolled her eyes. More snickers.

Ken scowled before scanning the box.

Katie turned to Elena, an up-and-coming artist at Cedar Bay Puzzles who reminded her of Selena Gomez, right down to her gorgeous singing voice. Although she already knew the answer, for the benefit of the others she asked, "Are either of these yours?"

Elena grinned and slowly nodded. "The 1,000-piece is mine. I guess I've got a thing for snowmen. Ian Trembley did the ski lodge, which is why it's so gorgeous. The man is truly the master of the craft."

"Even though it's above this petty officer's pay grade," Tony Foligno, the proud owner of the only Subaru dealership on Whidbey Island, employed his usual naval jargon, "I think the snowman is better. But that's just me."

Elena nodded. "That's very kind of you, Tony. Total nonsense. But kind."

"Let's stop the chit-chat and get going." Ken pressed a pudgy finger against his phone. "Okay everyone, we start . . . now."

"Great," Katie said. She and Elena quickly opened the plastic bag inside and the two of them began to separate the interior pieces from the frame. It was always best to establish the border before trying to put together anything else.

* * *

"Thank you, everyone," Katie said, gathering her notes.

As puzzle builds went, this one had progressed extremely well. In addition to the artistry, everyone seemed to like the piece design, even though they were challenging. Elena said she even got confused in spots, but that was a result of a couple of the colors in the background looking exactly the same. Ken had offered his favorite critique: "Several of the pieces appear as if they could be perfect in more than one spot, making it difficult the closer the puzzle got to completion." Then again, he would say that for a puzzle with only one hundred pieces. Ken was a perfectionist when it came to the diversity of the piece design, but no matter how many permutations a puzzler may take to solve a puzzle, sometimes you just can't avoid having similar pieces around at the end.

Katie's primary takeaway was that both new puzzles passed the proof-of-concept test, especially the 1,000-piece. They were challenging enough, but not too much for the casual puzzlers. The pieces snapped into place as perfectly as she'd hoped. And the images, oh wow, were they beautiful. She'd recommend that both be tooled up for mass production. The rest agreed.

"Who's up for Cynthia's?" Hannah asked. Cynthia's was the premier diner in town, and though it appeared to be a greasy diner for the tourists, it surprisingly delivered great food. It had quickly become the tradition to eat there after a meeting.

Elena and a few others murmured about having to get up early for work the next day. That left Katie, Tony, Hannah, Mildred, and Ken.

But something was off. Elena always went to Cynthia's.

"You're not going, Elena?"

Elena gave her an uneasy look. "No. Why?"

"No particular reason. We'll just miss you, that's all."

Elena shook her head as she gathered her things. "I've got some . . . things to do. Maybe next time."

"Everything okay?" Katie asked.

Elena nodded but was hardly convincing.

"I hope whatever it is works out for you," she said, concerned and disappointed. To Tony, Hannah, Mildred, and Ken, she said, "See you all there," as she headed for her car.

She got in and started the vehicle with the puzzle prototypes still on her mind. They were clearly the best of the bunch since she restarted the group.

"Thank God," she said. With Tony driving Mildred, the group's four cars pulled out of the library's back parking lot like a small caravan taking the mini-tour of everything Katie thought you needed to see in Cedar Bay.

They headed west on Second Street for a block, past Island Coffee and Bakery. On sunny days, when Katie passed with the windows down, the smell of one of Connie Constantine's island-famous crumb cakes made it almost impossible to keep driving without stopping in.

They took a quick left onto Vienna, past Whidbey Books, a place where Katie spent far too much time and money. They took a quick left on Main Street, passing the Palace Theater and Movie House and JJ's Sandwich Shop, the latter being Katie's sole source of weekday sustenance.

Finally, the four cars pulled into Cynthia's parking lot, which was nearly full, much to Katie's surprise. The restaurant was one of the many downtown establishments to be blessed by a gap in the tree line behind it, offering a clear view of the water. She took the farthest spot away to give the others a shorter walk against the quick bursts of gusty wind and the wet ground. Ever the gentleman, Tony held the door open for her when she reached the building. But when they were all inside, their progress came to a halt.

Cynthia's was packed. The tables along the windows—Katie's favorite spot—were stuffed with teenagers in hoodies and athletic gear. The rest of the restaurant teemed with locals, and a few tourists craning their necks to enjoy the scenery, which even with the rain and mist was breathtaking given the expanse of the sound. In the distance, a ferry cut a path to Kingston to the west. Katie wished she could magically teleport half the people in the restaurant directly onto it.

She asked the others, "How can it be so busy at this hour?"

"Yeah," Hannah said, pointing. "And who let those people sit in our seats?"

Violet, their usual waitress, a tall, sturdy woman about Dad's age, strode over the spotless gray-tiled floor from the pie case, which today featured marionberry and strawberry rhubarb. While the others on the waitstaff employed electronic tablets to capture their orders, Violet was old school. Pencil tucked behind her ear and her paper notepad both at the ready. She instantly reached out to give Katie a hug. "I'm so glad you're back in Cedar Bay."

Katie chuckled. "It's been six months, Violet."

The waitress tightened her grip. "At my age, it seems like it's only been a day. I bet it seems like that to your father, too."

"It's like a conspiracy with you two."

"You have no idea how much happier he is with you here," Violet said, pulling away. To the others, she said, "Sorry, folks. Your booth should be ready in about five minutes. Those people are just finishing up."

"Who the heck are they?" Mildred demanded in a tone only someone her age could get away with.

Violet pushed a strand of hair away from her face. "Youth football game. This is the team from Oak Harbor or Coupeville. I can't remember which." She lowered her voice. "We can't get rid of them fast enough. They must be the cheapest tippers I've ever seen."

Tony leaned in. "If you boot 'em out of here in the next five minutes, we'll cover all their tips."

Violet winked. "You're on."

Mildred sank down on her walker bench, while Tony escaped outside to smoke a cigarette. The rest of the puzzle crew stood at the entrance.

Katie eyed their booth, which was actually several tables lined up in front of a long bench that ran against the restaurant's back wall. Then she brought her hand to her cheek like she always did before solving a puzzle.

She imagined who would sit where, trying to figure out who would fit in which spot. Usually, the puzzle crew was larger and they took up most of the tables. Tonight, they'd only need the big one in the middle. So she imagined Tony and Ken against the far wall. Mildred on the right end of the table, on her walker, allowing Tony to stretch out his long legs on the other side. Katie and Hannah facing the men, with Hannah to Katie's left, since Hannah was left-handed. Done. Just another puzzle that Katie couldn't resist solving. It was a passion she'd gained from her mother as a kid that had only accelerated with Mom's passing.

"So," she said, after she was finished. "Thanks for tonight. My boss, Neal, will be relieved to hear we have a few winners for this year's winter series."

Ken smugly sniffed the air. "I'm relieved he's finally listening to my suggestions. Last week's puzzles were garbage."

"*Our* suggestions," Hannah corrected. "And let's not be so harsh. Last week's weren't as good as tonight's, but they were hardly garbage."

"They were hardly good," Ken said. "I think Ian is starting to slip."

"It doesn't matter," Katie said, not wanting to go there. "All Neal cares about is producing beautiful puzzles that are fun to assemble, and I think both from tonight check those boxes. It's even more exciting that Elena designed one of them."

"If you say so," Ken said.

Katie scratched her chin. "Still. Didn't you think something was off with Elena?"

"What do you mean?" Hannah asked.

She shrugged. "I don't know. I was really hoping she'd come. But something seemed to be bothering her."

Hannah shook her head. "I didn't notice anything."

"Me neither," Ken said. "The only thing I'm noticing is my empty stomach." He threw a glance over at their table. "Good. They're standing up."

The three stepped aside as four adults and five young boys all pushed past.

"Excuse me!" Mildred hollered at one of the boys who got too close. He ignored her but the mother quickly apologized on his behalf. Mildred grumbled her acceptance.

"You guys ready?" Violet asked, snatching her pencil from behind her ear and flipping open her notepad.

"Starved," Tony said, coming back in.

"Me, too," Mildred echoed, while Tony helped her up.

Katie, on the other hand, wasn't sure how she was going to eat anything. She rested her chin on her fist and gazed out at the ferry, wondering why Elena really wasn't there.

Chapter Two

The next morning, Katie drove into work down a two-lane road, through a thickly wooded area made up of a mix of pine trees and tall cedars, with some of the cedars beginning to flag. Her house was about a mile west of downtown but only a block north of the water. Some of the trees along her route were so close to the road that it was like she was driving through a forest. She often drove these roads below the speed limit to drink it all in, having missed the tranquil terrain for so long.

The woodlands thinned as she neared downtown but when she turned left onto Kinder, the thick trees returned three blocks away, surrounding the Cedar Bay Puzzle Company like a soft, warm blanket with more than a few yellow, brown, and red leaves floating helplessly to the ground.

She turned into the gravel parking lot, the rocks crunching beneath her wheels. The structure that greeted her was itself a puzzle. Three separate differently shaped buildings snapped together with jigsaw-like precision, with interlocking doorways and hallways to hold everything in place.

The front, the CBP store in which they sold puzzles, knickknacks, and fresh-brewed coffee, was a converted old schoolhouse, like something you'd see in *Little House on the Prairie*, with white wood siding and even a bell on top that only rang on New Year's. A barely used heavy wooden door connected the store to the office building, a wide, one-story wooden rectangular structure. The far back, where the magic really happened, was a 25,000-square foot metal building that housed the printing machines, the cutting machines, and the robots that transformed the designers' visions into the thoroughly loved games they distributed around the world.

Katie steered around the store to the employee parking alongside the office building.

She said hello to the petite CBP receptionist, Nancy Xiao, who let her know that Neal McMurray was looking for her.

"How'd last night go?" he said, putting his thick-rimmed glasses on.

Neal's office was a puzzle museum, eschewing pictures for puzzles hanging on the walls, ranging from new to old, big to small, with CBP's award-winning puzzles positioned prominently. And when his blinds were open, as they were now, the picturesque tree line that surrounded the building acted as a backdrop to the beautiful display. Just like his dad had designed it when he ran CBP.

Katie took a seat in front of Neal's handcrafted wooden desk and pasted a wide grin on her face. "Last night went great. It went better than I could've possibly imagined. Even Ken begrudgingly agreed that we've got two hits on our hands. Everybody loved them both."

"Really?" He paused. "Elena's, too?"

"Elena's especially."

"Good to hear. I thought so as well, but wanted to be sure. At the rate she's going, she could replace Ian as our top artist in a few years."

"How well will that go over with Ian?"

"How well does anything go over with the most temperamental artist on the planet?"

"Touché."

"How about your design for them both? The group was good with the thickness? The pieces interlocked okay? Didn't disassemble easily?"

She showed her palms. "Relax. It's all good. They loved them both."

He leaned back in his chair, locking his fingers behind his head. "You just keep getting better and better at leading the product design team. Maybe even better than your mom."

"Oh, come on."

"No, really. I loved your mom, but she was pretty conservative. Your team uses bolder color line cuts than we used to. You make the process of putting the puzzles together fun and interesting, without being impossible. I'm not the only one who's noticing."

"I appreciate it. My team will keep doing their best in designing them, and you keep doing your best in selling them." She checked her watch. "Before I leave, there's something I want to run past you."

He straightened. "Am I going to like this?"

"Depends. There's one person who definitely won't."

He sighed. "Our nomination for National Designer of the Year."

"Come on. You can't be surprised. Elena's earned it and to be frank, Ian's designs just haven't been as good this year."

He leaned back and folded his hands on his chest. "We've been nominating Ian for the last twenty-five years."

"And he's never won once. Elena's puzzles are a breath of fresh air. She's employing styles the industry has never seen. You know it and I know it. I think she can win."

Neal tossed her a worried frown. "And I think Ian will go ballistic. He considers the nomination his birthright. He may never win the award, but he's treated like a celebrity at the annual convention. This will be another big blow to his ego. You know he already doesn't love having you as a boss."

"He hasn't been shy about that."

"This could push him over the edge."

She shrugged. "What edge? It's not like he's going to quit."

Neal leaned forward. "At Ian's age, they call it retirement, and given the money he's made here coupled with the equity my father gave him when times were tough, he can retire very easily."

"You think he's going to retire?"

Neal sighed. "I think he's going to be very unhappy when I tell him. I expect a lot of yelling and more than a few threats."

She sat up. "Threats?"

He patted the air. "Empty threats. Like quitting or suing or kicking in the printing press. Nothing for you to worry about."

Katie stood, relieved that Neal was going along with her recommendation.

"Thank you, Neal. You won't regret it."

"I might, but that's okay."

She threw him a salute as she headed for the exit.

She slung her purse over her shoulder and zipped her North Face rain jacket over her fleece, then backed into the front door to open it. Outside, the air was crisp and clean. It wasn't raining, which could always change on a dime. The sun shone brightly through the broken clouds, reflecting off Puget Sound behind the businesses along Main Street. Another aspect of Cedar Bay she refused to take for granted: the beauty of the water and what it meant to this community.

It was ten minutes to twelve, the exact time she always left the office for lunch for her daily trek, a task that included a quick stop at JJ's Sandwich Shack to retrieve her two standing orders: a roast beef sandwich on rye with a side of potato salad for Dad and turkey on wheat with a cup of broccoli cheese soup for her. And two Diet Cokes. After which, she'd make the two-block trek to the library to spend what time remained of her lunch hour with Dad.

The walk to JJ's was short—three whole blocks away along Main Street's mist-slicked sidewalks. Though others from the office would drive, she always walked. Warm or cold. Rain or shine. Today, her journey was into a soft breeze. She hugged herself as the salty wind blew back her hair and looked up, her gaze landing on the Cedar Bay Marina, which rested majestically at the bottom of Main Street, and then upon the bay itself, its pure blue water glistening. A helmeted bicyclist headed toward her from the opposite direction, up the hill, waving enthusiastically.

"Hey, Katie!" he said.

"Hey, Tom! Great day for a ride!"

"Always a great day for a ride," Tom said, dipping his head as he passed. "Enjoy your lunch!"

She would, she thought.

Marching toward the Palace, she glanced up at the marquee. The local production of *Mamma Mia* was set to begin in two weeks. She and Dad had front-row tickets to the first Friday night show—one of his many perks as the town's librarian.

Katie then opened the door to JJ's.

"Good morning, pretty lady," JJ, the owner and sandwich wizard, said when she walked in.

"You're such a flirt, JJ."

"If I was thirty years younger . . ."

"And if you weren't married to the most patient woman in the world."

He lowered his voice to a conspiratorial whisper. "Don't let her hear you say that. It'll go straight to her head."

"I tell her that every time I see her, and she always wholeheartedly agrees."

He mockingly grabbed his chest. "You wound me, Miss Chambers."

JJ Van Pelt, a sturdy man with his trademark flannel shirt and jeans, bulging forearms, and thinning salt-and-pepper hair, had set her order next to the register, on time, like always. He and his wife, Judy, had opened the shop ten years ago, after he'd retired early from Boeing. The shop was only open from eleven to three on weekdays, but every resident, as well any tourist with a decent guide, found their way here during that window. Katie handed JJ a twenty. He tried to give her change, but she pointed to the tip jar. He tried to slip the change into her bag. She pulled the bag away before he could.

Same dance, as always.

Before she could turn, a familiar voice called out, "Good afternoon, JJ."

She froze.

"Good afternoon, Mr. Crozier," JJ said, raising his thick paw to wave.

Mr. Crozier, huh? She shut her eyes. Gulped hard.

She hadn't heard his voice since the week before she left Cedar Bay for college. A voice whose last words to her were, "It's not you. It's me."

It was him, all right. When she'd headed to school in Fort Collins on a partial scholarship, he was heading to school in Boston on a full scholarship, and he didn't have the courage to even *consider* a long-distance relationship. It'd been a wound that cut so deep at the time, she'd feared it could never heal.

But it did heal. It took years. Nearly seven years, to be exact. Four college boyfriends and a bachelor's in graphic design from Colorado State University later, she finally proclaimed that she was over him. She'd moved on.

Now the mere sound of his voice was all it took for that wound to reappear.

She turned and forced a smile.

"Wow," Connor said. "It's you."

She nodded.

JJ let out a snort. "I'll be in the back if you need me."

Katie and Connor stared at each other as the deli's lunch rush filed in. She wanted to say something pithy and important. Flustered, she reached out her hand as if reconnecting with an old work colleague. "Hi," was all she said.

He tossed her a knowing grin. "You're going to have to do a lot better than that, Kate."

* * *

Katie waited outside near a recently occupied picnic table adorned with freshly cut daisies—Mrs. JJ's special touch—

while Connor retrieved his order. The clear blue sky would've been something to enjoy if she hadn't been completely distracted by Connor's unexpected presence.

She'd known it was only a matter of time. That eventually she'd have to face him. But it hadn't happened for six months, and she'd foolishly convinced herself that she could avoid him forever. In a small town. Where people all shopped at the same places. Where everyone knew everyone's business.

What the heck was she thinking?

Connor strolled out of JJ's as confident as ever.

"Why didn't you wait inside where it's warm?" he asked, each arm hugging a tall paper sack.

"You feeding an army?"

"If you consider the guys I work with over at the fire station an army? Then yes." He nodded at her paper sack. "Taking that to your father?"

"How did you know that?"

He scoffed, "It's Cedar Bay, Kate."

She wanted to ask him who was keeping tabs on her, but he was right. It was Cedar Bay. It wouldn't be hard to guess. It was probably the same people who constantly reminded her that he was still single but who were unable to uncover why he'd returned to Cedar Bay after graduating near the top of his class in Boston.

She threw a glance in the library's direction. "Look, Connor, I'm late."

"Me, too," he said softly, his gaze piercing through her. He had more to say and so did she. But this wasn't the time, and they both knew it. "Tell your dad I said 'Hi.'"

"I will."

She turned and walked away, the bitter wind slapping her in the face as she did.

* * *

Five minutes later, she approached the library and its main doors parted automatically. Inside, she wiped her feet. She instantly spotted Amy Richardson, Cedar Bay's children's librarian, arbitrating a conversation between Dewey and a chubby-cheeked boy no older than four. Dewey, a red, furry puppet sporting a Seahawks T-shirt, was explaining how big boys liked to read, but Katie wasn't sure the kid was buying it. Outside of her library duties, Amy also ran the local acting group that performed at the Palace Theater and Movie House. As a result, she approached her job with the children like she approached the stage. Everything was a performance.

Katie threw Amy a wink as she walked by, which Amy returned without breaking character.

"Soup's on," she said as she walked into her dad's office. She set his sandwich on his desk.

"You're late," he said, taking a seat behind his desk. He unwrapped his sandwich. "Connor Crozier, huh?" he said with smirk.

"It's not funny, Dad." Word traveled fast.

He raised his hands in surrender. "I'm not laughing," he said, which was a lie. "Does he still call you Kate?"

She leaned back, crossing one leg over the other. "I'm not having this conversation."

He raised his eyebrows and shrugged. "We both knew you were going to run into him someday. Maybe something good will come of it."

"Come on, I—"

She was about to say more when Booker, the library's official cat, strolled in like he owned the place. The petite Russian Blue leaped up onto the desk, glanced at Dad, and meowed.

"I'm just saying." Dad tore a chunk of roast beef from his sandwich and held it out. Booker eagerly snatched it and chowed away. "It's not like Cedar Bay is bursting with a bevy of eligible bachelors. And you're not getting any younger."

"Dad! Can we change the subject, please?"

"If that's what you want," he said, failing to wipe the smirk off his face. "Enough about Connor Crozier, for now. How'd last night's puzzler group go?"

Finally, a conversation she wanted to have. She reached out and scratched Booker behind the ears. "It went great."

"How great?"

"The puzzles passed with flying colors, but . . ." She sipped her drink.

"But?"

"Something was off about Elena."

"Off how?"

"Hard to say," she said, setting the drink down. "She didn't come to Cynthia's afterward."

"That's hardly cause for alarm."

"I know. I just . . ."

"Well," Dad said with his mouth full. "She's got a lot going on."

She froze. "What do you mean?"

"Um . . ." Dad took another bite of his sandwich and shrugged.

"Come on, Dad. Out with it."

He pointed to his full mouth.

She folded her arms. "I'll wait."

He swallowed. "You know how it is with you kids." He sipped his soda. "You're all just go, go, go."

"You said *she's* got a lot going on."

"Didn't you say she inherited that old farmhouse up north, toward the base, from an aunt?" he asked. "Isn't she renovating that with some friends into an artist's retreat?"

She eyed her father. He was right about the farmhouse. That was something Katie had told him last week, but that wasn't what he meant. This was something else, and if she had time before she needed to return to work, she'd grill him about it a little more.

* * *

Later that night, Katie arrived home at six. Dad was still at the library, working more hours than he should. But he loved doing it, and the powers-that-be who oversaw the library loved him for doing it. If only they showed their appreciation by paying him more.

She hung up her rain jacket and her fleece in the mudroom. Kicked off her shoes. Went to the kitchen, where she filled her teapot and lit the gas stove. She then trekked to the living room to water her Xanadu philodendrons and her grape succulent. Maybe if she could cement this routine in her head, she could keep from killing her plants like she repeatedly did in Denver.

After living on her own for ten years in Colorado—four years at school in Fort Collins, including the summers, and six years working for a downtown Denver independent publisher, first as a graphic designer before getting promoted to the head of product design—moving back after mom's death to work for the puzzle company and be near Dad when he needed her was a no-brainer. She'd found a cute one-story baby-blue twelve-hundred square-foot cottage to rent about a mile west of downtown. It came with hardwood floors that still needed a little TLC and a stack-stone fireplace that was perfect during the chilly winter nights. The best part, though, was the view of the water from her back porch, between the Gonzalezes' garage and the Milligan's house, which both backed up to the Sound.

Although she'd originally planned on living alone, those plans had changed for the time being. Every centimeter of Mom and Dad's two-story Cape Cod house on the outskirts of town was suffocating Dad. He struggled with the overwhelming volume of memories of Mom strewn about the place. And it also convinced her to let him move in with her. Temporarily. As long he agreed to share the place with the family's latest addition: her cat, Whimsy. He agreed, as long as he could bring his phone number from the family home.

Whimsy's latest trick was to jump up on the floral-print couch, knead his paws into her legs, and then position himself between her and the television. Then he'd try to catch a little shut-eye. Normally, she'd pick him up and set him off to her side, but this time, she stroked his soft fur and stared at the blank television screen.

Two minutes later, she moved Whimsy off to the side and picked up the remote. More often than not, she and Dad would try to knock out a 300-piece puzzle before bed. Without him home, she was about to start binge-watching a new show on Netflix when the landline rang. She shook her head and rolled off the couch, much to her—and Whimsy's—dismay. Using a landline again was not something she'd ever get used to, but Dad had insisted, if only to keep their old phone number.

"Coming," she hollered on the third ring, picking the receiver up in the kitchen on ring number five. "Chambers' residence."

Nothing.

"Hello?"

Click.

Huh. Must've been a wrong number.

Then it rang again.

"Chambers' residence."

Click.

"This is ridiculous."

There used to be a way to call a number back, by pressing *6 or something. Before she could, it rang once again, and this time she didn't bother with the pleasantries.

"I don't know who this is, but if you keep this up, I'm calling the police."

"Even if I'm the one paying for the phone?" Dad said.

"Why didn't you say anything the first two times you called?"

"What first two times?"

"Someone just called twice and hung up."

"Probably some kids having some fun."

"I think prank calls went out of favor with the invention of caller ID, which most normal dinosaurs who still use landlines have, and cell phones. Speaking of which, wouldn't it be easier if you just called my cell?"

"It would be if I didn't have to check mine to find out what your number is. This number I've known for thirty years, and I can dial it while sitting at my desk."

She was never going to get him to change, but that didn't mean she was going to stop trying.

"Are you coming home soon?"

"Do you need me to?"

"No," she said, not so convincingly, worried about him staying out so late.

"I'll be home in a few hours. I need to place four or five last-minute book orders, and I have to get Amy some colored construction paper for tomorrow's story time."

Katie sighed. This was just the type of thing that caused him to work so many extra hours. "Can't Amy get the paper herself?"

"Not if she wants to use the library's account, she can't."

She shook her head. He definitely deserved a raise. "Drive safe," she said. "Main Street is still a bit slippery from the rain."

She hung up the phone and started toward the sofa when Whimsy arched his back and the teapot began to whistle. A second later, there was a knock at the door.

Chapter Three

Katie opened the door just as a gust of damp, cold wind blew in.

"Elena?"

Elena Larsson stood on the porch with her hair pinned up and wearing a cable-knit sweater, jeans, and a pair of tennis shoes—something she never did when she came to the group. She usually arrived at the library looking like she was heading out to a club, making it difficult to notice Katie had five years on her. But not tonight. Tonight Elena looked even younger than her twenty-four years.

And there was something else she never wore.

A worried face.

"Come in," Katie said. "Let's get you out of the wind." Stepping back, she eyed the growing fog, worrying about Dad driving in it.

Rubbing her hands together, Elena tossed her gaze behind her. And only after she appeared satisfied there was no one around, she stepped inside and wiped her feet on the mat.

Katie shut the door, expecting Elena to say something. Anything. But the younger woman hugged herself tightly and frowned. After several awkward moments, Katie motioned toward the couch. "Can I get you something? A glass of water? A cup of tea?"

Elena rubbed her hands. She peered over Katie's shoulder. Not toward the couch, but rather toward the hall leading back to the bedrooms.

"Elena?"

"No. Thank you. That's very kind of you."

As if knowing the conversation needed some encouragement, Whimsy approached their guest, rubbed his chin against her leg, and started purring. Usually, he was able to elicit *some* kind of response from a newcomer. A compliment. A pat on the head. But after Elena ignored him, he gave up and strutted to the kitchen, burying his head into what food was left in his bowl.

Katie gestured at the couch again. "Would you like to sit down?"

Elena faced the living room and narrowed her eyes, as if this was the toughest decision of her life. Then she looked down at her tennis shoes and shook her head.

"I can't stay long."

Katie folded her arms. "Don't get me wrong. It's great to see you, Elena. But it's a bit of an odd night for your first visit to our house, given the fog and all. Is there something wrong?"

"Is your father home?"

Katie recoiled before putting her hands on her hips. "My father?"

"Yeah. I need to speak with him."

"Why?

"It's a personal matter."

Katie cocked her head, wondering how a personal matter of Elena's could possibly interest her father. "He's still at work."

More handwringing. Another shake of the head.

Katie studied Elena. Although the two women worked together, or rather, Elena worked *for* Katie and they'd seen each other nearly every day for the past six months, they'd discussed very little with each other beyond a critique of a puzzle and the normal pleasantries. Even at Cynthia's, Elena largely stayed quiet, appearing to want to hear other people speak more than wanting to contribute herself.

"Do you know when he'll be home?"

Katie shrugged. "I just spoke to him a few minutes ago. He said he'd be back from work in a few hours. But you never know. If you want, I can give him a call?"

"No," Elena said a little too quickly. Then composed herself. "I appreciate the offer. I'll stop by the library. It's on my way home."

Before Katie could say another word, Elena rushed out the door. "Thank you," she said as she hurried off the porch. She hustled down the walkway and jumped into her car. In the blink of an eye, Elena was almost completely out of sight.

And Katie was totally confused.

* * *

At half past ten, Katie clutched her phone in one hand and held back the front curtain with the other. The fog had grown so thick she couldn't see across the street. She told herself she'd give him five more minutes before racing to the library and finding out what the heck was going on.

Dad had said he'd be home in a few hours, and that was four and a half hours ago. Since then, she'd called him no fewer than ten times, on both his work phone and his cell, without an answer or a callback.

Normally this wouldn't have bothered her. Dad wasn't required to check in with her, and she never checked in with him. It was the strongest part of their relationship. The trust. But the strange visit from Elena Larsson changed everything. At first, Katie had been able to shrug it off. Dad had a knack for assisting anyone with just about anything if they'd asked. All the better if he could help one of the crew.

But not when it kept him out late with the poor visibility from the fog.

Not good for anyone.

She picked up Whimsy and stroked the top of his head as she continued to glare out the window. A pair of headlights approached.

"Oh good," she said with an exhale. But her optimism was short-lived as the car drove past the house without so much as slowing down.

"That's it, Whimsy. I'm heading out."

She slipped on her rain jacket and a ball cap with the Cedar Bay Puzzle logo embossed on it. She grabbed her keys and rushed out into the rain.

* * *

Hurrying toward her Outback, she pressed her key fob and the car's doors chirped. She stepped into a puddle as she opened the driver's side door, when another pair of headlights approached her, this time from the opposite direction.

"Please, please, please."

But the car continued on.

She pulled out and drove toward the library. Her headlights barely pierced the wall of fog that had replaced the misty rain. She turned right onto Main Street, where she saw close to nothing.

She was the only car on the road, but she kept her speed below twenty. Swiveling her head, she hoped to catch a glimpse of something that might explain Dad's delay.

As she approached Cynthia's, she scanned the parking lot for Dad's new Altima. Sometimes he liked to go there with the library gang after work. But no luck this time. Three cars in all. None of them were his.

She shook her head and drew in a breath.

As she approached the front of the library, she slowed down even further. It was dark inside, but that didn't mean Dad had left. He could still be in his office. If so, his car would be parked in the back.

She hit the gas and turned right at Vienna a little faster than she should have.

"Uh oh."

The car hydroplaned. She turned into it, like she had so many times before, and tried to slow down even more.

The rear of the Outback clipped a mailbox standing along the far side of Elm Street. She pumped the brakes until she came to a complete stop, just short of hitting a parked car head-on. She gripped the steering wheel and let out a long breath. Squinting into the fog, she eyed the mailbox, then stepped out with a groan to assess the damage, careful not to step in a deep puddle.

A small divot of wood had been scraped clean out of the base.

Before getting back into the car, she spotted someone up ahead, crossing the street from the parking lot behind the library, barely visible in the fog. Had they seen her lousy driving and were about to call the police? That's all she needed, Connor responding to the call and seeing her bedraggled on the side of the road. But then she returned her focus to her task. Finding Dad.

She hopped back into the car and pulled into the parking lot. Like the rest of Cedar Bay, it, too, was damp from the mist, except for Dad's parking spot. That was still completely dry, indicating that Dad had left only recently. She hated the idea of him driving home when the fog was this thick.

She pounded the heel of her palm against the steering wheel. It was late, it was wet and foggy, and she couldn't find her father. She prayed he'd finally gone home, but her overactive imagination pictured the worst. Him dead in some ditch. Or in a kidnapper's basement being subjected to torture. *Thanks, Hannah.*

At this point, she could either drive aimlessly around town, desperate to find him, or return home and hope he was there. A gust of wind shook the car, making the decision for her.

This was no time to be out on the roads.

* * *

She slowed as she neared the house. But then she heaved a heavy sigh of relief.

Dad's car was in the driveway.

When she got in the house, she kicked off her shoes, hung her damp coat and cap up on the rack. Dad was pouring himself a beer. He tossed her a smile and gave her a one-armed hug.

"Where have you been?" she asked. "I've been worried sick."

"Crazy day," he said with a shake of his head. "Crazy day."

"Long day is more like it. What could possibly be so important that you couldn't come home before now?"

He sipped his beer and shrugged. "Just a few last-minute things that I wasn't expecting."

"Like Elena Larsson?"

He froze with the beer halfway to his lips.

"She was here looking for you, Dad. That was around six."

He set the glass on the kitchen table and jammed both hands into his pockets. "She came by the house, did she?" He went to the kitchen window. "She didn't mention that."

"What *did* she mention?"

He turned. "All I can say is that she's dealing with some personal problems and I've agreed to help her."

"Until ten thirty?"

"No, no," he said, shaking his head. "She was gone by eight. Her visit just put me further behind schedule, that's all."

"What could you two have talked about for two hours?"

He eyed her in a way that begged for compassion. "Like I said. It's personal. You'll have to trust me on this one."

"I do trust you. Implicitly. But . . ." But that didn't stop her from worrying.

He set down his beer, kissed her on the cheek, and patted her on the shoulder. "Get some sleep. We'll both feel better in the morning."

She wasn't going to sleep, and she didn't think she was going to feel better anytime soon. At least he was safe, though, and that was all that mattered.

* * *

The next morning, Katie woke up exactly at seven o'clock to Whimsy licking her ear. Dad always said Whimsy was as reliable as an alarm clock. She could've used that in Denver.

She rolled out of bed with a groan, took the hottest shower she could stand, and slipped on her favorite pair of jeans and an Aran sweater she'd bought in Seattle last month during one of her rare shopping sprees. As she slipped on her ankle boots, Whimsy beamed up at her expectantly, like he did every morning. She hadn't taken two steps before he started corralling her toward the kitchen.

After filling his bowl, she fixed herself a cup of coffee. She took a sip, pulled back the kitchen window's curtain, and shook her head. Dad's car was gone. The roads looked damp, but the fog had lifted, and the sky was full of gray but no rain clouds. He always left before her. But today she was hoping to have the opportunity to talk to him first.

No matter how hard she'd tried to pry Elena's secret out of him the night before, he didn't budge. Eventually he'd snatched the TV remote from the coffee table, turned up the volume of the Kraken's preseason hockey game he'd recorded, and declared the conversation over. And that was that.

So she'd fixed herself a cup of chamomile tea, wrapped herself in a Berber blanket, and sat out on the back porch. Since moving back, this had become her fortress of solitude. The perfect place to meditate and let her troubles float away. She drew in a calming breath and let her gaze land on the sound in the distance, its gentle waves twinkling in the moonlight. A lone sailboat crossed the channel and she raised her mug for its safety. It was chilly but not cold. The tea warmed her plenty as the chamomile's floral aroma was locked in a fight-to-death-battle with the lavender lining the window boxes behind her to her right and to her left.

Of course, the lavender never lost and she wasn't going to lose either. Just like Dad saying that their conversation about Elena was over.

Because it wasn't.

She closed her eyes and let her mind drift away.

* * *

Thirty minutes later, she shrugged on her REI windbreaker and set out a few catnip toys for Whimsy—her insurance against him wrecking yet another couch arm. She slung her backpack over her shoulder and reached for the kitchen door when her cell phone rang.

It was Neal McMurray. Her boss.

"Hey," he said, dragging out the "ey" part, like he did when he was about to deliver bad news. "You haven't left your house yet, have you?"

This wasn't good. "My hand's on the doorknob as we speak."

"Are you dressed work casual by any chance?"

She let go of the doorknob and set her backpack on the floor. "Let me guess. Marjorie called in sick and she can't go to the toy distributor conference in Seattle today."

"Your mom always said you were a smart one. Except it's not Marjorie who's sick. It's her kid. But close enough."

"And you're not sending Trent? Why?"

"Because Trent went instead of your mom last year."

"And?"

"And that's why I was going to send Marjorie."

Mr. Charming strikes again. "Count me in," she said.

"That's super. I appreciate it."

She checked her Apple watch. Seattle was about ninety minutes away, depending on the ferry schedule from Clinton to Mukilteo, and then the drive south into Seattle. She would be up to her elbows in stuffed animals and puzzles until after five and wouldn't get home until close to seven.

Her interrogation of Dad during their lunch date would have to wait.

She sent him a text, letting him know she wouldn't be coming by.

* * *

Later that night, around seven thirty, she passed the Welcome to Cedar Bay sign. The conference wasn't the slog that she expected. Neal told her that all she had to do was schmooze a little, take good notes, and not tick anyone off like Trent had. Instead, she shook hands with nearly every person in the place—competitors, distributors, and suppliers. Each one expressing their condolences, sharing how they'd admired her mom and how much she was missed.

They weren't alone.

For all the love expressed for Mom, there was one odd competitor who took the opportunity to complain about Cedar Bay Puzzle's upcoming fall series. The unhinged man, Harold Beck from Tacoma Toys, was quite emphatic that he thought the series' artistry was derivative. Too derivative. He was so worked up that he almost outright accused CBP of hacking into his computer system and stealing some of his artwork.

Katie, on the other hand, thought he was crazy and politely excused herself as soon as possible.

Despite all that, she hadn't forgotten Dad's late night and planned on interrogating him about Elena Larsson again. This time she wasn't going to let him off the hook so easily.

She turned onto Ambleside Drive, their road, and slowed.

The house had no garage, just a small shed at the end of the driveway. As a result, she usually parked in front, while Dad parked his new Altima in the driveway. But that would be difficult now.

Because a police car was parked in front of the house.

She hurried in through the side door.

"Dad?" she called out.

"In here."

She didn't even bother to put down her backpack or hang up her windbreaker. When she entered the living room, she found two men standing, wearing serious faces.

Dad and Lieutenant Daniel Crozier.

Dad had known Lieutenant Crozier—Connor's dad—since they were kids in school, like everyone in town in their fifties and sixties. But while they were friends, she'd never known the lieutenant to visit the house.

Crozier had a notebook out and his hat under one arm while Dad was scratching the back of his head. This wasn't two old friends having a chat. This was something serious.

"What's going on?" she asked.

The two men exchanged glances. Crozier tipped his head toward her father.

"It's about Elena," Dad said.

"What about her?" she asked.

Crozier answered. "She's dead, Katie. Her body was found this morning a few blocks from the library."

Dad dropped his head.

She brought her hands to her face. "Oh my God. What happened?"

Lieutenant Crozier shook his head. "Dunno. I was hoping your dad could shed some light on it."

"What's this have to do with you?" she asked Dad.

He blew out a heavy sigh. His eyes met hers. "Apparently, honey, I'm the last one who saw her alive."

Chapter Four

Katie studied Lieutenant Crozier. This was the man who used to take her and Connor to Oak Harbor for the weekend. Who taught her how to fish, sort of. That didn't really stick because the only thing she ever caught was a cold and a shoe.

And although she hadn't spent much time with him in years, she still knew him well enough to know that the sour look on his face wasn't good.

"What are you thinking, sir?"

He shrugged. "What can I tell you? It looks bad."

"What looks bad?" she said, her voice rising as the implications began to hit her. "You think *he* did it?"

Dad reached out to comfort her but she stepped away. "No. You guys need to be straight with me." She eyed her father. "Elena's dead?" Her gaze then landed on Lieutenant Crozier. "And you think my dad did it?"

The lieutenant raised a hand. "He's only a suspect, Katie. I'm not here to arrest him, but I am here to tell him not to leave town and not to talk to anyone about the case."

Whimsy appeared and looked up at all three of them before going to Lieutenant Crozier and rubbing against his leg.

"No!" Katie hollered, bending down to pick up the large cat. She stroked his back and admonished him. "That's not a nice man."

"Katie," Dad said, trying to reach out again and again, failing, but this time, she made sure he wouldn't be able to reach Whimsy.

"Lieutenant Crozier, I think you should leave."

"I have some more questions. I can do it here, or we can do it down at the station." He faced Dad with a pleading gaze, as if to say, "Can you talk some sense into her?"

"Give us a second, Dan," Dad said, this time taking Katie's arm and lightly dragging her into the living room. "What are you doing?"

She set Whimsy on the coffee table. "Do you even pay attention to the cop shows we watch? This is how a suspect gets into trouble. The cop gets all nice until you say something incriminating and bam! The next thing you know, he's—

"It's Dan, honey. I've known him for a hundred years."

"And I dated his son, who's just like his dad, who can turn on you just like his dad, and leave you miserable for ten years."

Dad snorted a laugh. "Come on. You don't think this has something to do with you and Connor, do you?"

"No, Dad," she said, stroking his arm. "It's about you. It's about me. It's about Mom. I know you feel guilty about Mom, and I don't want that to turn into guilt for something you clearly didn't do. So let's just tell Lieutenant Crozier your alibi and send him on his way."

Dad's frown tightened.

"What?"

"That's the thing we were talking about before you showed up."

"What thing?

"The thing where I don't have an alibi."

* * *

After seeing Lieutenant Crozier out and telling him to be careful driving because she just couldn't help herself, Katie went to the kitchen and started a pot of tea. Dad sat at the kitchen table, as instructed. Whimsy sat atop the table, despite his instructions. Katie took the other seat and waited for the kettle to boil.

"Okay," she said, bringing her hands together in prayer. "I want to hear this before your interview with Lieutenant Crozier tomorrow, so start from the top."

"What can I say?" He reached out and petted Whimsy's head, which was rewarded with a warm purr. "Elena shows up at the library around six thirty, or maybe it was seven. I don't know, I was busy, if you recall."

She crossed her arms and looked away. "That doesn't make sense. She left here around six, and it barely takes five minutes to get to the library from here."

"I'm telling you what happened." He tilted his head up and flashed her a fatherly smile. "Can you let me finish?"

"Okay, okay," she said, raising her hands in surrender. Then she pretended to button her lip and nodded for him to continue.

"As I was saying, she came to the library around six thirty, and I could tell right away something was wrong."

Katie was about to speak, but Dad pretended to button his lip but with force. She mouthed, "Sorry."

"Anyhow. Her left eye looked puffy and it wasn't from crying."

Katie gasped, which was really her way of saying, "Someone hit her?" Elena's eye wasn't puffy when Katie saw her at the house last night.

He nodded. "I think so. You see, there's this guy she's been seeing."

She raised her hands. "I can't do this. What guy?"

But the teapot whistled.

"Saved by the bell," Dad said.

"Go on. You know every question I'm going to ask anyhow."

She retrieved a box of tea bags from the cupboard above the stove and to the right. Found her and Dad's favorite mugs. Hers was covered in puzzle pieces, and his said "Keep calm and ask a librarian." She wished she could get even close to calm right now. She turned to him and said, "Go on."

"She's been dating this guy. Won't tell me who. But they get together at weird hours and he can only talk to her at certain times."

She poured the steaming water into the mugs. "He's married."

"That's what I think, but she wouldn't confirm it."

After dropping the tea bags into their respective mugs, she returned to the table. "Can I ask you something?" She set the mugs on the table and took her seat. "Why was she telling you all this?"

He shrugged. "We're friends?"

She furrowed her brow. "Since when?"

"Since before your mother died but after she got sick."

She sat back in her chair. "Don't tell me—"

"Hey! Don't go there. And the answer's no. We were just friends."

But she didn't like the way he said it. "What aren't you telling me?"

He sighed and pushed the mug away. "Amy Richardson thought it was more than that."

"She thought you were having an—"

"Don't say it."

"An affair, Dad. An affair. Let's use our words. If you weren't having one, why is it a problem?"

"You know how this place is. Word like that gets around, you can't put out the rumors with a fire hose."

She bit her lower lip before asking slowly, "Did it get around?"

"Why do you think Dan was here?"

She turned her face as if she'd been slapped. Whimsy raised his head as if he knew what was going on. The thought of Dad having an affair while Mom was still alive was simply unimaginable. Except, in a way, it was. It must have been so hard for him. So lonely. Giving Mom every spare moment he had to keep her comfortable only to have her die in a stupid accident.

Who helped him as he was struggling? Who helped him with his emotions? Katie didn't, because she was a thousand miles away, and she still regretted not coming home sooner. Oh God, maybe Elena—

"Hey," Dad said, snapping his fingers. "It didn't happen."

"You're positive?"

Even Whimsy threw him an accusing stare.

"It didn't happen. What did happen is this other guy. I don't know who. And . . ." He paused and ran a hand across his face. "I think he was physical with her."

She lowered her voice to a conspiratorial tone. "Are you saying that they were, you know?"

"Please don't say it." He dropped his head into his hands. "I can't believe we're having this conversation."

She grinned. "Don't worry, Dad. Mom and I had the talk, oh, I don't know, twenty years ago?"

He sighed. "That's not what I mean."

Then she got it. The black eye. "You think he hit her."

Dad nodded.

"And you didn't tell anyone?"

"I promised I wouldn't. A promise I shouldn't have kept, I know. I explained that to Dan, but I could tell he wasn't buying it."

"That's because he's a jerk like his son."

Dad shook his head. "They aren't jerks." He took a deep breath and exhaled loudly. "Look, there's more I need to tell you. Elena and I didn't just talk when she came to the library. We argued."

"About this guy?"

"I noticed her eye when she came in, but no one else did. She was clearly trying to hide the bruise with makeup, and she didn't run into a door." He let his point hang in the air until it rolled over Katie like an avalanche.

"Someone thinks it was *you* who hit her?" she said, nearly lunging out of her seat.

He motioned for her to sit back down, which she did. "Dan is just doing his job."

"Okay," she said, picking up her mug. "Okay." She gulped down the tea so fast it burned her throat. She tried to shake it off. It didn't work. She rushed to the drawer next to the sink, opened it up, and pulled out a pen and a legal pad. "Here's what we're going to do."

After sitting back down, she opened the pad and began to write. "Suspects," she said, underlining it several times. "Number one. Affair guy."

"What are you doing?"

"What do you think I'm doing? We're going to solve the case. You, me, and the puzzlers. They'll be great at this."

Dad stood. "Now wait just a minute."

"Nonnegotiable, Dad." She wrote the number 2 and then a name that broke her heart to write: Dad. "Lieutenant Crozier thinks you're a suspect. The best way to change his mind is for us to find Elena's killer."

"Katherine, please. We don't even know if she was murdered. It could have been an accident."

"No," she said. "Elena was my friend, too. And my coworker. And a member of our group. The puzzlers owe it to her to find out what happened, and if she was murdered, I owe it to you to get you exonerated."

He frowned. "Or you might just end up sending me to the electric chair."

* * *

Having spent the past two hours staring at the ceiling, ping-ponging between worrying about Dad and feeling horrible about Elena, Katie finally lifted herself out of bed at six fifteen. She stretched, lifting her arms high, and wished that last night was just a horrible dream, but no such luck.

She rushed through her shower, threw on her clothes, and slipped her hair into a ponytail. Fashion was taking a back seat today.

Dad, not wanting to miss a minute of work, had left extra early, about an hour ago, before the library opened as agreed upon with Lieutenant Crozier, for his interview. He promised to tell Katie the result as soon as he could, but she was not to bug him. That was after Katie had tried until the wee hours of the morning to get him to confess more about Elena, but he refused to budge.

Meanwhile, she was a wreck. According to her watch, she'd slept two and a half hours and she was surprised it was that long. She'd tossed and turned for hours, and when she'd finally managed to sleep, she'd had nightmares about Dad going to prison.

She was so worried about her father that she skipped breakfast and didn't even make a pot of coffee. Instead, she decided to head to the office early, even though sunrise was still a half hour away and she would arrive before Neal. He was always the first to arrive and the last one to leave every day, but not this morning.

After feeding Whimsy and petting him for the daily minimum of two minutes, she grabbed her things and headed for the door. She locked the door behind her and pulled out her phone to call Ken Gorman. Of all the members of the puzzle crew, she knew Ken with his legal logic would at least know where to start figuring this out.

"Do you know what time it is?" Ken growled in a whisper.

"It's half past six," she said, pressing her phone against her ear and tossing her purse into her car with her hair becoming wet in the misty rain. "More importantly, it's time for the early birds to get the worm."

Ken grunted, "Am I supposed to be the worm in this scenario?"

"You're supposed to be my brave eagle. But first I have some terrible news."

She told him about Elena. And Dad.

"Holy cow," was all he could say several times. When he was done, he asked, "How's Jim?"

She pressed the ignition button and the call transferred from her phone to her car.

"He's better than he should be. He should be freaking out like I am. The last thing Lieutenant Crozier said to me before he left last night was, 'Everyone's a suspect, Katie. But I'd be lying if I said your dad wasn't at the top of my list.'"

Ken whistled as she raced through a slick intersection and a yellow light.

"So they think it's murder and not an accident. Is there anything I can do?"

"Is there anything a puzzle master like you can do? You tell me."

He moaned and something jostled on his end of the phone, like he was getting out of bed. "For heaven's sake, you're as bad as your mother."

"I'll take that as a compliment. Does that mean you're willing to help?"

"Hang on."

While she waited for Ken, she parked in her usual space at CBP. Hers was the only car in the lonely, semi-lit lot. The building was pitch black inside. Any other day she'd be too frightened to enter the building all alone, but this wasn't any other day. And despite her hectic schedule, she would have to work around it if she planned to keep her dad out of trouble.

"I'm back," he said. "Marcia's still sleeping, and the last thing I want her to hear is the harebrained scheme I suspect you've concocted. But let me say this first."

"It better not be negative." She entered her keycode for the building, hurried inside, and turned the lights on. "This isn't a time to be negative."

"No. It's a time to be honest. Painfully honest. Look, Katie. Jim's a great man and I'm sure he did nothing wrong. But we do puzzles. We do not solve crimes, if there is even a crime to solve."

"Maybe we should."

Ken let out a heavy sigh. "Dan Crozier's been doing this since before you could walk. He's fair and he knows what he's doing."

She set her purse by her desk, slipped off her jacket, and powered up her desktop. "Forgive me if I'm not in a trusting mood when it comes to the Croziers."

"Is this because you ran into Connor yesterday?"

"You heard about that?"

"It's Cedar Bay, Katie."

Ugh. "Let me put this another way. Solving a crime is like solving a puzzle. You find a bunch of pieces that don't look like they fit, and then you test and you plan and you act until the pieces start to fall into place and you have your answer."

He sighed.

"You don't believe me."

"I believe we're making a big mistake. Dan Crozier does not like people interfering with his business or, worse, making work for him, and he tends to take his anger out on people who do."

"We! You said we!"

"I'm also saying that we need to be careful. Let's do our best not to broadcast our intentions and if we do find something material, we'll share it with Dan in a professional, legal manner. Crossing the t's. Dotting the i's and all that."

"You got a deal. You won't regret it."

"I already do."

"Okay, first things first," Katie said. "There will be an unscheduled, mandatory meeting today of the South Island Jigsaw Crew at noon at JJ's. I'll text Mildred and Hannah, even though Hannah probably won't be able to leave school. You take care of Tony."

He snidely asked, "Will there be a puzzle?"

"Yes. It'll be the hardest puzzle we've ever tried to solve."

Chapter Five

Katie hadn't been at her desk for more than ten minutes when she heard a door open. She popped her head out of her office doorway and spotted Neal angling toward the break room. By the time she reached him, he was already sitting down at the small round wood table in the middle of the room, drenched in fluorescent light, blowing steam from his coffee.

She was about to ask him why he was in so early until she saw his puffy red eyes.

"I take it you heard."

He nodded, cradling the cup in both hands. "Daniel Crozier called me last night."

"What time was that?"

He shrugged. "I don't know. Late. Maybe eleven? Kristy and I had just gotten back from Seattle."

That was after the lieutenant had left Katie's house, but not by much. She took the seat to Neal's left, terrified that Lieutenant Crozier had implicated Dad in some way.

"What did he say?"

Neal leaned back and slouched in his chair, still cradling the coffee. "That Elena was dead, and it appeared she was murdered. That they'd found her near the library. He was just beginning his investigation, and he's going to want to talk to everyone here."

"And you said?"

He raised an eyebrow. "Is this an interrogation?"

"Just curious."

He looked back down. "I told him fine. Why not? It's not like I can stop him." Neal dipped his head, bit his lip, and held his gaze on the swirling steam.

She rested a hand on his forearm. "It's going to be okay. We're going to find out who did this."

He arched an eyebrow. "We?"

"It's just an expression."

"Actually, it's not. But I don't care." He drew in slow, contemplative breath. "Dan also asked me to secure Elena's desk. No one's to touch her computer or go through her drawers or even sit in her chair."

"Is that a problem?"

He sighed. "I was hoping to have this conversation with you under much different circumstances."

The hairs on the back of her neck prickled, but she said nothing.

He lifted his gaze to meet hers. "I fired Elena yesterday, while you were at the trade show."

Katie blinked. Then shook her head. She must've heard him wrong.

"Wanna try that again?"

He brought the cup to his lips with a shaky hand and took a sip.

"You heard me."

She leaned in. "You fired her? My employee, Elena, one of the best up-and-coming puzzle designers in the field? You fired *that* Elena?"

He set the cup back down. "That's the thing, Katie. I don't think she was one of the best up-and-coming puzzle designers. I think some guy at Tacoma Toys is."

Her stomach growled and her eyes were droopy. She went to the counter and fixed a coffee with extra cream and even some actual sugar for a change. She sat back down in total disbelief.

"Why would you think that? Are you trying to tell me that you think Elena is a *thief*?"

He nodded. "The puzzles your crew tested on Sunday? They were designed by some guy named Harold Beck."

"Beck?" She jumped to her feet. "That's the smarmy guy I met at the show. He accused us of stealing their designs, but I didn't believe him. Don't tell me you do."

At that moment, someone new entered the break room. Someone else who felt the urge to begin their day earlier than usual. It was Marjorie, Neal's very tall sister.

Whereas most of CBP's employees showed up to work looking like they'd just gotten out of bed, right down to the occasional fuzzy slippers, Marjorie, like Katie, took a more professional approach, which included perfectly fitting jeans, a bright red blouse, and pair of Taos Soul Lux sneakers, so comfortable that they allowed her to walk the factory floor over and over again without looking like she'd trudged a mile along a gravelly beach.

Neal looked up at Marjorie, appraised her and nodded. Then turned his attention back to Katie. "Beck sent lawyers here around noon. That's really why Majorie here couldn't go to the show. I apologize for the misdirection, but I didn't want you to know in case you ran into someone from Tacoma Toys, which you did. And it was Beck."

"You think I would have said something?"

He cocked his head.

"Yeah, I definitely would've said something," Katie said, "especially after that idiot Beck got in my face."

"Anyhow," Neal said, "I needed Marjorie here to study the technical aspects of their designs. She agreed."

Marjorie nodded slowly. "It's true. Elena stole them."

"That's great news!" Katie said.

Now it was Neal's turn to stand up. "Are you crazy?"

She put a hand on his shoulder. "No, I mean, sorry. Yes, I am crazy. Totally losing my mind. I didn't sleep a wink. Because what I didn't tell you is that Lieutenant Crozier was at our house last night before he called you. Dad had to go to the station early this morning to be interviewed."

"Why at the station?"

She looked around. The early morning crowd had grown considerably—from the three of them to ten. She swallowed hard. Struggled to find the words.

"Because Lieutenant Crozier thinks my dad did it."

* * *

It was just before noon. Katie had spent the morning with one eye on her work and the other on what she assumed to be Elena's murder. She was late for her lunch routine because she hadn't heard from her father yet.

She tried Amy Richardson for the umpteenth time.

"He's still not here, Katie. And it's not much fun trying to run this place without him."

She hadn't shared her concerns with Amy. It was bad enough she'd done so with her co-workers in such a public fashion. "I'm sure he'll get there soon. Just please, please, please have him call me as soon as he does."

Her stomach growled on cue, telling her it was time to go to JJ's. She snagged her purse and headed to the door, but not before stopping by Neal's office. She was about to knock *on* the open door when she noticed Ian Trembley sitting across from her boss.

"Katie," Neal called out before she could get away.

She popped her head back in. "Nothing urgent. It can wait."

Ian turned to face her. He was a scratchy middle-aged man, desperately trying to cling onto his youth. With his long, unkempt hair and his endless supply of black concert T-shirts, he looked more like a college student than a professional who was trying to get ahead. But despite his casual attire, his attitude about his career was anything but casual. Of all the people on her team, Ian had the biggest problem with her being hired. He thought he was entitled to the Vice President of Product Design position given his many years of service and wouldn't hesitate to tell anyone who would listen. The problem was that the other members of the team threatened to resign if he got the job, with Elena being the most vocal. Which was why it didn't surprise her that while everyone in the office seemed to be vacillating between crying and working, Ian looked positively pleased with himself.

"Any word from your dad?" Neal asked.

But knowing how unhappy Ian still was having lost the job to her, she couldn't take her eyes away from him. There was something off about his happiness. It was as if . . . *No,* she chided herself. *Don't go there.* Despite his surly demeanor, she'd known Ian Trembley for years. Before Mom's death, they'd even gotten along. No way was he a murderer.

"Katie?" Neal said.

"Uh. Dad. Right. No, haven't heard anything yet."

She crossed her arms and cut a quick glance toward Ian. The smugness on his face unnerved her. To Neal, she said, "Who knew you fired Elena?"

Neal sat back. "Me, Marjorie, HR, and Elena, of course."

"I didn't hear about it until today," Ian added.

"Today?"

He looked puzzled.

"I'm sure it's nothing, Ian." To Neal she said, "I'm heading to lunch."

"Be back by two. That's when Lieutenant Crozier is coming."

Ian turned back toward Neal. "I'm not going to be here for that."

"You're going to be out again? You realize that with Elena gone, we've got four puzzles we need to redesign?"

"I got a-a doctor's appointment that I can't move."

"I'll let Crozier know," Neal said in a sour tone. "But you and I need to get hustling on these new designs or we're going to miss the window to get them put into production." He looked at Katie. "Let me know if you hear anything new about your dad, okay?"

"Will do," she said.

With that she nearly ran all the way to JJ's.

When she got there, Ken had already arrived, as had Mildred.

"Tony will be here in five minutes," Ken said.

Katie waved at JJ but took the seat next to Ken. "I know what we have to do."

"I have to eat," Mildred said, loud enough to be heard over at the ferry dock miles away.

"Did you both order? It'll be my treat."

Tony strolled over with his bushy eyebrows and his hooded, black South Island Subaru rain jacket, and plopped himself next to Mildred. As always, he didn't have a hair out of place. Rumor had it that he was pushing fifty, but he didn't look a day over forty. "Good genes," he'd say when asked. But everyone knew it was the hours he somehow put in at the gym, in between running the dealership and helping Mildred. "What's this about a free lunch?" he said.

"I'm buying."

Once everyone had ordered, Katie went to the counter and picked up and paid for her and her father's standing order as well as Ken's, Tony's, and Mildred's.

Back at the table, she found Tony holding his phone for her to see. She could see Hannah, with her wire-rimmed Harry Potter-style glasses, staring back at her.

"Hey, Katie," Hannah said.

"Shouldn't you be in class?"

Hannah shook her head, the light intermittently bouncing off the silver stud in her nose as she did. "It's lunch period and I got a pass from Miss Winston to go outside."

"That's great," Katie said. "I know what we have to do."

"Maybe you should tell us what's going on first," Mildred said.

Katie replayed the story she told Ken that morning, but with a new twist.

Following a round of oh-nos and my-Gods, the group went silent.

Tony unwrapped his sandwich. “You think Ian Trembley did it?”

“No,” Katie said, shaking her head. “Well, maybe. But that’s not the point. We need to create a list of suspects.”

“Isn’t Lieutenant Crozier going to do that?” Tony asked.

“Not if he’s sure my dad’s guilty. He’ll think he’s got an easy bust and not bother to look anywhere else.”

Ken stroked his long salt-and-pepper beard. “An easy bust, huh? I see we’re already using the lingo.”

She playfully elbowed him and said, “Oh, hush.” Then she leaned in. “What I’m saying is that seeing Ian sitting there all smug and satisfied made me think that he could be a suspect. He hated Elena because he knew that she was emerging as the company’s top designer, which would have given him a motive. He said he didn’t know that Neal fired her until today, so what if he jumped the gun and killed Elena too early?”

“That’s crazy,” Mildred said before diving into her egg salad sandwich. Tony nodded his agreement.

Ken wrung his hands. “Except it’s not.”

All three stopped whatever they were doing and turned to him.

“Katie’s laid out a perfectly reasonable supposition.” He rested his hands on top of his belly. “I see where you’re going now. We don’t have to solve the crime. We only need to create a list of plausible suspects so Crozier will have to pause before rushing to judgement with Jim.”

“Thank you,” Katie said with a nod. “That’s exactly what I think we should do. So.”

“So,” Tony said.

"So. Let's pretend we have a puzzle," she said. "What should we do?"

The others went silent, each wearing serious expressions while pondering the question. It was as if she could see the gravity of the situation descending upon the crew. Well, not all of them.

"We find the edge pieces," Mildred teased, breaking the silence.

"That's right!" Katie said. "That's what we're doing." She took out her phone, opened her notes app, and typed as she spoke. "Creating a list of suspects is like finding the edges of the puzzle. Suspect one: Ian Trembley. Okay, who else?"

"Your dad," Ken said.

She shot him a dirty look.

He shrugged. "I'm just saying. He is a suspect. Heck, right now, he's not just an edge piece. He's a corner piece. We have to consider him, even if it's only to exonerate him."

It hurt her to do it, but she typed *Suspect 2: Dad*.

Her heart clenched, but it wasn't just because of what she'd written. A familiar face had entered JJ's and it wasn't someone she wanted to talk to today.

"Hi folks," Connor said as he breezed in, sporting a navy blue CBFD hat with a smattering of rain on top. She was surprised to see that his friendly smile didn't reach his eyes. Most wouldn't notice, but she could tell. He looked positively troubled. The other three said their hellos, but Katie only nodded. Connor seemed to take the hint and kept walking toward the counter.

"That's it?" Tony said, arching a playful eyebrow. "Not even a hello?"

"Where were we?" she said.

"We were ignoring the fact that your ex-boyfriend just came in and you didn't so much as give him the time of day."

Katie studied the others, seeing the curiosity on each of their faces except Mildred's. She was too focused on her knitting, which was when she did her best scheming. Then—

"His father!" Katie blurted out. She lowered her voice. "His father thinks my dad is a murderer."

Ken furrowed his brow. "And that's Connor's fault?"

"Can we just focus, please? Now, who else could've done it?"

Ken whisked away some crumbs from his sweater. "At this rate, we have to include Connor Crozier because Katie doesn't like his dad."

Katie shot him a look.

"Sorry," he said. "That was too much. Back to the puzzle. Other than Ian, did Elena have any enemies?"

"Good question. The answer is yes." She started typing again. "Suspect three: Harold Beck."

"Who's Harold Beck?" Tony asked.

"He works for Tacoma Toys. I met him at a trade show yesterday and he got up in my face because he thought we were stealing their designs. What if he learned Elena was the thief? That gives him motive, doesn't it?"

All three nodded.

Mildred took a bite of her sandwich but suddenly stopped. "Does she have a boyfriend?" Mildred said, crumbs flying everywhere.

The two men looked at each other and shrugged.

Katie took a sip of Diet Coke.

"Katie?" Ken said.

"I'm not sure you'd call him a boyfriend, but my dad thinks she was having an affair with a married man."

"Was that man your dad?" Mildred said and then swallowed. Tony grabbed Mildred's hands and shook his head. Mildred simply shrugged. "It's possible."

"No, it's not."

Ken turned to her again, but this time with a knowing but sensitive stare.

"It's because he's not married," Katie said. "He's a widower."

She typed *Suspect 4: Mystery Boyfriend/Married Man.* "Okay, we have four suspects. Ian, Harold Beck, this mysterious married man and . . ." She coughed. "My dad."

Speaking of Dad, she sent Amy Richardson another text. *Any news?*

"So what now?" Ken asked.

"I think I should I meet with Lieutenant Crozier, go over this list and . . ." The others had stopped paying attention to her and were staring to her right.

"Can we talk?" Connor said.

Even though she could feel him behind her, staring at the back of her head, she refused to turn to face him. "Can't you see I'm busy?"

Tony slid out of his chair. "Great plan, Katie. I think we're done."

"Yep," Ken said, eyeing his watch. "I gotta get back to work."

"I can stay," Mildred said.

"No, you can't," Tony said, helping her to her feet.

Katie frowned. "Chickens," she muttered.

* * *

Outside of JJ's, the clouds had moved on and the sun was drying the Cedar Bay streets.

"We meet again," Connor said.

"My dad's waiting for his lunch." She held up the bag. "It's getting cold."

"It's a cold sandwich."

"Then it's getting warm."

He put his hands in his pockets and kicked the ground. "I heard what happened."

She put a hand to her ear. "What's that? Someone's cat is caught in a tree? I know just the man for the job. You're needed, Connor, as am I."

She started to walk away, but he grabbed her arm. She glared at him.

"Let go."

"I wanna help."

"You wanna help?" she scoffed. "Tell that to your dad."

He let go. "I'm serious. I know about your dad. I overheard you guys talking in there. All I'm saying is that I want in. I want to help exonerate your dad."

She narrowed her eyes. "What aren't you telling me?"

"What do you mean?"

"You're acting like you know something. Did your dad arrest my dad?"

A car sped past before he could answer.

"No. He hasn't. In fact, your dad left the station about twenty minutes ago."

"Then why hasn't he called me?"

"You'd have to ask him."

"I'm asking you."

He threw his hands in the air. "How the heck would I know? All I can tell you is that it doesn't look good for your dad and I want to help."

Her watch buzzed with a text. *He just arrived.*

"I gotta go. If I need help, you can be sure that you would be the last person on earth that I ask."

He looked wounded. She knew him well enough to know that he was trying to hide it, but he hadn't changed. Connor revealed everything about him through his gaze. And right now, that gaze was telling her that she'd hurt him. Some other day, that might have made her feel bad.

But not today. Not when his father was trying to put hers in prison.

Chapter Six

After leaving Connor outside JJ's, Katie marched into the library carrying Dad's lunch, but she wasn't as interested in delivering his order as she was to learn what happened down at the police station.

"He's in his office," Amy offered without Katie asking.

"Thanks."

She threaded her way through the rows and rows of books, avoiding the urge to stop at the new releases, until she found Dad at his desk gazing at his computer monitor, which she was sure was either dark, blank, or full of information he didn't much care about.

"I thought we had a deal," she said, setting his lunch in front of him.

"That was a long time ago."

"It was this morning."

He kept his head down, struggling to get the next few words out. "This morning is almost a lifetime ago."

"Look up at me."

He complied.

"Where have you been?"

"I told you."

"No. It's a five-minute walk from the police station. It took you twenty."

He leaned back in his chair. An angry expression crossed his face. "Do you have people spying on me?"

"Not intentionally, but it's a small town. Remember?"

He let out a sardonic laugh. "I guess this is my day for interrogations."

"You didn't answer my question."

"I went for a walk. Okay? It was a long morning. Dan asked a lot of questions and frankly, I couldn't answer most of them, so I strolled around town because I needed to clear my head."

She took the seat across from him. "What did Lieutenant Crozier say?"

He allowed himself a smile. "I'll never get over how much you look like your mom."

"Come on, Dad."

"Seriously. Even when you're angry with me." He laughed. "Especially when you're angry with me, it's like she's here. It's the eyes. And the nose, I suppose."

"Thank God I got her nose."

"We agree on that."

She let some silence linger between them. Then asked, "What'd he say, Dad?"

He stared up at the ceiling and rested his hands on his lap. "It's what he didn't say. He didn't say I was a suspect, I guess they don't use that term anymore. He didn't say I was going to be arrested. All he said was, 'Don't leave town.'"

She brought a hand to her chin. "Which means he thinks you are a suspect and you might be arrested."

He nodded, sat up, and fished his roast beef sandwich out of the sack. "I believe they call it a person of interest. How's the potato salad today?"

"JJ didn't say."

"That's odd." He peered at her lap. "Where's yours?"

"Are we going to talk about your conversation or not?"

He sighed and swiveled his chair to face her dead on. "What do you wanna know?"

"How about the truth?"

"Okay," he said, setting his unwrapped sandwich down. "He grilled me about Elena. And I mean everything. He focused on this mysterious supposedly married man that Elena was involved with and tried everything in his power to trick me into saying it was me."

"Why would he do that?"

"Because according to him, Elena's killing was a crime of passion. Whoever did it had some sort of emotional attachment, and since she was killed near the library and the library surveillance system clearly shows me leaving the library around the time of her death."

"Did you leave the library?"

He looked away.

"Dad?"

"I got something out of my car. An overdue book I'd forgotten to bring in."

"Did anyone see you?"

"Just the cameras."

"That's good, right?"

He dug his fork into his potato salad and shook his head. "It was too foggy. The cameras caught me leaving the building but didn't catch me opening the car or leaving the car. There's a gap of about ten minutes."

"It took you ten minutes to get a book?"

He shoved a forkful of potatoes and into his mouth and didn't say a word.

"Dad?"

He picked up his Diet Coke, sucked the straw hard, and set it back down. "You're starting to sound like Dan."

"I'm not trying to. I'm just trying to figure it out."

"It's okay," he said with a wave. "It's a fair question. If I'd known someone was getting murdered at that moment, I'd have hurried back inside. Instead, I sat in the car and finished the book. Wait a minute."

"What?"

"What do you mean you're trying to figure it out?"

"I'm trying to figure out who did this. You don't think I'm just going to sit here and let that man put you in jail."

Dad lowered his head and his voice. "Stay out of this, Katie. This is bigger than you and me. I've known Dan Crozier since Little League, and he's promised to keep an open mind."

"It sounds like he already thinks you're guilty. Everything he'll do from now on will be to confirm his hunch, not change it."

Dad played with his potato salad again.

She said, "That's why I have to help him."

"Help him? Come on, Katie. Let the man do his job. You do yours."

"I am doing mine. I'm trying to solve a puzzle."

She eyed the clock on the wall above his head. It was after one. Neal wasn't a stickler about how long his people took at lunch, but with Lieutenant Crozier coming to the office, he was liable to be pretty tense.

"Is there any good news?"

Dad shook his head. "Just the obvious."

"Which is?"

"I'm innocent."

* * *

Back at the office, Neal assembled the whole team into the break room, which could only comfortably hold about half of the CBP employees. It was a somber assembly as everyone moved quietly to the room and those who could fit packed into the cramped space. The rest spilled out into the hallway.

Katie leaned against the counter in front of the coffee pot. The whole place was on pins and needles. As a few stragglers found their way near, what began as a quiet crowd turned into nervous murmurs, then all-out conversations. Some loud. A few angry. This gathering was falling apart before it even started.

Neal and Marjorie tried to calm them, but it was no good. Between the shock of Elena dying and the certainly of Dad's guilt, thanks to Katie's big mouth, more than one person wondered why they should have their day disrupted at all.

Neal stood at the edge of the room, patting the air. "Come on, guys. Let's settle down." But it was no use. Then someone let out a whistle that could've cut glass.

"Thanks, Maurice," Neal said. "Now, as I'm sure you'll all aware by now, we lost a valuable member of our family last night."

"I thought you fired her," Lalo from the loading docks said.

Neal's head dropped. He took off his glasses and rubbed his eyes. "That's not what we're here to talk about."

"But you did fire her, right?"

"It's complicated. What I can say is that it is true that Elena was not officially a CBP employee at the time of her death."

Janet from accounting chimed in. "Why did you fire her, Neal?"

He put his glasses back on. "That's a topic for another day, Janet. Right now, we're focused on Elena's death and who might have caused it."

"Is it true she was shot?" Richard from color engineering chimed in.

"I heard she was strangled," someone shouted from the hall.

"Guys," Neal said, raising his hand. "I can't get into specifics because I don't know the specifics. All I know is—"

"Less than we do, apparently." Richard wasn't letting it go. "I thought they already knew who did it." He cut a glare Katie's way. "I'm sorry, but that's what I heard." He returned his attention to Neal. "Is that true, or do you think one of us did it?"

Neal's shoulders dropped. Katie knew him well enough to know that he hated this and if he could, he'd leave. Confrontation wasn't his strong suit. Firing Elena had to be the hardest thing he'd ever done. Finding out she'd died hours later probably broke him. For a minute, Katie wondered if he could've been a suspect, but if he did kill her, why go ahead and fire her earlier in the day? Besides, he already said he and his wife were out in Seattle, and seeing his face right now, he couldn't have done it. He wasn't that good of an actor.

Katie wanted to say something to defend her dad, but that would only make things worse. She crossed her arms and bit her tongue, wishing this whole meeting would come to a merciful end.

Neal started to speak over the employees' agitated voices, each one seeming to have an opinion of what was going on, but Marjorie cut him off.

"Folks," she said, taking Neal's side. "We're telling you everything we can, which isn't much. We're sorry. But this is a police investigation, and we've agreed to be as cooperative as possible without totally disrupting our day."

"I think that ship has sailed," Janet said. Others let out a morbid laugh.

"Then it's our job to steer that ship back into port. Lieutenant Crozier will be here in thirty minutes. He'll likely take a tour and then begin asking each of you questions. We don't know what he's going to ask, but we expect you to be as truthful as possible because despite any issues Elena may have had, we want justice served. That's all for now."

Nobody moved. It was as if they were expecting more but Katie couldn't imagine what, because she wanted to get out of there as fast as possible.

"Seriously, guys," Marjorie said. "That's all for now. If you have any additional questions, my door will be open." Then she gestured for everyone to leave.

The crowd hesitated at first but then began to disperse. A few said hi to Katie as they passed, but just as many tossed her uncomfortable glances. She simply smiled, balled her hands into fists, and watched her coworkers leave in silence. She needed to keep calm before sharing her suspect list with Lieutenant Crozier, wishing she had a few more names to add.

* * *

It was close enough to five for Katie to decide to leave the office. She didn't know if she'd ever had a day where she'd accomplished so little. At least work wise. She'd spent most of the afternoon texting with Ken, Tony, and Hannah. Mildred didn't have a mobile phone, which was probably for the best.

Ken and Tony took turns talking her out of confronting Ian Trembley at work, advice that she'd followed, sort of. She'd manufactured several reasons to stop by Ian's desk and ask him a series of innocuous questions, looking for anything she could use in her presentation to Lieutenant Crozier. Unfortunately, the only thing close to an admission of guilt was Ian's insanely good mood. And for some reason, Lieutenant Crozier never got around to talking to her. Connor's dad made the rounds and seemed to have spoken to everyone else, but her. What was the deal?

After powering down her desktop, she stopped by Neal's office before reaching the front door. She poked her head in.

"You doing okay?"

"I've been better." He was staring at his monitor, but she could tell it was just that. Staring. He took off his glasses and rubbed his eyes. "This wasn't the day I had planned."

"This wasn't the day any of us had planned. Did Lieutenant Crozier say anything informative before he left?"

Neal shook his head. "Nothing. I wonder why he bothered. He couldn't have been here more than a couple of hours. He talked to me and Marjorie, a few people on the dock, and we gave him a tour. He barely touched Elena's cube, which isn't a surprise. It wasn't like she left anything there."

"Did he talk to Ian?"

"Why would he talk to Ian?"

"I'm just asking."

He narrowed his eyes. "You're never 'just asking.'"

"I just think it's weird that he immediately zoomed in on my dad and isn't interested in anyone else who could have done this."

"Who else did you have in mind?"

She spread her arms and shrugged.

"No," Neal said, leaning in.

"Maybe."

Neal's face paled. "Do you think Ian could've done this?"

She shrugged. "I don't know. But he and Elena had a history. I can't think of anyone she argued with more than him. I just think that's worthy of a few questions. That's all."

Neal raised his hands but looked down at his desk. "At least the lieutenant is out of our hair. That's all I care about for now."

He may be gone, but it's not over, she wanted to say. *Far from it.*

* * *

Katie checked her reflection in the Cedar Bay police station door before opening it. Despite having lived here most of her life and having dated Lieutenant Crozier's son for four years, she'd never stepped foot into the building.

She took a deep breath and held it for four seconds.

"Here goes nothing." She opened the door and . . . she stepped right into it. "Ouch."

As luck would have it, an impossibly young police officer was leaving just then. He held the door open for her. "You okay, ma'am?"

Ma'am? "I'm fine. Nothing hurt but my pride."

"Can I help you with something?"

"I'm here to see Lieutenant Crozier."

"Is he expecting you?"

She shook her head. "I don't think so."

"I'll take you to him."

"Thank you."

As they walked through the station, she couldn't help staring at the young man, wondering if he was old enough to shave, let alone protect the Cedar Bay community.

They stopped in front of an office with a frosted glass window and a plate making it clear whose office it was. Lieutenant Daniel Crozier.

The young man sporting rimless Warby Parker glasses—his badge said *Tallon*—waited for Lieutenant Crozier to look up from his phone call before making a sound. When the lieutenant finally did, he failed to hide his displeasure at seeing Katie waiting in front him.

"I'll call you back," he said and then hung up.

"What can I do for you, Miss Chambers?"

She pulled out her list. "The question is, 'What can I do for you?' And the answer is, a lot."

Officer Tallon's head snapped up, but Lieutenant Crozier dismissed him with a glare and offered Katie a seat.

"I assume this is about the Elena Larsson investigation."

"Good guess," she said before sitting down. She pulled her list out of her bag. "My crew and I have been working on a suspect list." She handed it to him.

"Your crew?" he said, putting on his reading glasses and studying the paper.

"Yes. The South Island Jigsaw Crew. My mom started it years ago. We meet every Sunday to review puzzles and grade them for the company. Every Sunday except when the Seahawks have a night game."

"Oh," he said with a nod, not looking up from the list. "I'm familiar with that."

"I do have one question."

He looked up.

"I'm curious why you didn't ask me anything today."

He folded the list, set it down, and rested his arms on his desk. "We spoke last night, and I spoke with your father at length this morning."

"Have you learned anything interesting so far?"

"We don't comment on an ongoing investigation."

"Do you have any questions regarding our list?"

He glanced down and shook his head.

"Are you looking into any of those people?"

"Like I said—"

"You don't comment on an ongoing investigation."

"Correct, but we do appreciate whenever a citizen takes the initiative to help us, so your crew's efforts are greatly appreciated."

"But you're not going to do anything with it."

His nostrils flared. "I didn't say that. If we find something useful, we run it all the way down. I'm pretty confident that we have our man."

"If you have your man."

He cleared his throat. "If you have something to say, Miss Chambers, please say it. I appreciate candor."

Someone coughed behind her and she turned, only to find her father being escorted across the room by two uniformed officers, his hands cuffed behind his back.

Tears pressed behind her eyes. She didn't want to fall apart, not here. Not in front of Lieutenant Crozier, but she could feel that she was losing that battle. But when the lieutenant tightened his scowl, that was the last straw. The tears started to flow.

"I'm sorry you had to see that, miss."

"It's Katie, Lieutenant. Not miss. It's Katie Chambers! You've known me my whole life. You've known my dad your whole life. Why are you treating me like a stranger? Why aren't you taking anything I'm saying seriously?" She went on from there, accusing him of every horrible thing in the book. It was a tantrum for the ages.

He must've been clenching his jaw super tight because the veins popped out of his neck. It didn't matter. He could get as mad as all get-out for all she cared. Because she'd decided right then and there.

She was going to lead her own investigation, whether he liked it or not.

Chapter Seven

When Katie went outside, it was like the whole world had changed. The air felt colder. The clouds had grown thicker. It looked like it could rain at any minute, not that this was new. In truth, the thing—or the person—that had changed the most was her.

She looked back at the door, her eyes blazing with anger and her hands balled into fists. They wouldn't let her see her dad, let alone talk to him. Even his impeccably dressed attorney, Carlton McQuire, Esquire, barely gave her the time of day. "I'll take care of it from here. I'll let you know if I need your help with the bail bond." With that he turned on his well-oiled heel and left her in the dust, completing her transformation.

Gone was the good little girl who did what she was told, who followed the rules. Well, she didn't always follow the rules, but she'd always followed the big ones. No more.

Her car was back at the office but she headed in the other direction, toward the one place she'd avoided since returning to Cedar Bay. The fire station. It was only a block away from the police station, on the other side of Kinder Drive.

Clutching her bag to her chest, she marched into the wind, ignoring the voice in her head screaming for her to turn around. She ignored it because this was no brush fire. This was no cat in the tree. This was her dad, he was in trouble, and she was going to get help from the last person on earth she wanted to see.

Both garage doors were open, revealing two shiny red fire engines. Since he had an in with the old fire chief through his dad, she and Connor used to ride the trucks when they were kids when there wasn't much happening, which was pretty much all the time. Those were only a few of her fond memories that Connor hadn't ruined.

A firefighter leaned against the engine on the right, smoking a cigarette. Another guy she'd gone to school with. Austin Xu.

Austin smiled and flicked the cigarette away. The fire hazard he'd just created was not lost on her.

"Crozier!" he hollered with folded arms. "You've got a guest!"

Connor approached from behind a fire engine, jamming his hands into his pockets. "I take it this is about our dads."

"Have you talked to yours?"

He threw her a quick shrug. "A little. He doesn't say much, but I can read between the lines."

"Well?"

He sucked in a breath and looked away.

Her chest tightened. She mustered the courage to ask him, "Do you think my father did it?"

He sighed, folded his arms, and stared at the ground. After way too many beats, he shook his head. "It doesn't sound like your dad, but men sometimes do strange things when a woman's involved." He sheepishly peered up at her. "Case and point."

"This isn't about you and me. This is about him. It's about your father's obstinance."

Connor scoffed, "I can't argue with that." He lifted his head and let his stare bore into her eyes. He hadn't done that in years. "What do you want, Kate? Just come out and say it."

"Okay," she said, her head damp, again. Her bag clutched against her chest, again. Her heart writhing in turmoil over Connor Crozier. Again. "I need your help."

"My help doing what?"

"You know."

He shook his head. "Say the words, Kate."

"Fine. I need you to help me prove that my dad is innocent, and your dad is wrong."

"See? That wasn't so hard, was it? You just forgot one word."

"And what word is that?"

"Please."

Chapter Eight

With all the craziness that'd gone on over the past forty-eight hours, Katie had completely forgotten that it was Wednesday. Normally, she'd have dinner with Dad, someplace special on Wednesdays, maybe even ferry over to Mukilteo and have dinner at Ivar's Mukilteo Landing. Tonight, however, it was just her and Whimsy, and Whimsy was in a mood. Then again, so was she.

It was after six o'clock, and the clouds made it darker than it should've been. She brought Whimsy's food dish up to the kitchen table so she wouldn't feel so lonely as she ate her reheated chicken noodle soup.

Being alone probably wasn't the best idea, but she didn't want to bother anyone. Connor had offered to come by, but as the words were leaving his mouth, she could tell he didn't mean it. Or if he did, he didn't really want to. Or if she was completely wrong about his offer, she probably hadn't been as receptive as she should've been.

Whimsy licked his dish clean and then spread out on the table, surrounding her bowl. Katie's soup was half-eaten, her stomach too twisted to accept another drop.

Katie brought out her iPad and even though she'd relinquished her list to Lieutenant Crozier, it wasn't like she hadn't memorized all of the names.

Ian Trembley.

Harold Beck.

Mystery Married Man.

Dad.

She studied the names. Secretly, she hoped it was Harold Beck because he'd been such a jerk when she ran into him at the toy distributor conference, but down deep it didn't matter. All she really needed to do was find a suspect who raised enough reasonable doubt for Lieutenant Crozier to let Dad go. At least, that's what television and those mysteries she liked to read had taught her.

Suddenly there was a sharp rap on the door, so forceful she jumped in her chair. Even Whimsy was curious enough to turn his head toward the door, if not lift it.

She had half a mind to ignore it. She didn't want to talk with anyone, but that wasn't her style and maybe it was important.

"Just a minute." She got up and pulled the front window's drapes aside but didn't spot a car. Maybe it was a prank. She hoped so. But then she peered through the peephole and let out a pent-up breath.

"Hey," she said, opening the door.

It was Hannah. "I hope you don't mind that I put my bike on the porch."

"You can bring it in the house, if you'd like."

"Nah." Hannah reached her arms out for a hug and Katie pulled her in. "Something tells me you could use one of these."

"You have no idea." She stepped back to allow the teen in. "Are your parents okay with you visiting the house of a suspected killer? I'm sorry, I mean a person of interest?"

"They think this whole thing is a bunch of crap." Hannah went to the table and scratched Whimsy behind his ears. "That said, they've heard some things."

Katie gestured for her to take a seat at the kitchen table, but before she even sat down, there was another knock on the door. Katie frowned and Hannah shrugged.

"Don't ask me," Hannah said, clearly lying.

"Surprise!" It was Tony and Mildred on the doorstep, posing as if they'd just won an Olympic gold medal.

"Hey guys, come on in. Sorry, but Hannah beat you here by a minute."

"We brought food!" Mildred proudly yelled, clinging to her walker.

"The missus made a lasagna," Tony said, picking up a carrying case. "Before my mom passed, she taught my wife the recipe, so it's pretty darn good, even by my standards, which as you know, when it comes to food, are insanely high."

"Oh, yum," Katie said. "I've got a spatula in the drawer next to the fridge we can use to serve it."

"No need," Tony said, holding up the case. "It's a turnkey operation. It just needs a little heat."

Katie turned to Hannah and said, "I guess we should move to the living room until everyone else arrives." Hannah picked up Whimsy and headed toward the couch.

Katie was about to offer the three something to drink when there was another knock on the door.

"Come in, Ken," Katie said.

He entered with a fistful of refreshments. "How'd you know it was me?"

"Process of elimination," Katie said, waving her hand across the room.

"I brought some Diet Coke, some Fresca, and some IPA." He turned to Hannah. "That's not for you, young lady."

She shrugged. "Fresca works."

Katie stood in the middle of the house, watching her friends take over. Ken taking over the fridge. Tony manning the stove. Hannah babysitting Whimsy and Mildred knitting away while doing her best to offer moral support. It was kind and it was sweet, and Katie would've been brought to tears with gratitude if it weren't for one thing.

They were following the exact same script they'd followed after Mom died, right down to the IPA. The only thing—or person—missing was Dad, and that made it all the worse.

After managing the stove for the lasagna, Tony came up and gave her a hug.

"How'd it go with Connor?"

She didn't bother asking him how he knew she'd spoken to Connor. "He agreed to help."

"We're gonna need it," Ken said.

"What do you mean?"

He put his hands on his wide hips. "I'm hearing stuff."

"What kind of stuff?"

Tony answered instead. "Probably the same stuff I'm hearing."

"Me too," Hannah added.

"You too?"

"Well, my parents. They shared some things."

"About my dad?"

"About Elena," Mildred said in the lowest voice she could possibly muster.

"You should sit down," Ken said.

The five of them surrounded the wooden coffee table. Hannah, Whimsy, and Ken on the couch. Tony in the stuffed chair at one end, with Mildred sitting in her walker to his right and Katie in the stuffed chair at the other end.

"Who wants to go first?" Tony said.

Ken raised a hand. "I'll go first." He took a breath and blew it out. "Word is that Elena was pregnant."

"Pregnant?"

All four heads nodded.

"That's why my folks heard."

"So it's the mystery married man." Katie held up her iPad. "Number three on my list."

The others shot uncomfortable glances among them.

"What?"

It was Ken's turn. "Your dad went with her to the ob-gyn."

"He what?"

But no one answered.

She sank in her chair and rested her hands on her thighs. Her head swimming with the implications. "You don't think . . ." But she couldn't bring herself to finish the question, and no one felt the urge to answer.

She sat up. "So you do think?"

Tony raised both hands. "We don't think anything. We're just gathering data."

"And working the problem," Hannah said.

"Right," Ken said. "For the moment, we're dealing with rumors and speculation, and our job is to convert them into facts and motives and do everything we can to find Elena's killer."

Tony, Mildred, and Hannah nodded. Katie joined them, as did the timer from the kitchen.

She began to stand up, but Tony motioned for her to stay.

"I got this. You sit. Relax. Take your mind off things." Then he took everyone's drink order.

She didn't make the point that talking about this was hardly taking her mind off things, but she did appreciate the sentiment.

While Tony searched her kitchen for plates and utensils, the rest of the crew continued their discussion.

Katie said, "Ken raises a good point. It's not enough to find a suspect. We also have to determine their motive." She opened her iPad to her list and added a column. "Let's start with Ian. I think his motive is straightforward. Professional jealously. He's been the top puzzle design dog for years, but Elena's been nipping at his heels."

"Except she hasn't, from what I hear," Hannah said.

Katie cocked her head. "Do your parents tell you everything?"

Hannah grinned. "Now that I'm solving mysteries? You bet."

"Which leads us to Harold Beck."

Ken looked over her shoulder toward the kitchen and nodded. He got up and joined Tony, the two of them returning with plates of lasagna and salad.

"I hope you don't mind eating in the living room," Tony said. "The missus would have me hogtied if I did this at our house."

Katie shook her head. "Dad and I do it all the time. I like it this way, frankly."

Tony fetched everyone their respective drink orders and returned to his seat. "Harold Beck," he said, sitting down. Katie shared the 411 on that piece of work.

"His motive is similar to Ian's," Ken said. "Professional jealousy?"

Hannah shook her head. "Not really. This dude's problem seems more intense than that. He's pissed, not jealous. It's about the stealing."

"Good point," Katie said. "Revenge, then."

The others nodded.

"Jealousy. Revenge. That leaves our mysterious married man."

"If she was pregnant, a married man might go to any lengths to keep her from having that baby."

"If he's a big jerk," Mildred said.

Katie nodded. "Too true. But if they were having an affair, it could be anything related to that. Maybe Elena threatened to tell his wife. Maybe the rumors were hitting too close to home."

"Either way," Ken said, "this guy has to be at the top of our list, but how do we go about finding out who he is?"

Katie looked at the others and said, "There's one person I can ask."

* * *

The next morning, work was exceptionally difficult for Katie. Word had gotten out about her father's arrest and some people seemed to be transferring his perceived guilt onto her. As a result, her productivity plunged from poor to nearly nonexistent overnight.

She drifted through meetings, zoned out talking on the phone, and walked the factory with no goal in sight. Given the turn of the emotional tide, she found it easier—read, with less guilt—to focus her energies on the crew's new mission. Operation Free Dad.

If she were being honest with herself, the crew had fallen short of their goal last night. They didn't uncover the motive of one suspect, her dad. None of them said it, but you could see it cooking behind their eyes, the faint possibility that her dad had gotten Elena pregnant and then killed her. But it was impossible, absolutely impossible. They knew it and so did she, if they stopped thinking of Dad as a puzzle and more as a person. That said, she couldn't come up with a motive for him. If she couldn't, how could Lieutenant Crozier? All signs pointed to Dad helping Elena, not wanting to hurt her, even if he was being elusive about some of the details.

Thankfully, she only had one more morning meeting to endure before lunch, before pseudo-accidentally running into Connor. The daily design meeting. It'd been canceled yesterday, for obvious reasons, so the team had a lot of catching up to do.

It was eleven o'clock. She was the last one to enter the Rainier Conference Room, a room with wood paneling and a decade-old conference table that was more often referred to as the Time Warp Room. Neal's dad had decorated it in the seventies, having curated various Whidbey Island knick-knacks, ranging from fine wood carvings from the sixties to seashells from both Double Bluff Beach and Penn Cove that Neal and his father had gathered when Neal was a kid. Taped to the wall at the far end of the room, a watercolor poster showed a big red *S* and *Seattle* written in the letter along with the logo for the Seattle Metropolitans, Seattle's first professional sports team and the first American team to win the Stanley Cup.

Katie parked herself along the far side of the table, along the wall with the blinds. The overhead lights were turned off, and the blinds were closed halfway. Just enough to allow light into the room but dark enough to see the screen that showed the three people working virtually from home.

What made this meeting different from the other meetings was the presence of Ian. Until now, he'd somehow managed to dodge her. Every time she'd found an excuse to pass his cubicle—which happened so often people probably thought she had a bladder problem—he was nowhere to be found. She was tempted to ask Neal about it but didn't want to show her hand and reveal that her workday mostly consisted of trying to talk to the person she considered her number one suspect.

Another thing that made this meeting different was that it was her meeting. She was in charge of it, despite being wholly unprepared. Emotionally and professionally.

"Okay," she said, laying her legal pad to the right, setting her pen on top of it, and propping her iPad up in front of her. She logged in and tapped the screen until she reached her status sheet, sharing her screen for the virtual attendees. "Let's start with Project Onyx. Obviously, there are some concerns there, given what's transpired over the past few days."

"Are we going to address the elephant in the room?"

The voice came from the speaker that sat between them. She looked up at the large screen plastered across the far wall. Todd Marchand, the type of guy you preferred working from home given his unpleasant disposition, had his digital hand raised.

"Which elephant is that, Todd?" she asked.

The three others in the room, including Ian, threw an "Are you kidding me?" look her way.

"What? We can't use the current design so, obviously, we need a new one."

"Because Elena stole it," Todd said. "But that's not what I'm talking about."

She looked at Todd in the top right corner of the screen and then back at Ian, who wore a satisfyingly smug expression on his face. He and Todd got along. In fact, Ian might've been the only person in the whole company who got along with Todd. It made her wonder if Todd's surly line of questioning was actually Ian's, and he was using Todd as his surrogate.

"Anything you'd like to add, Ian?"

"No, siree," he said with a wide swing of his head.

"It seems like you do."

He shrugged. "Todd brought it up. Not me."

"Yeah," Todd said, growing even more indignant. "And if she stole Onyx, what else did she steal? And more importantly, who'd she steal it from? Again, not my point. My point is—"

"I hear you," she said, tugging on her earring. Somehow the team only knew half the design-stealing story. That the designs were stolen but not from whom, which was probably for the best.

"You know," she said, "Todd raises an interesting issue." She picked up her pen and tapped it against her chin before facing Ian. "Where were you Monday night?"

His eyes widened. "Excuse me?"

"Katie, I meant your dad," Todd said. "I wanted to talk about your dad."

She ignored Todd, holding her gaze on Ian. On the inside, she was trembling. She'd never confronted anyone at work like this, especially someone with as much seniority as Ian. She may have been his boss, but she didn't have his influence.

Nonetheless, she couldn't let that stop her. One mental image of Dad wearing those cuffs was all it took.

"I was wondering if you were here, you know, in the building, working on some new designs."

"You think I helped her steal the designs?"

"No, not at all. I'm—"

"Wait. You think—"

"Of course not. I'm just trying to determine where you *were*. I mean, if you were here, in the office. Working. The cameras could confirm that. And if that's the case, that could really bail us out. You know . . . with the new designs."

Ian eyes blazed with hatred. He knew what she was doing.

"I was home. Checking flights for this year's national convention, if you really must know."

She couldn't believe he'd said it. It was almost an admission of guilt. "What makes you think you'll be going to the convention this year?"

He pushed back from the conference table. "What are you playing at, Katie?"

"What I'm playing at is . . . is . . . is that we need a new design. Heck, we need several new designs. Fast. Preferably, one that isn't stolen."

And you, my friend, have all the motive in the world and an alibi that I could drive a truck through.

Todd chimed in. "So, are we going to talk about Elena being a thief or not?"

Katie shook her head. "No, Todd. We aren't."

"And why not?"

"Because according to Lieutenant Crozier, we can't comment on an ongoing investigation."

Chapter Nine

At half past noon, Katie was on her way to JJ's when a lump formed in her throat as she realized she was only going to order for one. She did her best not to look at the library as she passed it. She couldn't bear the thought of what Dad must be going through.

But she would find out later in the day.

Adding insult to injury, the weather had turned perfect. The sun was directly overhead and not a cloud in the sky. According to the bank clock on the corner, the temperature was a wonderful sixty degrees. Or as Dad called it, sweater weather.

Inside, JJ's was more crowded than usual and given the number of heads that swiveled in her direction, the reason hit her quite quickly. The only saving grace was that no one actually said anything to her, especially a reporter, which would've really teed her off.

As she approached the counter, JJ mournfully reached behind himself and grabbed one of the two sacks sitting on the counter. And one of the Diet Cokes.

She reached into her purse for her credit card, but JJ waved her off.

"This one's on the house, honey."

"That's not necessary."

"Yeah, it is. And this one?" He jerked a thumb over his shoulder. "Will be ready when your dad is."

She gulped hard, swallowing an ocean of tears that were ready to flow. Her encounter with Ian and Todd had left her so calloused, she hadn't prepared herself for the kindness that JJ was giving.

Feeling the room's eyes on her, she hesitated before turning around. But then a hand attached to a very strong forearm reached in, grabbing the sack.

"I'll carry this for you, if you don't mind."

She nodded, losing her emotional battle as two tears trekked down her cheeks.

Like a bodyguard, Connor led her out of the restaurant. The previously peering eyes found something else to focus on, lest they endure the wrath of one of Cedar Bay's most popular first responders.

"Thank you," she said outside on the sidewalk. "I don't know how much longer I can take this."

"Yes you do."

She recoiled. "What's that supposed to mean?"

"It means that you'll be able to take it for however long it takes."

"How long what takes?"

"However long it takes to find Elena Larsson's killer and exonerate your dad."

She sighed. "What makes you so sure?"

"Simple. You don't have a choice."

They walked in silence toward the fire station. They'd always had the ability to communicate without speaking; he knew she needed a place to eat, and she knew the only option that wouldn't break her was the station, where he could control the environment, assuming no alarms sounded.

They walked in a side door of the brick building, straight to the station's dining area.

"Where is everybody?" she asked.

"They've already eaten."

"So they just disappear?"

He sent her a supportive smile. "They do if I ask nicely."

Instead of eating inside, they went out back, and as soon as Katie stepped outside, her jaw fell. The fire station had a better view of the sound than Cynthia's. The backyard was a mesa rising above the other lots, bordered by cedars with nothing but beautiful blue water straight ahead. A seagull raced overhead toward the water, and she watched it until her gaze landed on two sailboats racing across.

"Incredible," she said.

"Best-kept secret in Cedar Bay." He gestured toward one of the small wooden picnic benches near the edge. Of course, it had the best view of all.

After taking a seat, she unpacked her lunch and sipped her Diet Coke. "Want half a sandwich?" she said, offering it, a breeze blowing her hair in front of her face.

He patted his stomach. "Like I said. We already ate."

Despite the never-ending twists of her stomach, she was surprised how hungry she was. She pulled her hair behind her ear and practically guzzled her broccoli cheese soup from the bowl and wolfed down half her turkey sandwich in three bites.

"Don't forget to chew," Connor teased.

"Nice," she said.

He folded his hands in front of himself on the table. "I have some news."

"Oh?"

He nodded. "I've discovered the identity of the mysterious married man."

"Get out."

"Get in."

"What?"

"Never mind," he said with a wave. "It's some guy from the mainland."

Her shoulders sank. "That narrows it down."

"It does if you have a name."

She braced herself for the answer.

"Ever heard of a guy named Harold Beck?"

She dropped the last bite of her sandwich. Lettuce and turkey flew.

"You're not serious," she said.

"Why would I make that up?"

"Seriously? Harold Beck is the last person Elena would be involved with. He hated her guts. He was the one who accused her of stealing designs from Tacoma Toys."

"That's the guy. I got it confirmed by two different, independent sources."

"How?"

"A man never tells."

She lightly punched his arm. "This man always tells. So spill."

"Let's just say there's a fraternity among firefighters. I douse your flame, you douse mine. Anyhow, that's not all."

"Please don't tell me this has to do with my dad."

"This has nothing to do with your dad. It has everything to do with Elena breaking up with Harold on Sunday night."

Katie leaned back in her chair. "Wait," she said, her head snapping to face him. "That's the night she begged off of going to Cynthia's. I thought it was strange at the time, but that must've been why. She already had plans to break up with him."

She gobbled the last bit of her sandwich and washed it down just as quickly.

"This is wonderful," she said, quickly sweeping the crumbs from the table and into her hand. "I don't know how to thank you." She stood and tossed her trash away.

"Where are you going?"

"*We're* going to tell your dad so he can set my dad free."

He held a hand out. "Woah, woah, woah. Slow down."

"Why? You just said it yourself. He's the guy. He has motive. Revenge. He has opportunity, because . . . I don't know. Because he did. Anyhow, that's enough for reasonable doubt."

She tried to hurry past him, but he caught her around the waist. She looked into his eyes and for the tiniest moment, she forgot that ten years had passed.

"Please let me go." She pulled away and headed for the door.

"It's not enough, Katie."

That stopped her cold. "You called me Katie."

"It was the only way to get your attention."

She drew in a few calming breaths. As her pulse slowed, she realized he was right. It wasn't enough. It wasn't even close to enough. It wasn't even more than what she had on Ian Trembley. But it did convince her of one thing.

They were making progress. And she had hope.

* * *

Back at the office, Katie breezed through the aisles like she was walking on air. Harold Beck. He was the guy. She knew it. All she had to do was convince Lieutenant Crozier, and Dad would be off the hook and life could return to normal.

She sat down and started a group text with the crew, bringing them up to speed and telling them the good news.

Is Connor in the crew now? Hannah asked.

That's not the point.

It sounds like he's in the crew, Tony wrote.

Focus, people. I think we have our man.

It sounds like you have your man, Hannah wrote.

Katie gripped her phone tighter and growled.

I gotta go, she typed and then put her phone away.

Before digging into work, she placed a call to Carlton McQuire, Dad's attorney who was, unsurprisingly, out of the office. The last thing she'd heard was that a bail hearing was supposed to be later today, but it wasn't set in stone. When she asked McQuire's assistant what was happening, the woman with the deep voice said, "Miss Chambers, you can be certain that Mr. McQuire is doing everything within your rights and his power to make sure you father receives the justice that he deserves."

Which Katie interpreted as code for "I have no idea, you'll have to ask him."

"Is the bail hearing still happening today?"

The woman didn't answer.

"Hello?"

"Patience, my dear. I'm checking Mr. McQuire's calendar, which I'm sure you can imagine is simply chaotic."

More silence.

"I'm sorry, I don't see anything about a bail hearing today."

Katie thanked the woman and hung up.

Putting her phone away, she tried to focus on work but wasn't getting far. Suddenly, an email notification popped up on her screen.

Subject: Fw: Lousy Puzzles

Thought you should see this. I already forwarded to Neal.

It was from Susan Zhang in marketing. Susan was the wizard with website design, search engine optimization, email marketing campaigns, landing pages, and all that stuff that Katie was happy someone else did. Susan was also an avid reader of mysteries, thrillers, and the occasional rom-com who depended on Dad for ideas to increase her to-be-read pile.

Katie scrolled down and found an all-caps, no paragraphs, stream of consciousness rant about CBP's crappy puzzles and their even crappier designs and if the company had any brains they'd fire the bubble-headed beatnik in charge of them.

Katie scratched her chin and read the email again, slowly shaking her head. "Bubble-headed beatnik" had to mean Elena, who loved her late-sixties sartorial style. The email could've been something, or it was simply a prank. The bad news was that the internet was filled with hateful people who liked nothing more than tearing things down. Still, it—

"Everything okay?"

She nearly jumped out of her chair. She quickly closed the email and looked up to find Marjorie towering over her.

"Sorry. You scared me. And yes, everything is fine."

"Just checking. Since Elena's death and with all of these rumors flying, it hasn't exactly been easy for anyone around here. Most of all you, I would suspect."

"Good choice of words."

"I'm not following."

"Suspect."

"I'm still not following."

"It's nothing," she lied. "Is there anything I can help you with?"

"Actually, there is. Mind if I sit?"

Katie nodded.

Marjorie took the seat across from Katie's desk. "Now," she said, showing her palms, "I don't want you to freak out, but we're going to have some company soon."

"Company as in a customer, or company as in Lieutenant Crozier again?"

Marjorie shook her head. "Neither. Company as in a competitor."

Katie's chest tightened. She set her phone on her desk. "Which competitor?"

"Remember way back when I told you not to freak out?"

"It was thirty seconds ago."

"Seems like an eternity because you look like you're going to freak out."

"I promise I won't."

"Anyhow. You remember Harold Beck, correct? I believe you met him at the show."

Katie cocked her head. "Please don't tell me."

"Remember your promise."

"That was before—"

But shouting from the direction of Neal's office interrupted her.

Everybody's head popped up, including hers and Marjorie's. Neal's door slammed.

"I thought I was the one who wasn't supposed to freak out."

Marjorie was staring at Neal's office and biting the inside of her cheek when she said, "You stay here."

Not on your life, Katie thought.

The two women hurried toward Neal's closed door. When they got there, Marjorie turned and shot Katie a look as if to say, *I thought I told you to stay?* Katie turned and pretended to give someone the same look behind her. Marjorie wasn't amused.

On the other side of the Neal's door, two men were shouting, although Katie couldn't make out the words. Marjorie grabbed the doorknob but didn't twist it.

"What are you waiting for?" Katie asked.

"A break in the action."

Katie reached down, turned the knob herself, and pushed open the door. The two men, Neal and Harold Beck, froze as they stared in her direction.

"How come I wasn't invited to this party?"

"You!" Beck said, jabbing a finger toward her. "You're the one from the show." He faced Neal. "She was the one I talked to. I tried to explain—"

"Tried to explain what?" Katie was incredulous. It took all the self-control she had not to step forward and kick this clown—the man she thought murdered Elena, the scumbag who sent her father to jail—right in the groin. Instead, through a clenched jaw and with a calm voice, she said, "You yelled and screamed at me like a madman—just like you're yelling now—about how we were a bunch of thieves. How we'd stolen your designs. You name it, you accused us of it."

He ran a haggard hand through what was left of his thinning hair. "That was supposed to be confidential."

"Confidential? People in Spokane were telling you to keep it down."

Katie pushed her way into the office with Marjorie on her heels.

Beck got in her face and raised a finger to her nose. "It's all your fault. You're the one who got her killed."

"Me? What are you talking about?" Katie looked around him, at Neal. "He's the guy, Neal. He's the guy who killed Elena. They were having an affair. He was feeding her designs. She got pregnant and then, the other night, he followed her to the library, waited until she got outside, and . . ."

Beck's eyes widened and his jaw dropped.

"Killed her. An innocent man would say that I'm wrong." She reached into her pocket for her phone, which, unfortunately was still at her desk. "Neal, can I borrow your phone? I need to call Lieutenant Crozier and have him come here and arrest this pig."

"Now, wait just a minute," Beck said, raising a finger. "She wasn't . . . I didn't." With a look of terror, he turned to Neal. "What is this crazy woman talking about?"

Neal bit his lower lip and put his hands on his hips. He shook his head. "I wish I knew."

Beck backpedaled and Katie filled his relinquished space. "Admit it. You were having an affair with Elena Larsson." She grabbed his left hand and pointed toward the wedding ring. "Did your wife know?"

"Katie, that's enough," Neal said.

"He did it, Neal. Isn't it obvious?"

"He was just here complaining about Elena stealing his designs."

"He's deflecting. Isn't it obvious? He knows we're onto him, so he comes here to point the finger at Elena so we won't look in his direction." To Beck, she said, "I'm not falling for it."

"You . . ." But it was almost as if she could see the wind leaving his sails. The once pompous, obnoxious man was deflating before her eyes. "It's true," he said, barely above a whisper.

Katie was too stunned to speak. She turned to Neal and Marjorie, who were just as wide-eyed as she probably looked.

After an uncomfortable silence, words began to tumble out of her mouth. "I'll . . . um . . . we'll . . . um call Lieutenant Crozier. Do you want to wait right here?"

Beck gestured to one of the chairs facing Neal's desk. "Do you mind?"

"Be my guest, I guess."

Beck sat and rested his elbows on his knees. "I suppose it's gonna get out, especially if Ms. Nosy here knows." He stared at his feet. "It's true. Elena and I had a relationship."

"You mean affair."

He looked up. "Yeah, fine. If that's what you want to call it. But I loved her. That's why I was helping her with her designs."

"You mean feeding her your designs and then accusing us of stealing them."

He sighed. "My company did some recon and got ahold of your latest work, the stuff coming out in a month. They recognized it right away and this morning, they threatened to fire whoever did it. So, yes, I was deflecting. I thought if I could convince you that it was Elena who stole our designs and not the other way around, I might be able to save my job."

"What about the baby?" Majorie asked in horror.

He shook his head. "There was no baby. False alarm, but that did put a lot of things in motion."

"Like murdering her," Katie added.

"No," he said, having the audacity to appear offended. "More like marrying her." He pulled a small box out of his pocket and popped it open. "I was planning to propose this weekend."

"What about your wife?" Neal asked, finally deciding to join the conversation.

"It was only a matter of time. The only thing left for us to do is file the papers, and at this point, we'll probably flip a coin as to which one of us does it first."

"If you were getting a divorce, why did you murder Elena?" Katie asked.

He leaned back, shock written across face. "Are you kidding? I didn't murder Elena. In fact, I wasn't anywhere near Cedar Bay that night. I was alone, in Kirkland. I arrived early for the show."

"Did anyone see you?"

"Katie," Neal admonished.

But Beck was squirming in his chair. She wanted to go in for the kill and let this guy have it, but Neal's face said otherwise.

An awkward silence hung among the four of them, until Beck finally broke it.

"I didn't do it, Miss Chambers. But if I ever get my hands on who did, he'll wish he was never born."

She couldn't tell if he was speaking the truth or putting on one helluva performance.

Chapter Ten

That night shortly before six thirty, the puzzlers met at Cynthia's at Katie's request. She was the first to arrive. Violet spotted her from across the restaurant and met Katie almost as soon as she entered the building and threw her arms around Katie and squeezed.

"What are you doing here?" Katie asked.

"Daniela called in sick," Violet said, letting go. "And I could use a few extra bucks." She cast a mournful look. "I am so sorry you and Jim are going through this."

"It's a nightmare," Katie said, trying not to get too emotional.

"I don't see what your father ever saw in that woman."

"What woman?"

"That Larsson woman. I don't think that means he killed her, but if the rumors are true . . ."

Katie froze. "I don't know what you've been hearing, but you know darn well that's not true."

Violet looked both ways like she was about to race through a stop sign. "I know it's not my place to tell you this, but he hasn't been the same since your mom died. There are days when he would come in for his usual breakfast, and it was like talking to a stranger. I'm sorry."

Katie found herself getting upset, but she wasn't sure if it was directed at her dad or at Violet for telling her this.

Violet didn't look too pleased, either. She almost looked as mad as Katie. Especially the way she said, "I like Jim, but I think he started making some bad decisions." She paused and smiled. "Look, I hope for his and your sake, it is just a misunderstanding, and Lieutenant Crozier uncovers the truth. Honestly, even though he was struggling, I can't believe he would ever harm someone, let alone kill them."

Katie nodded, wondering if she'd missed the signs of how much her dad was really struggling.

"If there's anything I can do, you just let me know. Anything that happens in this town eventually gets discussed here. Consider me a part of your crew."

"I appreciate that, Vi."

Violet smiled and set a gentle hand on Katie's shoulder. "Do you want your normal table? It's Thursday night, so it's not that crowded. You can sit pretty much anywhere you'd like."

"Anywhere we can have some privacy would be great."

"I've got a table in the back with nobody for miles."

"That'd be fine."

Katie took a seat against the far wall, doing her best to shake off Violet's comments. Had her dad not been honest with her when she'd talked to him on the phone, telling her he was fine? She never regretted for a second moving back home, but what else was he hiding from her? She would take it up with him in the morning, the earliest she was allowed to visit him.

Hannah was the first to arrive, full of youth and energy. She gave Katie a hug before taking a seat across from her.

"I heard you had a run-in with that Beck guy."

"Do your parents have bugs planted everywhere in town?"

"What can I say?" She shrugged. "People talk."

Violet returned with everyone's drink orders, even the three who hadn't arrived yet. Both Katie and Hannah thanked her.

"Oh," Hannah said, "Tony and Mildred were pulling in when I walked in. No sign of Ken yet."

Katie shook her head. "Shouldn't you be at a party? Or a basketball game? Or something with your friends?"

"And miss this?" Hannah sipped her Pepsi. "This stuff is way more interesting than high school."

Katie lowered her voice. "I don't know if Harold Beck did it, but if he didn't, that only leaves us with Ian Trembley."

"I thought you were pretty confident about him."

"I was positive about Harold, so let's just say my confidence is a little shaken."

Tony and Mildred slowly made their way toward the table.

"You couldn't have found someplace closer to the door?" Mildred shouted loud enough for the cooks in the kitchen to hear.

Hannah nearly spit her Pepsi and Katie tried her hardest not to laugh. When Tony finally got Mildred seated, Katie explained herself.

"As Violet just reminded me, everything that happens in this town is discussed in here and then passed on like currency. I'd like for that not to happen with our conversation."

"So you're saying we need to be quiet," Mildred said, again loud enough for the cooks to hear her.

Katie sucked in a breath and counted to four. "Yes," she said as she exhaled.

"Sorry, team," Ken said, wringing his hands. "Nature called."

"That happens a lot at our age," Tony added.

With all five of them seated around the table, Katie brought everyone up to speed regarding Harold Beck.

"Are you sure he's telling the truth?" Tony asked.

She shrugged. "I don't know. I couldn't tell, and my boss was less than happy that I accused the guy in his office. Probably worried about getting sued."

"Given that Beck confessed to helping Elena with her designs," Ken said, "I don't think Neal has anything to worry about."

Mildred merely raised her eyebrows.

Before Katie could agree, Violet was back.

"Don't mind me," she said.

Katie didn't mind. She trusted Violet with almost anything, except for gossip, of course, which was why all discussion of the investigation stopped.

"Do we want to order?" Hannah offered.

Even though it wasn't their usual night to be there, they each placed their usual order nonetheless. Violet almost seemed disappointed. "I was hoping for a challenge," she said before she left.

Katie continued, "I was telling Hannah that right now, the only other suspect we have is Ian Trembley."

Tony picked open a creamer cup and dumped its contents into his coffee. "What's his motive?"

"Professional jealousy? Revenge?"

"You seem sure about that."

She shook her head. "I'm not sure about anything at the moment. I was so certain that Harold Beck did it that I stopped thinking about Ian."

"Rookie mistake," Ken said, buttering his bread. "You'll learn."

Violet returned with another server, wearing plates on their arms. They distributed everybody's orders. The other server nodded and returned to the kitchen. Violet asked if that was all and everyone nodded.

"So what's the plan?" Mildred said, managing to keep her voice to a low roar.

Hannah sipped her Pepsi and then set her glass down. "I think we only have two options. Find more suspects, or nail Beck or this Ian guy to the wall."

Katie stared at her plate and played with her eggs. Hannah was right; those were the only two options. Or were they? Katie wanted to find Elena's killer, but she wanted to exonerate her dad more. She sighed. That made her sound like such a terrible person.

"I vote for more suspects," Ken said.

Tony and Mildred nodded.

Katie was about to agree when three people entering the restaurant caught her attention. Lieutenant and Mrs. Crozier. And Connor. She tried to look away before any of them noticed her staring, but she was too late. Connor was too fast.

The other four turned to see what had grabbed Katie's attention.

"The plot thickens," Tony said with raised eyebrows.

One of the servers started to bring the Croziers her way until Violet intercepted them and guided them to a table on the other side of the room, the servers' stand blocking Katie's view of them completely.

"Anyhow."

"What about Connor?" Ken said.

Mildred leaned in. "You think he killed Elena?"

Tony buried his face in his hands to keep Mildred from seeing him laugh.

"Now that would be cool," Hannah said before catching herself and turning a guilty stare toward Katie. "I mean, you know. Interesting. Surprising. Plot twist!" She shook her head. "Never mind."

"What I mean is," Ken continued, "maybe Connor can help us. The whole firefighter fraternity thing."

Katie hated to agree. "He might be able to find out if Beck really rode the Mukilteo Ferry that night. Beck also said he stayed at his house in Kirkland. Maybe Connor can check on that, too."

That still didn't seem like enough. She agreed with the team. They needed more suspects. She checked her watch. It was only seven o'clock. The library was still open. One thing she hadn't checked was the library's surveillance tapes. Maybe there was something on there that the lieutenant overlooked.

While the rest took a break to eat, she texted Amy Richardson. *Can I come by in thirty? I'd like to check something out.*

A thumbs-up quickly appeared on her phone.

She threw a glance in the Croziers' direction, landing on Connor, who met her gaze looking hurt. Lieutenant Crozier, in his civilian clothes, stood and approached her table.

"So," he said, standing behind Mildred, hands together in prayer. "This is your little puzzle group I've been hearing so much about."

The five of them exchanged glances, probably looking guilty as sin.

"It is," Katie finally said. "The South Island Jigsaw Crew."

"Interesting. Interesting." He was wringing his hands now and looked around the table. "One question." He looked directly at Katie, who decided it was a good idea to shut off her iPad. "Where's the puzzle?"

"We do the puzzles in the library. We come here afterward to talk about the puzzles."

"Ah, so you finished a puzzle earlier today."

Everyone looked concerned except Ken, who looked like he was about to lose his patience.

"Get to the point, Dan," he said, startling everyone except Mildred, who merely sipped her coffee.

"Well, *Ken*. I'm receiving reports that you five are getting yourselves mixed up in something more than a puzzle, and I'm here to tell you I want it to stop."

"Well, *Dan*. If you were doing your job properly, we wouldn't have to be doing what we're doing now, would we?"

Katie sat there wide-eyed. She'd never heard anyone talk to Lieutenant Crozier that way. Not even Mrs. Crozier when she was mad. Even when Katie talked to him the other day, she'd managed to be respectful, but then she remembered the lieutenant's bulging veins, like the ones she saw now, and thought maybe she wasn't as respectful as she thought.

The lieutenant took a few breaths. It looked harder than it should've been. Then he leveled a gaze on Ken.

"Let me put this another way. If I find any of you inserting yourselves into a certain investigation, I will have to charge you with obstruction of justice. Is that clear?"

"Crystal," Ken said. "Unless you've stopped. Because if you've stopped, there's nothing for us to interrupt. Right?"

"Don't push me, Ken."

Mildred dug something out of her purse and handed it to Lieutenant Crozier. Rather loudly, she said, "Here's a mint. Your breath could drop a dinosaur."

* * *

After Lieutenant Crozier left their table, they all agreed he could do something unsavory to himself.

Violet returned with a pot of coffee, but she didn't seem interested in pouring any.

"I don't like that man," she said. "I know I should keep my mouth shut, but what he's doing to Jim is just terrible. If there's anything I can do to help, Katie, you just ask."

The other four all looked Katie's way. She didn't need to be a psychic to know what they were thinking.

"Could you keep an ear to the ground? Let me know if you hear anything that can help my dad?"

In one swift move, Violet set the pot on the empty table to Katie's right and grabbed a chair.

"I'm not one to gossip," she said. "But I hear things."

"Not you, Violet," Tony teased.

But Violet ignored him.

"I heard . . ." She looked around with a conspiratorial grin. "I heard Elena was stealing designs from that other company. What's their name? Over on the mainland."

"Tacoma Toys," Katie said, her enthusiasm waning.

Violet pointed at her. "That's the one. I bet one of those guys really did it and found a way to pin in on your dad." She threw a glance over her shoulder, toward the Croziers. "Do you want me to say something to him?"

Katie raised her hands. "That's okay. I appreciate the input. But if you hear anything *else*, you'll let me know?"

Violet stood up. "You'll be the first person I call." She grabbed the coffee pot and moved on to another table across the room.

Hannah propped her chin on her hands. "Well, that was a letdown."

"Not entirely," Ken said. "We just added the biggest pair of eyes and ears to the cause. You never know. She might just be the one who breaks the case wide open."

Katie looked toward the Croziers again. She hoped Ken was right, but hope was in short supply at the moment. What she needed was action.

They each paid their bills and as the others started for the door, Katie asked Ken to stay behind.

"What's up?"

"How good are you with surveillance tapes?"

"About as good as I am playing cricket."

"You play cricket?"

"Not at all, but it's a lot like baseball. I think I could figure it out. What's on your mind?"

"My dad said Lieutenant Crozier reviewed the library's surveillance tapes and the only person he saw was Dad."

"And?"

"Well, maybe he didn't look hard enough."

Ken shrugged. "It's a long shot, but I wouldn't put it past him. He seems like he's in an awfully big hurry for this to go away. When do you want to go?" Then he added, "You aren't worried about Lieutenant Crozier's obstruction of justice threat?"

"Not as much as I am about my father spending the rest of his life in prison." She nodded behind her. "Let's hit it. Amy Richardson's waiting for us in the library's video surveillance room as we speak."

Chapter Eleven

Ten minutes later, Katie was standing in a small closet, hovering over Ken's shoulder while Amy Richardson scratched Booker's soft, gray fur as she sat to Katie's right with the cat on her lap.

Violet's accusation about Dad having an affair with Elena weighed on Katie. He'd already denied it and she'd assumed that'd put it to bed, and though Violet was known to be the town gossip, she wasn't known for being wrong.

Katie focused her attention on Amy's monitors. She felt a little guilty for not inviting Hannah, Mildred, and Tony, but to answer Ken's question, she was a little worried about Lieutenant Crozier's threat and the fewer people she involved publicly, the better.

Ken performed like an old pro when it came to manipulating the controls on the video feed. "Almost there," Amy said.

"Is this the first time you've looked at this since the murder?" Katie asked.

"More like the hundredth. Hopefully you've got better eyes than I do."

"I hope so, too." She leaned in close to Ken, who paused the image. "Amy, tell me what I'm looking at."

Booker dropped out of Amy's lap, and she pointed at a spot on the screen. "This is Elena coming in the back door at around six thirty. At least, I think it's Elena, because she's wearing sunglasses."

"Dad said that she was hiding a black eye."

Katie couldn't imagine how Elena received a black eye during the thirty minutes between Katie's house and the library, but there were almost thirty minutes missing from Elena's life and Katie knew that was important. She gulped. Unless Elena got the black eye visiting her dad . . . But if she got the black eye from her dad, why was she wearing sunglasses at night?

Ken kept working the controls until a new image appeared. Amy said, "Here she is going upstairs, ignoring Booker, which was rude. And now." Ken paused the picture.

"She's clearly going into your dad's office and then he closes the door."

Katie folded her arms. "All this does is prove that Elena was here and that she talked to my dad. It doesn't prove that he killed her."

"Okay, this is where it gets boring, so Ken, can you fast-forward it?"

"Boring how?" Ken asked.

"Wait, stop right there," Amy said as Ken paused it. "Here's your dad coming out of his office. He gets a couple of cups of coffee and comes back. Okay, Ken, keep going." She turned to Katie and said, "and they're in there for three hours. That's what I mean by boring. Jim comes out once or twice for a quick pit stop, I assume, but other than that, nothing else happens."

Ken shook his head and stroked his beard. "No cameras in the office, I take it?"

"No. Apparently the City Council drew the line there. Anyhow, we're getting closer to nine thirty and . . . watch." Amy pointed. "Here's the door to her dad's office opening. Elena steps out. No sunglasses. Black eye in plain sight. She runs out the back and disappears into the night. Jim runs after her."

Katie covered her mouth when her dad appeared on the screen looking haggard.

"This is your dad heading down the stairs and out the back door. Check the time stamp." Ken punched a few keys. A new image appeared. "Check the new time stamp. It's the same. Now . . ." The video rolled. Katie watched her father go outside, into the fog and rain. Within seconds, he was only a blur walking toward what was probably his car but it could've been a white horse for all she knew.

"That's all I have," Amy said. "Forty minutes later, he walks back in with a book in hand, tosses it into the return bin, and then he leaves for good."

Ken said, "The time stamps have not been manipulated, or any of the footage been tampered with. This is all accurate."

Katie brought her hands to her face as her mind swirled. Forty minutes was a long time to read a book in the cold. For an instant, she let her mind wander to the rumors of her dad and Elena and shivered. *No,* she told herself. *Not a chance.* Dad was a lot of things, but he wasn't a teenager.

Then something struck her. If Dad and Elena were lovers, maybe that could exonerate him as the killer.

Get it together, kid, her dad would say when she got this way. *Focus on what's in front of you.*

"What about the other cameras?"

"What other cameras?"

"Don't you have any in front or along the side of the building?"

Ken turned to face her. "What are you looking for?"

"When I drove here that night, the roads were really slick and I lost control. I was on . . ." She swiveled her head. "I was on the west side of the building, along Vienna, and I saw a figure moving toward the building, but I couldn't make out who it could be. Maybe one of the other cameras can."

Amy frowned. "We only have the one in front. Nothing along the side."

"This figure had to come from somewhere."

Amy looked puzzled, and Ken shrugged and hit a few buttons. A new video appeared. It showed the front of the library, but the angle was wide enough to almost reach the corner where Katie lost control.

"When did you see them?"

"Hmmm. I left my house at ten thirty, but with the weather, I drove pretty slow, so maybe ten forty? I think my dad had already left or was about to leave."

"Okay. Ken, start it at ten fifteen and run it fast."

The three watched the video allegedly fast-forward, but the only thing that changed was the rain, which intensified. But then there was a blur.

"Stop it!" Katie said. "There I am. I can see my Outback off to the right. Back the video up."

Ken did as he was told.

"There!" Katie said. "Do you see that person? On the south side of Main?"

Ken leaned forward until his face was almost against the screen. "Well, I'll be darned. How the heck did you catch that?"

Katie shrugged. "I just did. Run it slowly now."

The figure crossed Main at Vienna but then stopped, turned around and crossed Main again.

"Are they drunk?" Amy asked.

"No," Katie said. "They're nervous." She checked the time stamp. Ten seventeen. "This is after Elena was murdered but before I arrived."

Ken turned and put a hand on her shoulder. "I don't think this is anything, Katie. I'm with Amy. This person could be drunk or bored."

She brushed his hand away. "Roll it some more."

The figure crossed Main for a third time and disappeared off the right side of the screen.

"Rewind it again. This time, go back to nine thirty, before Elena was murdered."

"Whatever you say," Ken replied.

The video rolled again, fast-forwarding. A few more cars crisscrossed Main. Nobody walked in front of the library until—

"There!" Katie said pointing. "Top-left corner of the screen. That looks like the same person."

"Or it might be a raindrop on the camera."

"No, I don't think so." She asked Ken, "Can I drive?"

"Be my guest."

Katie took Ken's seat. The controls were pretty self-explanatory. She ran the video backward until the figure was all the way to the left of the screen. Then she ran it forward, even slower this time.

"Would you look at that?" She ran her finger across the screen. "The person is intentionally avoiding the camera. It's as if they know its range." She ran the video some more and sure enough, the figure arced around the screen just far enough to avoid being detected.

"They're casing the library." She turned to face Amy. "Can you or Ken bring up the hallway cameras again? I want to be able to show where my dad was when all of this was happening."

Ken reached over and after a few clicks, he pointed at a familiar face. "Here he is going into his office . . . But I have to admit, I'm not sure what this proves."

"I don't, either. At least not yet. But I'm gonna." She stood up and faced Ken and Amy. "I believe this is suspect number four."

* * *

Ten minutes later, Katie thanked Amy and said goodbye to Ken.

In front of the library, she studied Main Street. It was dead for a Friday night, except for the theater, which seemed to be doing a booming business.

She didn't know what she was looking for. Maybe a clue. Maybe some inspiration. Or maybe . . . She gasped. There they were. The figure from the video, casing the library again.

"Hey!" she hollered. In hindsight, not the brightest way to sneak up on someone.

The figure ran toward Vienna, on Katie's left, but then disappeared south on Vienna.

Katie started to run but just as she did, a car decided to nearly run her over. Not on purpose. That's just what she got for not looking.

She rounded the corner down Vienna hoping to catch up to the figure, but she stopped. There was no one in sight. And it was dark. The day's sunshine had given way to a thick blanket of dark clouds. The hairs on the back of her neck tingled, telling her to run the other way, and she obeyed. She didn't stop running until she reached her Outback in the library parking lot.

Ten minutes later, she pulled into her driveway. The house was so dark and lonely that she hurried to the side door until a voice called out, "Hey, Kate."

A silhouette of Connor approached, at least she hoped it was Connor. After so many years in Colorado, she was still getting used to how dark the cloudy nights got on Whidbey Island. Much darker than on the mainland. Way darker than Denver. The lack of any light pollution coupled with the absence of streetlights made it positively pitch-black after seven. So she fished her mace out of her bag just in case.

"Don't come any closer."

"Or what? You'll blind me?"

It sounded like Connor all right, but that didn't put her mind more at ease. Just the opposite.

"Or . . . Keep talking, but don't come any closer."

"Okay, how about why did you ignore me at Cynthia's?"

"Lots of people know I was at Cynthia's. Tell me something no one else knows about me."

"Well," the voice said. "There's this birthmark—"

"Shut up." She lowered the mace and stepped closer until she could make out Connor's features in the dimly lit drive. "What are you doing here?"

"That Hannah girl said you wanted to talk to me."

"When did that happen?"

"Outside Cynthia's, after you and Ken Gorman raced out of there."

A soft breeze blew between them and she shivered. The smart thing to do was to invite him inside so she didn't catch pneumonia, but instead she asked if he wanted to sit on the back porch.

"Are you going to be warm enough?"

"I'll go make tea."

"While I sit alone on the porch."

"That's the plan."

"It's not a great plan."

She agreed. It wasn't a great plan, and for an instant she considered changing her mind. What could it hurt to have him come in? There wasn't any need for the two of them to sit outside and freeze. Plus, it would've made her feel safer in the well-lit house. That was certain. But it would've also stirred up the heavy emotions she'd been swallowing all day. Emotions that she'd buried a long time ago. Still . . .

"Kate?"

"Yeah, um. I'm sorry, but it's probably for the best." She pointed to the back of the house. "I'll meet you there."

She entered the mudroom, flipped on the lights, and wiped her feet on the mat. Instead of taking off her jacket she put a scarf on, kicking herself for not telling Connor to go home. Her pulse was racing, even more than when she was watching the video of Dad at the library.

Her mind bounced between not wanting to deal with Connor and not wanting to be alone in the house, not after the day she'd had.

Upstairs, she turned on every light until it was as bright as a carnival. She even lit the back porch for poor Connor.

"I'll be right there."

Whimsy feathered his way around her legs, a not-so-subtle reminder of her duty. After filling the teapot and turning on the stove, she fed the little beast, all the while throwing glances toward the back of the house.

Part of her wished Connor would come in without asking, but he wouldn't do that. Too polite. Or maybe his father had beat into his head that entering a house without being asked was breaking and entering.

"Seriously," she shouted. "It'll only be a minute."

She brought her fingers to her temples and silently said, "Boil. Boil. Boil." But the water wasn't having it.

Finally, the whistle sounded. "Thank God." And minutes later, she was going out the back door with two teacups in her hand.

"Sorry about that."

"Don't be," he said, rocking in the chair, the porch light washing over him. "I enjoy the cold."

She handed him one of the cups and took the seat next to him. "I suppose that's because you have to deal with so much fire."

He laughed as he brought the cup to his lips. "Yeah, that's it."

The two stared forward, rocking slowly, saying nothing. She was tempted to take out her phone and play Spotify to break the awkward silence.

"Did that information about Harold Beck help?"

She nodded. "You were right."

"I wasn't right. I was merely passing along what I'd heard."

Katie sipped her tea. "It only half-helped. Yes, he was having an affair with Elena, but he claims he was in Kirkland when she was murdered."

"Hmm."

"Hmm, what?"

"I can probably help with that."

"Really? How?"

"I can check the ferry logs. See if his car was on it."

"What if he just took Deception Pass? Going two hours out of his way seems like a small price to pay for an alibi."

He snickered.

"What's so funny?"

"You. I never thought I'd live long enough to see the day when you started thinking like a cop."

"Oh, hush."

They rocked a few more minutes in silence, each occasionally sipping their tea.

"How's your dad?" he finally said.

"I don't know. Ask yours," she shot back with a bit more bile than she intended.

He sighed. "I did."

She stopped rocking. "And?"

"He's okay. Safe. There'll be a bail hearing on Monday."

"What happened to today? Or tomorrow?"

"Don't know."

"I do," she said, blowing the steam from her cup. "Your dad got it pushed to Monday so my dad has to rot in there over the weekend."

"That's not fair."

She started to argue with him, but it was true. It wasn't fair. And if she were in a better place, she'd apologize.

"Here's another thing. Violet told me Dad was having an affair with Elena."

Connor snorted. "She must be losing it."

"You don't think it's true?"

"Don't tell me you do."

She hesitated, then shook her head and sipped her tea. "Still."

"Still nothing," he scoffed. "I know Jim. That's not his way."

She turned. "What do you mean, you know Jim?"

He faced her. "I know your dad, and I'm telling you he's not that type of guy."

"What type of guy is that?"

He stopped rocking. "Are you mad at me?"

"No. I just . . . whatever. I'll ask him again tomorrow."

More uncomfortable silence passed between them, until he said, "This is nice."

She spit out her tea and laughed. "You gotta be kidding me."

"Maybe a little. Perhaps we should change the subject."

With her anxiety starting to get the best of her, she had a better idea. "How about we keep the subject, but change the topic."

"Deal."

Then she told him about the video at the library, forgetting to stop talking when she got to the part about the figure from earlier in the evening. Connor was out of his chair in a nanosecond.

"Get inside."

"What?"

"You heard me."

"Uh. Fine." She stood without spilling her tea and opened the back door. She stepped inside, fulling expecting him to join her. "What are you doing?"

"I'm calling someone," he said, still standing on the porch.

"It better not be your dad."

"Hey," he said into his phone. "It's me. Can you arrange protection for someone?" Pause. "Katherine Chambers." Pause. He eyed her. "Yes. That Katherine Chambers." Pause. "Do I need a reason?" Pause. "Someone threatened her earlier tonight. No, I don't know who it was, but with her father spending the weekend locked up, I thought the least we could do is help her."

"Get in here," she said.

This time he complied. Whimsy rewarded him with a sniff of his boots.

"Bad cat," she said, picking up the tabby.

Standing in her foyer, Connor kept the phone held up against his ear.

"Nobody?" he said. "No, I'm not asking him." He bit his lip. "I'll think of something else. I appreciate you trying." He lowered his phone and sighed.

"What was that all about?"

He put his hands on his hips and spread his feet apart. It was as if he couldn't help looking like Superman, although she preferred Spider-Man. He was cuter and a lot less full of himself.

"Here's what we're going to do."

"Slow down, cowboy. Let's not make Space Mountain out of this molehill."

He eased up on the Superman routine. "Do you think your dad did it?"

"Of course not," she spat. "Why do you think I'm doing this?"

"So you think the killer is still out there, possibly the person you saw outside the library that night and again tonight?"

She hugged herself. "What are you getting at?"

When he approached her, her muscle memory kicked in and she reached out to hug him. Until she caught herself. He laughed. "What was all that? A new yoga pose?"

She returned to hugging herself. "Go back to whatever you were saying."

"I was saying . . . we should make sure all your windows are locked."

"I'm sure they are, but I'll double-check."

"We'll double-check. And the doors."

She gestured at the front. "It's just this one, the one to the mudroom, and the one to the back porch."

"The lights stay on. I want this place to look like Times Square."

"Times Square?" she scoffed. "Pick your favorite place. Disneyland."

He smiled.

Katie thought about it for a second. "With all the lights on, how am I going to sleep?"

"Want me to buy you a mask?"

She shook her head. "What else?"

"You're not going like this one."

"If you think you're staying here, you have truly lost your mind."

He raised his hands. "I'll be on the couch. I promise."

With that, she pushed him toward the front door. "You can stay on your couch. I'll be fine here by myself."

"Be reasonable, Kate."

"Stop calling me Kate." She opened the front door. "I'll be fine. If anything happens—"

"You'll call me."

"I'll call 911."

He pursed his lips and let his gaze bore into hers, which would've been cute as hell under different circumstances, but this was a sign that he disagreed with her completely. The problem was that she didn't disagree with him at all. She would've loved for him to stay there. It would've made her feel a heck of a lot safer for him to stay there. But she couldn't let him stay. She just couldn't, and there wasn't a way for her to explain why that would open up a Pandora's box of feelings—good, bad, and ugly—that were best left dead and in the past.

"Call me," he said.

"Not a chance."

"Fine," he said, fully surrendering. "You can't say I didn't try. If my morning Google feed has a screaming headline about an obstinate woman getting murdered in her sleep, I'll know I did everything I could to prevent it."

She pushed him out the front door. "Go." Then without warning to her or him, she reached out and gave him a peck on the cheek. "I do appreciate it, but I'll be fine. Whimsy will protect me."

They both looked down at the cat sprawled out on the floor near his food bowl.

"I feel better already," he said.

Chapter Twelve

The next morning, Katie woke up early again—not as early as yesterday, but early for a day off, which she told Neal she would take right before going to bed last night.

It was seven AM. The sun was rising above the mainland. The sky was partly cloudy, and according to her phone, the weather was a balmy fifty-eight degrees.

Out in the living room, the house was only slightly warmer but still completely lit. After feeding Whimsy and cleaning his cat box, she turned off all the lights and opened the shades. When she opened the large one to the left of the front door, she swore.

There was a car parked out front, but no one was in it.

Cautiously, she opened the door and peeked her head out. The porch light was still on, and—

She said, "You gotta be kidding me."

There was a lump under a blanket on the porch chair.

The lump twitched and then a head peered out from under the blanket.

A groggy voice said, "Good morning."

"What are you doing here?"

Connor threw the blanket off and stretched his arms wide and let out a loud yawn.

"Not sleeping very well. That's for sure."

"I told you to go home."

He combed his hair with his hand and widened his eyes, which caused him to yawn again, which caused her to yawn. "Technically, you said I couldn't stay in your house. This isn't in your house."

She opened the door wider. "Get in here. You've gotta be freezing."

He yawned again and checked his watch. "I'd love to, but my shift starts in thirty."

"You're going to work?"

He stood and folded the blanket. "We don't have bankers' hours like you do."

She didn't bother to tell him that bankers work on Saturdays, but only because down deep she was so touched by what he'd done.

"The least I can do is make you some coffee to go. I've got a Keurig. It's no trouble."

He cradled the blanket in one arm and rubbed his eyes with his free hand. "That's a kindness I'll accept."

"Wait here, then."

She ran to the kitchen. Debated over the hazelnut or the dark roast. She couldn't remember which he liked. Or maybe it was the Donut Shoppe. *Oh, just pick something! He's out there freezing!*

On the porch, she handed him the coffee. "You can keep the mug."

"I don't want to be in your debt. I'll return it to you nice and washed." He blew on the steam and took a sip. "Plus, that'll give me another excuse to come over. Speaking of freezing . . ."

"Never mind my chattering teeth. I'm used to this. I lived in Colorado for ten years, remember."

His eyes told her that he remembered. And that he'd taken the comment as a shot at him. Was this how it was always going to be? Reliving the past? Both of them reading into every word or comment? He'd done something incredibly nice, and she'd killed the moment without so much as trying.

"I'm sorry," she said.

"Don't even think about it." He adjusted the blanket under his arm and held up the mug. "Like I said, I'll wash this and get it back to you as good as new."

"What about the other thing?"

"You mean Harold Beck's alibi? I have a buddy on the Mukilteo Ferry as we speak, sweet-talking the captain to let her check out the logs."

"Her?"

"Buddies can be a her, you know."

He raised the mug one last time and walked down the porch's stairs. Her gaze followed him all the way into his car and down the road. Leaving her with a mixture of feelings that included guilt, shame, pride, and probably other stuff that she had no intention of admitting to herself.

Closing the door, she heard a noise behind her and spotted Whimsy at the window, his eyes peeled on Connor.

"Don't you start," she said.

* * *

Two hours later, she was at the last place she'd ever expected to be in her life: the Cedar Bay jail. On the bright side, it wasn't a very busy place, a testament to how safe the city was.

Officer Tallon escorted her to Dad, who was sitting in a dimly lit room that had two chairs and a table, with Dad handcuffed to the latter. Tallon then told her to let him know if she needed anything; he'd be right outside the door.

As much as she wanted to hug her dad, it was against the rules. As was hitting him, which was also on her mind.

"How's Whimsy?" he asked, still in his clothes from the other day.

"That's all you have?" she said. "Not, 'Hey, how are you? What are you doing to get me out of here? Did you hear I had an affair with Elena after all?'"

He shook his head. "I told you. Elena and I were nothing more than friends."

"Someone with a lot of credibility says otherwise."

"The only other one with *any* credibility on the topic is dead, Katherine." He slumped in his chair. "Who can I thank for this morning's good cheer?"

"I shouldn't say."

He said nothing.

"Fine. It was Violet."

Then he did something she didn't expect. He burst out laughing.

"What's so funny?"

"You're listening to Violet now?"

"She knows everything that happens in this town."

He shook his head. "She knows a lot of things that happen and allegedly knows a lot of things that didn't happen, and this is one of them."

"You're saying she's lying?"

He briefly looked away. "I guess I'm saying that she's not very discerning about the things she overhears, and sometimes she lets her jealousy get the best of her."

Katie straightened in her seat. "Her what?"

"Come on. You can't tell me you haven't noticed?" Then he shook his head. "Maybe not. You've only been here six months and we rarely go to Cynthia's together."

"What are you trying to say?"

He sat back and spread his hands as wide as the cuffs would let him. His face turned aw shucks, like a little boy, like he would whenever Mom gave him a compliment or he was proud of something he'd done.

"Violet has . . ." He shook his head again and looked up at the ceiling. "I can't believe I'm saying this."

"She has what? A tumor? Cancer?"

"A crush."

"A crush," she said with a laugh. "A crush on who?"

He cocked his head, shrugged, and grinned.

"You?" She wished she hadn't laughed when she said it because she could tell it wounded him. "I'm sorry," she said, raising her hands. "That was mean. It's just . . . Violet has a crush on you? You? My dad?"

"I'm not Big Foot, Katie. Your mom thought I was a pretty good catch."

"That's not what I'm saying." She didn't know what she was saying, but she couldn't quite bring herself to accept this. "It's just weird, that's all."

"It's not if you think about it. I've known Vi for years. Your mom knew Vi for years. I think Vi thought it was her duty when your mom got sick to help me out. And she did. I probably gained ten pounds in six months. But when your mom died, I got the impression that Vi sorta, kinda assumed she was going to take your mother's place."

Katie put her fingers in her ears. "Ew, I'm not listening to this."

He sat back and folded his arms.

She took her fingers out of her ears. "Fine, I'll listen. But this is crazy, Dad."

The door opened behind her. She turned to see Officer Tallon.

"Everything okay in here?"

"According to your standards? Yes," she said, facing Dad again. "According to mine? Not even close."

Dad raised a hand. "Long story."

"Family stuff," she added, turning.

"Ah, okay. Um. Would you like some coffee? It's pretty awful. By Seattle standards, it's undrinkable."

She said, "That would be wonderful, thank you."

She waited for him to leave before returning her attention to Dad.

"It's crazy," she said as if the conversation hadn't been interrupted.

"It's not crazy. It's just a harmless, unrequited crush. I've explained that I'm not ready for a relationship, and she understands. She and I have stayed good friends."

"But she's convinced you were involved with Elena."

"I know. I've tried to talk her out of that. I thought I'd made progress, but apparently not. Are you convinced now? Or are we going to have this conversation again in a few days?"

She nodded. "I believe you, but I'm really hoping our conversation in a few days will be at home."

His head dipped. "I don't think that's gonna happen. Even Carlton's raising the idea of a plea deal."

"A plea deal? Are you listening to yourself?"

His eyes widened. "Have you been listening to me? Everybody thinks I did it. Everybody thinks I had an affair with her. They think I gave her a black eye. I don't have an alibi."

She leaned in and lowered her voice. "There are other suspects. I can't tell you who, but they're real."

"Is Harold Beck one of them?"

"You're finally admitting that he's the married man Elena was involved with?"

He shrugged. "I figure she won't mind, especially if it can get me out of trouble. Who else do you have?"

"Just people who might've had it in for Elena."

"Does that include Ian Trembley?"

"Have you bugged my phone?"

"He'd be my next choice. Their professional competition was a lot worse than they liked to lead on. In fact, when I saw her black eye, I thought he was the one who'd given it to her."

There was a knock on the door. The bespeckled Officer Tallon stepped in and handed her the coffee in a Styrofoam cup.

"You promise me this is terrible?" she said.

"The worst coffee you'll ever have."

"Is that so people won't want to come back here?"

"Hmmm. Probably."

Tallon left and she faced her dad again, who had a quizzical look on his face.

"What?" she said. "Come on, what is it?"

"He's good-looking, I'll give you that."

"Wait." She looked briefly behind her. "You think? No. Ew, ew. Why are we having these conversations?"

"You're the one flirting with the guy."

She sipped the coffee and would've spit it out if she were outside or in her kitchen. "Ack, he wasn't kidding. This is dreadful. I think that's my cue."

She stood, rounded the table, ignored the rules and hugged him.

He grinned. "I still think Connor is the right one for you."

"Dad!"

"Just saying. You'll come on Monday for the hearing?" he said.

"You couldn't keep me away."

* * *

She walked down Main Street to clear her head. The air was crisp but not cold, but it could threaten to snow if Mother Nature wanted to be that way. A steady breeze coming in from the west blew big, fluffy clouds across the sky. Thankfully, the fire station's doors were closed, so she didn't run the risk of running into Connor. But she thought that wouldn't have been the worst thing in the world.

It was coming up on lunch and although she didn't want to sit anywhere, she did like the idea of shaking up her routine by getting one of Cynthia's patented grilled chicken Caesar salads with the extra crunchy croutons that she liked so much.

She was a block away from the parking lot when she stopped in her tracks.

Violet was behind the building having a cigarette, pencil tucked behind her ear as always, but she wasn't alone. She was with Ian Trembley. Katie was surprised, since Violet usually didn't work on Fridays and Saturdays, so she shouldn't be here. Katie looked around for a place to hide that was close enough to hear the conversation.

She waited until there were no cars on Main and hurried to kneel between two parked cars in Cynthia's parking lot. She was close enough to smell the rancid smoke but not close enough to hear anything.

About to get up, she bumped into someone behind her.

"Hannah?"

Decked out in her bike helmet and Lycra bike attire, the teen knelt down and removed the stud from her nose. "Watcha up to?" she teased.

"Shhh. I'm trying to hear what they're saying."

"That was my plan, too. I was riding my bike past when I saw the two of them talking." She eyed Violet suspiciously.

Katie nodded at the stud in Hannah's hand. "What's with that?"

Hannah nodded upward. "I didn't want the sun reflecting off it and giving us up."

Katie looked around her. "Where's the bike?"

"I left it against the fire station wall. Wait here."

And just like that, she was gone, ducking behind the cedars toward the fire station.

Katie popped her head up and studied Violet and Ian through the windows of a Telsa. Violet was smoking away and Ian was talking a mile a minute. Katie wondered if he could've been the figure she saw outside the library, but there was no way of knowing. The figure was average height, which described Ian and plenty of people around there.

Speaking of figures . . . "Oh, my."

She spotted Hannah walking into Cynthia's but taking her good, sweet time. Violet and Ian were so engrossed in their conversation that neither paid her any mind. After longer than should've been possible, Hannah disappeared into the restaurant, while Katie focused her attention, wishing she knew how to read lips. But all she saw was Ian saying something that made Violet laugh. Then Violet saying something that made Ian laugh. The longer she watched the conversation, the less interesting it became. This wasn't any backroom scheming. It was two friends having a laugh. Violet knew everyone in town.

Dropping back down, Katie shook her head. This wasn't getting her anywhere unless . . .

"I'm back!"

Katie spun without yelling. "You scared the crap out of me."

"That was sort of my intention."

Katie took a breath. "Did you hear anything?"

"They're buds."

"What makes you say that?"

Hannah shrugged. "They were just smokin' and jokin'. I didn't hear a word about Elena or your dad."

"Do you think this is a dead end?"

"Depends on what you mean by 'this.' Does it prove Ian's guilt beyond the shadow of a doubt? Nope. Sorry. I wish it did. Does it prove that Violet and Ian are friends? Absolutely. What *that* means?" She shrugged. "I have no idea."

"That's something I'll have to ask Violet about, though she does seem to know everyone."

"Hey," a new voice said. "This one of yours?"

It was Connor holding Hannah's bike.

Katie and Hannah stood, just in time for Violet and Ian to see them and wave.

Connor dropped his head and said, "You guys really don't have the sneaky part of the job down pat yet, do you?"

Katie gently punched him in the shoulder. "No thanks to you."

Chapter Thirteen

Despite Connor's comment to the contrary, she was getting pretty good at the sneaky part of the job, thank you very much. As evidenced by the fact that she'd followed Ian Trembley from his house on the north side of town, to the Handy Man's Hardware store, to the Cedar Bay Market, to the drug store, without him once noticing.

Or without her learning much new.

Ian looked more haggard than usual, his hair so unkempt that it revealed the gray he'd been hiding, and his rumpled old Metallica T-shirt had definitely seen better days. He'd heard that Katie had planned on nominating Elena for the National Design Award. Neal had confirmed that.

But did that mean he killed her?

Katie hated to say it, but she hoped so. It would mean her father would come home, cleared.

After leading her on one of the most boring Friday afternoons on record, at 4:00 PM Ian appeared to be heading back to his house.

She'd been giving her crew a play-by-play of the day via text. However, Tony was the only one replying as Hannah had a soccer game, Ken's wife had dragged him to the farmers' market in Clinton to buy lavender candles, and Mildred hated using her phone.

After stopping at the light at Vienna and Main, two cars behind Ian, a horn honked. She turned to find Tony in his beloved blue '72 Corvette to her right. She rolled down her window.

"What are you doing?" she asked.

"You think I'm going to let you have all the fun?"

"This has been anything but fun."

"What's your OPLAN?"

"My what?"

"You're operational plan. Your war plan. My old XO at WINAS always said he wouldn't so much as brush his teeth without a plan."

She glanced at the light, which was still red.

"If Ian goes home, I'm going to call it a day."

"And if he doesn't?"

The light turned green and the cars ahead of her started to move.

"I'm going to keep following him."

They both drove in unison with their respective windows down. Tony hollered, "That doesn't sound like a very good plan!"

"Do you have a better one?"

He shook his head.

"Then it's the only plan we have!"

Up ahead, Ian took a turn she didn't expect. They were in a residential area, but the route didn't go anywhere near his house. Then he took another turn. And another turn. He headed into a lightly treed neighborhood filled with kids playing and parents watching from their porches.

A light drizzle began to fall and she turned on her windshield wipers.

She checked her rearview mirror just in time to see Tony salute her goodbye right before he bailed, and during that instant, Ian chose to pull over in front of a one-story house with beige siding and a worn shingled roof.

After taking her foot off the gas, the car slowed as she debated what to do. She could pull over, too, which would give her away. Or, she could drive on past, loop around the block, and hope he didn't see her. But before she could make up her mind, Ian made up her mind for her.

He'd jumped out of his car and was now standing in the middle of the street. He glared at her, almost daring her to run him over, which she would never do regardless of how tempting it was. Instead, she parked her Outback behind his Tesla and lowered her window.

Without saying a word, he marched up to her, rested his arm on her roof, and leaned in.

"Pretty soon I'm going to need to charge my car, so let's get this over with."

"Get what over with?"

"Get whatever the reason you have for following me around for three hours."

She got out of her car and noticed Tony's Corvette pulled over a block ahead of her, facing her direction. She was surprised how much it relieved her.

Ian must've noticed, too, because he looked behind himself and shrugged. "He can come, too, if he wants."

"That won't be necessary." She threw a glance at the house behind her and found an old man standing on his porch, looking quite unhappy about the excitement in the street. "Friend of yours?" she asked.

"I don't even know where we are. I was just trying to lose you, and this is where I ended up. So what's this about?"

She crossed her arms and worked up the courage to ask her question. "Where were you Monday night?"

He furrowed his brow. "What's that have to do with Harold Beck?"

"It has nothing to do with Harold Beck. It has everything to do with Elena Larsson."

"The thief?"

"I believe the term people use is 'victim.'"

"I prefer untrustworthy coworker who got what was coming to her. I was thinking about baking a cake for your father until I remembered that I don't know how to bake."

Katie couldn't believe her increasingly damp ears. Incredulous, she asked, "You're *glad* she's dead?"

"I'm glad the charade is over." He shook the rain out of his hair. "Can we continue this conversation someplace dry? Like in my car?"

"You must think I'm an idiot."

"On this, we agree. Anyhow, I told Neal from the start that Elena was a nontalent hack. She could've studied puzzle design for a hundred years and never have created those puzzles."

Katie swallowed. She wanted so much to come out and just ask if he'd killed Elena, but something told it was too soon for that. "What did Neal say?"

Ian threw his hands in the air. "What he always says. 'You're overreacting, Ian. You're too sensitive, Ian. You could use a little competition, Ian.' I don't mind competition. What I do mind is that bubbled-headed beatnik cheating, which was why—" But he stopped.

"Which is why what?" she said, her hair now dripping with rain. "Wait. Bubble-headed?"

"Never mind," he said, turning away.

"It was you! You sent that email."

"What email?"

"The person used that exact phrase. 'Bubble-headed beatnik.'"

"A lot of people use that phrase, and I don't know what email you're talking about."

"Nobody uses that phrase, except you and the person who wrote that email."

The rain fell harder, the sky grew darker, and the temperature seemed to drop ten degrees.

The old man on the porch put up his rain hood.

Ian stood biting his lower lip and balling his hands into fists. An anger etched across his face so intense it scared her. When he took a step toward her, Tony flashed his lights.

Ian lowered his voice to just above the din of the mist. "I don't know what you're up to or what your game is, but if you keep hassling me like this, you're going to rue the day you were born."

"Is that a threat?"

He threw a glance at the man on the porch before leveling his gaze on her. "It's a fact."

* * *

After word spread of Ian's threat, thanks to Tony's big mouth, the crew decided to do what it did best. Throw a party.

Someone, probably Hannah, thought that'd be the best way to keep Katie safe while not driving her crazy.

The place was Hannah's house, or rather her parents' house.

Luther and Alana Jackson were his and her doctors, general practitioners with an office two blocks north of Main Street. Katie wondered if they were also therapists, given how much dirt they dug up on Cedar Bay. Doctors Jackson were a better source of gossip than Cynthia's.

Their house was large, one of the largest on the island's western shore, a three-story house with huge windows to take in the view of Puget Sound. They could easily throw a party for a hundred, maybe more if they used the beach right off the porch. The crew's little gang of five were no match for the structure. In fact, they could play hide-and-seek and no one would be caught for hours.

After Hannah's dad took their drink orders, Hannah's mom, who could've been Michelle Obama's twin, walked into the living room with a plate of hors d'oeuvres.

"How about some bacon-wrapped shrimp?"

"Yes!" Katie said, reaching for the tray. "Thank you, Dr. Jackson. I'm starving."

The woman cocked her head. "It's Alana because, girl, I'm young enough to be your much older sister."

Katie grabbed the shrimp and wolfed it down, knowing Dad would kill her if she called this woman by her first name. Ken appeared to her right and took two pieces of his own.

He eyed her. "Don't start. One of them is for my wife."

Katie looked around. "Where is she?"

Ken tugged on his sweater. "Not here yet. Uh, oh. I guess I better eat both of them before they go bad."

Hannah's mom snorted laugh. "Don't be shy. There are a lot more where that came from." She turned her head. "Oh good, here's Luther with your drinks."

Hannah's dad, a tall, slender man with movie star looks and a Jamaican accent, held out two wine glasses. "White for the lady and red for the gentleman. And since both your hands are occupied with some of Alana's award-winning shrimp, I'll just put these right here." He set the drinks on the glass coffee table to Katie's left. "Now I'll get out of your hair and let you resume your sleuthing."

"Luther!" Hannah's mom scolded. "We're not supposed to know about that."

"Let's pretend I didn't say that," he said with a wink, before he put his hand on her back to guide her out of the room.

"You're awful chipper tonight," Katie said to Ken while snatching another shrimp before Hannah's mom got away.

Ken picked up his wine glass from the coffee table. "It's an act. Defense mechanism I learned when I first started trying cases. I was so overwhelmed by the implication of a trial, I'd crack jokes. And no, judges did not find that an attractive quality, which was why I stopped trying cases."

"Why are you overwhelmed?"

He took a sip of his wine.

"The better question is why aren't you?"

"Frankly, I'm more frightened of you spilling that red wine on the Jacksons' very expensive white couch. Let's mosey to the back."

They headed for the family room in the back of the house, where they stood beside a wide window with a beautiful view of the water.

Ken set his drink on a nearby glass table. "I'm serious, Katie. It isn't every day someone's threatened. Normal people go to the police with such things."

"Normal people aren't hated by the police."

Ken frowned.

"I'm serious," she said. "Lieutenant Crozier has it out for me and Dad for some reason, and I'll be darned if I know why."

"Maybe he thinks your dad did it?"

"That doesn't explain not wanting my help in case he's wrong. I tried to call him today to tell him about the threat, to tell him about the email."

"What email?"

"That's right! So much has happened, I forgot all about that until now."

"You could forward him the email."

"The company already did, and he still hasn't done anything."

"Oh, I see the problem," he said, picking up his wine glass. "Take it from a recovering defense attorney, cops never think they're wrong. At least not the ones in this county."

She turned to face out the window, letting her gaze land on the Point No Point Lighthouse across the channel.

"So you think I'm wasting my time."

He shook his head. "Ian Trembley's threat makes me think you're using your time quite wisely, albeit dangerously."

Katie took a sip of wine and shook her head. "I don't think he meant it."

Ken laughed. "You think he's a suspect in killing Elena, but he's not capable of following through on a threat to you. Do you hear yourself? What's Connor think about it?"

"Why would I tell Connor?" she shot back.

"Maybe in case he wants to sleep on your porch again?"

"Ugh," she said, looking for Mrs. Dr. Jackson so she could get her hands on more shrimp.

Speaking of Connor, she hadn't heard from him all day. Not that he was required to check in with her or anything, but she was more than curious about what he'd found out about Harold Beck. She took out her phone and flirted with the idea of calling him. Nope. Bad idea. She wasn't up for a conversation. She decided to text him instead but then thought better of that, too. He should be the one text her first, right? Weren't those the rules? And then she would wait the appropriate amount of time before responding so as not to make him think she was too eager. She pocketed the phone.

Heck with the shrimp. She needed a drink.

But as if on cue, her phone buzzed. It was Connor. *Don't be too eager.*

She ducked into the Jacksons' dining room.

"Katie can't come to the phone right now. She's at a party."

"Can you give her a message?"

"If it's short."

"Okay. Tell her that Harold Beck . . . is not the guy."

Her chest tightened.

"Hang on," she said. She ducked out the back of the Jacksons' house, down the stairs of their wooden deck, and onto the moonlit beach. Shells crunched beneath her feet as she walked along the water's edge.

She brought her hand to her forehead. "Tell me you're kidding."

"Nope. My friend checked the security camera feeds around the ferry logs, and there wasn't a car matching Beck's on board the ferry that day. He could have ridden as a passenger and paid cash, but then he would've needed to get around the island somehow. I was also able to confirm that he did stay in Kirkland that night, and the travel time between Clinton, Mukilteo, and Kirkland, even without traffic, is a solid couple of hours. And, there's video evidence that he was at the Kirkland Walmart at the time of the murder, and the GPS from his phone supports that."

"You got this from your fireman friend who's not a fireman?"

"Not all firemen are firemen, Kate. Some are policemen, too."

"Now you're just making stuff up."

"If you say so."

She wanted to tell him about her encounter with Ian Trembley earlier that day, but she didn't. He'd just worry and try to sleep on her porch again, which she didn't think she could endure.

So she thanked him and returned to the living room.

Feeling a lot more uneasy about Ian Trembley than she did five minutes ago.

* * *

Two hours later, the conversations grew shorter and shorter and the attendees looked more and more tired. No one appeared to be ready to wave the white flag until she did, so she did. Even Mildred toughed it out, though this was way past her bedtime.

Katie finished the last of her water. She'd switched from wine to water about an hour ago. Checked her watch so everyone could see her and said, "I think I should call it a night."

Murmurs of agreement quickly filled the air, especially from the Jacksons, who looked ready to hit the sack, even Hannah.

"You gonna be okay, Katie?" Tony asked, helping Mildred into her coat. "Need someone to stay with you tonight?" he teased.

"I'll be fine," she said but noticed the others eyeing each other, including Mr. Dr. Jackson. "What?"

Hannah said, "We've got you covered there."

"Guys—"

Ken raised his hands. "Don't look at me. My wife would kill me."

"I'm taking Mildred home," Tony said.

Which left Hannah and her parents sporting grins the size of Mount Rainier.

Katie frowned. "You didn't."

"*We* didn't," Mrs. Dr. Jackson said smugly. "The young man offered, and we all agreed."

All their heads nodded.

"And I suppose he is waiting on my porch as we speak."

"Freezing his butt off, I bet," Mildred cackled.

"Now," Ken said, admonishing her as if she were a child. "You go straight home, young lady. No stopping off to the malt shop to see your friends."

"Malt shop? Am I in a bad *Happy Days* rerun?"

"Hey," Ken said. "Watch your mouth. There's no such thing as a bad *Happy Days* rerun."

"Except after Richie left the show."

Ken nodded. "Yeah, those don't count."

"I'll be fine. I'll text you all the minute I see Connor on my porch."

"Don't bother," Hannah said with a grin. "He's agreed to text us first."

Katie said her goodbyes and gave hugs all around. Outside, the temperature continued to drop as the cold brought along a heavier mist, and more than its share of wind. She hurried to her car and got in. It wasn't a long drive to her house, maybe ten minutes, but given the day she'd had, she'd just as soon get home as soon as possible.

Cedar Bay traffic was light on this Saturday night, the mainlanders who'd ferried over for the early fall foliage having already departed. Traffic now was nothing like the bumper-to-bumper bottleneck the town experienced during the summer, when the days were long and 80 degrees was considered a scorcher. Then, the place was filled with tourists coming to enjoy the weekly farmers' market, the June Jazz festival, as well as the summer solstice festival, which included a bonfire on the beach, not far from her house. Then there was July and the Shakespeare in the Park festival, and the tourists flocking in to kayak and stand-up paddleboard their way around their southern coast of the island.

Nope. Nothing like that tonight. Tonight there was only one car behind her and nobody had approached her from the opposite direction. When she made it to the open road, she upped the speed to over fifty, keeping a tight grip on the wheel should she hit a puddle.

The road was extra dark; many of the streetlights weren't on, which bugged her. She increased her speed to fifty-five, only ten miles over the limit, should one of Lieutenant Crozier's people have been setting up a speed trap.

She found her gaze alternating between the road and the rearview mirror, tightening her chest even further with each glance. The car behind her was still there, matching her speed. She almost called Connor, but decided she was being paranoid. She should've been happy there was only one other car on the road in this weather.

According to the sign, the exit to her house, to all of downtown, in fact, was only two miles away. Less than two minutes at fifty-five miles per hour. She'd relax once she took her exit, being closer to civilization.

Raising her gaze again, she swore the car was closer now, but in a minute and thirty seconds, it wouldn't matter. She hugged the right lane, practically begging the guy to pass her, and let out a sigh of relief when she noticed his blinker. He'd graciously taken the bait, and her pulse slowed ever so slightly.

She slowed as the car came up alongside her. With the rain and the darkness, she couldn't make out what it was. It wasn't a big truck. More like an SUV.

"Go ahead," she said with a wave, as if the person could see her. Now her heart was pounding harder than ever. When she sped up, he sped up. When she slowed down, he slowed down.

Her exit was only another mile. Her plan was to avoid using her blinker and simply make the turn at the last minute to get away from this guy.

Barely managing to control her panic, she hit the call button on her dashboard. She said, "Call Connor Crozier" after the prompt.

But in the instant she said words, the SUV raced ahead and swerved into her lane.

"Geez!" she cried, quickly spinning the wheel to barely avoid the other vehicle. She thought she was safe, but then he veered over the line again. This time she turned the wheel too fast and the next thing she knew, the Outback started to spin. Her heart raced as she tightened her grip. "Stop, stop, stop!" she cried, as the world swirled all around her. She tried to regain control and the spin downgraded into a swerve, and just as she thought she'd avoided a major accident, the back of the car hit something hard and the next thing she knew, she was careening off the shoulder and the world was turning upside down.

"Hey, Kate," were the last words she heard before everything went dark.

Chapter Fourteen

When Katie woke up next, the Outback was on its edge, in a ditch, alongside the road. Everything was dark. Her seat belt was the only thing keeping her from falling into the passenger seat window.

She craned her neck to check the clock on the dashboard. It was nine o'clock. She'd been out for at least thirty minutes, and no one had come to rescue her.

Careful not to fall, she undid her seat belt but plunged to the other side of the car anyhow, which was pinned to the ground. She reached out and tried the handle, but the door wouldn't budge. She tried it again, but it still wouldn't budge. She contorted herself and reached back to position her feet up against the driver's side door and pressed upward, hooking her toe under the door handle and pulling it with one hard shove until it popped open. But then it shut again.

This time when she tried, she remembered to keep her foot in place to keep it from shutting all the way. Now the trick was to make sure that she could actually climb out, which she did.

Outside it was still cold, maybe even a little colder than before, with a soft rain. What clouds she could see in the darkness were thick and ominous. There were no streetlights lit. And she was down in a ditch about ten feet below the road, so it was unlikely any passerby would have seen her to make any rescue call. She checked her pockets but couldn't find her phone. It must be still in the car. She leaned back in and hunted around for it until finally, she spotted it in the back seat, up against the window, and wouldn't you know it, the screen was cracked.

She unlocked her phone and scrolled for Connor's number, but before she could even hit the button, a siren wailed. She turned and saw flashing lights approaching in her direction very fast. She assumed that they must have been heading elsewhere because there was no way anyone could have seen her, but she was greatly relieved as they slowed and pulled over to the side. There were two vehicles. A fire truck and an ambulance. No police car, which surprised her a little bit.

Several men jumped out of their respective vehicles and ran in her direction.

"Are you okay, ma'am?" the first man asked.

Ma'am? Seriously? She actually didn't know if she was okay. She was numb. The bile in the back of her throat tasted strong and bitter. Her muscles ached, but when she thought about it and did a scan head to toe, like she'd learned in her meditation app, she realized she was largely unharmed, maybe with a small bump and a scrape.

"I'm fine," she said.

"Well, let's get you checked out just to be safe," the second one said. "Can you follow me back to the ambulance?"

She agreed, but the first step was a doozy. She nearly fell right on her butt. Two of the men took her by the arms and carried her the rest of the way, her feet barely touching the ground. They sat her in the back of the ambulance, which was a little bit uncomfortable. One of them shined a flashlight in her eyes, moving it back and forth. Before she knew it, another one had a cuff around her arm checking her blood pressure. And yet another one hooked a monitor to her finger, checking her pulse, she assumed, which she didn't need to tell them was faster than she'd ever felt before.

By now, the crowd had grown to six. She didn't know where the other two men came from. She realized that some of them looked familiar. In fact, one of them she was sure she'd met at the station when she was with Connor. He must have realized the same thing at that moment as his eyes widened a little bit.

"You're Connor's friend. Aren't you?"

"That's one way of putting it," she said.

"Do you want me to let him know you're here?"

"That won't be necessary," a new voice said.

She turned to see Connor standing there, looking as scared as she'd ever seen him. She had the urge to reach out and hug him, and probably should have, and she could tell he had the same thought in his eyes, as well as exercising the same level of restraint. The other men must have caught on because they all looked at each other, and then an uncomfortable silence fell between them.

The man who checked her pulse appeared to be the guy in charge. He turned to Connor. "Overall, I think she's okay beyond the superficial scrapes and bumps. Blood pressure's fine. Alertness is good. Her pulse is high, which you'd expect."

Connor said, "We should still take her to the hospital, to be safe."

"That's not necessary," Katie said. "Like your friend just announced, I'm fine. All I need to do right now is go home and get a good night's rest."

"That's really not smart, Kate," Connor said. "And I think you know that."

"Maybe you don't know me as well as you think," she said.

"If you're asking if I know just how darn stubborn you can be? I think I've got that one pegged, and I think the other guys would agree."

She wanted to call somebody, but the only person that popped into her mind was Dad and, unfortunately, he wasn't taking any calls at the moment.

All of a sudden there was another siren. Another car racing down the road toward her. The vehicle was smaller than an ambulance. Definitely not a fire truck. It was a Cedar Bay police car. She hoped it was Officer Tallon, but she doubted she'd be that lucky.

She faced Connor. "Is this who I think it is?"

"He was the first call I made."

"Why? Does he wanna make sure I'm dead?"

"Don't be like that."

"God knows somebody wants me dead."

He recoiled. "What do you mean?"

"This wasn't an accident, Connor." She looked around and all six men were staring at her. She could read the disbelief in their eyes. "You think I did this? You think I lost control and just rolled the car into the ditch?" The silent exchange of glances told her it was true. "You can't tell from the front bumper? You can't see where somebody hit me?"

They all shook their heads.

"All we saw on the bumper was mud, but the cops can look into that," one of them said. They all turned to Connor.

"Don't look at me. I'm not a cop."

"But I am," his father said. He wore an olive windbreaker and jeans, the casualness of which totally threw her off. "How are you, Miss Chambers?" he said.

"Still with the 'Miss' stuff?"

He didn't reply.

"These nice men tell me I'm fine and I can go home just as soon as my Uber arrives."

The lieutenant looked at the men, who all shook their heads.

His expression darkened. "Have you been drinking?"

Her jaw fell. "Are you serious? Ian Trembley just ran me off the road, and you want to pin a DUI on me?" She unlocked her phone. "I was kidding before but I probably should reserve an Uber, or the next thing you know, you'll be arresting me for kidnapping the Lindbergh baby."

"The who?" one of the paramedics asked.

She shook her head as Lieutenant Crozier reached for her phone, which she quickly pulled away.

She scrolled through her contacts to one she hadn't planned on calling. Her dad's attorney.

"Hi, Carlton," she said. "No, Dad's fine. Well, actually, he's not fine." She glared at the lieutenant. "You already know he's in jail for a crime he didn't commit. But I'm here with our friend Lieutenant Crozier and given our recent history, I feel that it's in my best interest to have my attorney present before I answer any more of his questions."

* * *

Ten minutes later, Carlton McQuire rolled up in his hot-off-the-lot BMW. The rain had receded to a soft drizzle. Katie was leaning against the back of the ambulance, arms crossed, smoke pouring out of her ears having just been subjected to the indignity of a breathalyzer test, which of course, she passed.

Her head hurt and the rest of her body ached, but she didn't want to tell any of these guys that. Then again, her hurt head probably wasn't helping her make very good decisions at the moment.

"Hey there, party people," McQuire said as he approached. "What do we have here? A rave? A shindig? An after-hours big-bash? That's what we called 'em in law school."

"What we have is entrapment," Katie said. "And persecution. And police brutality."

"But we're going to assume that what we really have is someone in shock from a terrible accident and she doesn't know what she's saying," Connor added.

"Which makes it inadmissible in court. It's nice to see all that college money your dad shelled out has paid off," McQuire said.

Even in the cold, dark night, she could tell that Lieutenant Crozier was hot—and not just from McQuire's dig. The breathalyzer had turned up negative, which she'd tried to tell him would be the case. The six firemen and paramedics milled around their vehicles, clearly wondering what to do next. And to Connor's point, Katie wasn't at her best. She probably was in shock, a little, and probably should have kept her mouth shut.

Carlton went straight for the ditch, shiny shoes and all, and descended down the hill.

He was back in less than a minute.

To Katie, he said, "I take it a large gray vehicle drove you off the road?"

"See? I told you guys. It took my attorney ten seconds to figure it out. Why not you?"

The firemen and paramedics all turned away, appearing like they wanted to be anywhere else but there. Lieutenant Crozier and Connor simply shifted their stances.

To Carlton, she said, "It was Ian Trembley. He's the prime suspect after Connor told me that Harold Beck . . ." She stopped. Connor's eyes were as wide a saucers. "I mean . . ." But it was too late.

"You did what?" the lieutenant asked his son through gritted teeth.

"He helped a friend because you wouldn't," Katie said "Anyhow, we exonerated Harold Beck, which leaves Ian Trembley as the prime suspect in the murder of Elena Larsson. I may have had an interaction with Mr. Trembley and he threatened me. I also learned he sent an anonymous email to CBP complaining about Elena."

"Threatened you, how?" Carlton asked, throwing Lieutenant Crozier a sideways glance that made the lieutenant look away.

"He said I'd rue the day I was born if I kept bothering him."

Carlton spread his arms wide. "Dan, what are we doing here? Why is Jim Chambers in jail? Why are you hassling his daughter?" He looked around. "And come to think of it, did anyone even consider calling this young lady a tow truck?"

Lieutenant Crozier hooked his finger, gesturing for Carlton to follow him, leaving Katie with Connor.

"Well, this is fun," Connor said.

She wanted to respond with a witty retort, but she couldn't. Her nerves were frayed. Any courage or adrenaline or whatever had been pumping through her left her the minute Carlton McQuire arrived. Almost like when a kid gets home after a long day of school and falls apart at the first sight of Mom. But she couldn't fall apart. What little strength she had was going toward keeping her from shaking. From crying. From showing Connor any hint that she couldn't handle this situation, no matter how big of a lie that was.

But even as the thoughts rolled through her head, it was as if the words were scrolling across her forehead and Connor was reading each one.

She needed a hug, more than ever. Almost as much as the moment when Dad told her Mom had died. In fact, she couldn't think of anyone she wanted one from more than Connor, despite all the crap between them. Their history was their history, but he still knew her best. He knew how much this was torturing her. But he also knew how to keep his distance, for once. And to keep his mouth shut, sort of.

Carlton McQuire and Lieutenant Crozier returned wearing somber looks on their faces. McQuire spoke first, rubbing his hands together.

"So. Here's what we're going to do. A tow truck's on its way. It'll take Katie's car to Mel's over on 5th Street. Mel already knows it's coming, though he did not appreciate the lateness of my call. He knows it's part of an active police investigation, so he'll handle it with the utmost care. Katie?" He leveled a gaze at her. "These nice gentlemen to my right will be escorting you to the hospital, just to be cautious. I've already let the ER know you're coming and they have a summary of everything we know here so far."

"I thought I was gonna join my dad in jail for a DUI."

"Your test was negative, and Lieutenant Crozier was just doing his job. So you should cut him some slack. In fact, giving you that was smart not only on his part but for you as well."

Katie rolled her eyes, even though it made her head hurt, and looked away.

"Connor?" McQuire turned his head. "You'll meet them at the ER, wait until the doctors are done, and assuming they don't want to keep her overnight for observation, take her home." He returned his attention to Katie. "Lieutenant Crozier has agreed to have one of his men outside your house throughout the night as a precaution. You can decline this, but I suggest that you don't."

Katie thought that would calm her nerves. It didn't.

"What about my dad?"

"This has nothing to do with your dad."

"It has *everything* to do with my dad."

McQuire widened his eyes almost imperceptibly, but just enough for her to take the hint. *Shut up and let me do my job.*

"This is a police matter. The accident will be investigated to the fullest extent possible. I have every confidence that they'll find the person who did this to you."

Katie bit her tongue so much it hurt. Now that she was regaining control of herself, she felt like a jerk. Connor was probably right. She probably was in shock. And that's probably why she said the things she said.

"I'm sorry, Lieutenant Crozier, for the things I said. I was out of line."

He snorted a laugh. "Katie, if this is the worst thing anyone says to me on any given day, it's a great day."

Now the tears were back. He'd called her 'Katie.' She didn't know why that meant so much, but it did. It also signaled the seriousness of what she faced. This wasn't just about Dad anymore. It was about her, too.

Then she stared at her attorney, remembering that the price for Lieutenant Crozier's smile was going to be very, very high.

Chapter Fifteen

The next morning, she woke up before eight, which gave her less than four hours of sleep. She wanted to blame the pain, but that wasn't the culprit.

She went to the kitchen and fed Whimsy because he wasn't going to give her a moment's rest until she did. Then she gave him her customary two minutes of petting and fussing until he purred louder than a lawn mower. But it wasn't easy. Everything hurt. The seven stitches in her forehead itched. Getting thrown around in your car like a ragdoll will do that to a girl.

Her trip to the hospital had been largely uneventful, save for the aforementioned stitches. She lay on a gurney while Connor fell asleep in a chair. The doctor concluded she was fine, as she assumed, except for a mild concussion, which she didn't assume. So she was to be careful. "Don't overexert yourself. Drink lots of fluids. Get plenty of rest." She didn't exactly remember his instructions, but they were allegedly written down on her discharge papers.

That said, she and Connor didn't get out of there until close to four in the morning, something she would pay for during the next few days.

Beyond kowtowing to Whimsy's every wish, she usually liked to plan her weekends out with some level of detail, but there was nothing scheduled for today. Today was a change of direction. For the time being, she'd take her focus off Dad and put it where it belonged—on whoever had tried to kill her. She knew that's what it would take to free Dad.

As she daydreamed about how to go about that, there was a knock at her door. Given everything that'd happened, it could've been anyone. But when she opened the door, and a cold breeze smacked her in the face, she realized it wasn't just anyone. It was everyone. Ken, Tony, Hannah, and Mildred. Even Connor stood there, though he hung behind everyone else, down the stairs.

At first, she panicked. Something terrible must've happened to bring them all here. That fear was quickly washed away when she realized they all had something in their arms: breakfast.

Bagels, breakfast sandwiches, and some of the best coffee the South Island Café on Main Street had to offer. She felt so generous she briefly considered saving some for Officer Tallon so he wasn't subjected to that swill down at the jail.

Before she knew it, her kitchen buzzed with a flurry of activity. Hannah got out mugs. Ken went on plate patrol. Tony retrieved utensils. Connor helped Mildred to the couch, which she enjoyed immensely.

The only one not super enthused with the turn of events was Whimsy, who expressed his displeasure by spreading out in the middle of the foyer and throwing out the occasional meow.

An hour passed, then two. By then, the food was gone, and Whimsy had retreated into Katie's bedroom. They'd talked about puzzles, work, and last night's party at the Jacksons', which she found hard to believe had only ended twelve hours prior.

Over the course of the morning, they talked about everything except the one thing that was really on her mind: the accident.

In what could only be described as an overabundance of effort, or maybe some guilt, Connor loaded the dishwasher.

"This is a new trait," she said. "Learn this skill at the firehouse?"

"Actually?" he said, hitting the start button. "I did. We take turns. And speaking of which." He checked his watch. "My shift starts in thirty."

"Are you okay?" she asked.

"Me? What do I have to do with anything?"

"I don't know. You're acting funny, even for you."

He nodded toward the back door and she followed him out to the porch, where it was freezing.

The genial impression he'd given all morning quickly blew away with the wind.

"I don't know what I'm supposed to do here. I don't know what to say," he said.

"What on earth are you talking about? I think you're doing great. I don't know where I'd be without you the past couple of days."

"But that's the thing. Where exactly are we?"

Oh, crap. She folded her arms and walked to the east edge of the porch, staring at her neighbor's wall but not really staring.

"Katie, I'm not kidding. I don't know what's going on with us."

The wind began to swirl between the houses, kicking up the few leaves Mr. Ramsay had missed during his daily raking.

Without turning to face him, she said, "Nothing's going on with us. It's just, you know, life. Stuff happens and we have to deal with it. And that's what we've been doing this week. Dealing with stuff." She pretended to look at the watch that was still charging in her bedroom. "It's probably best that you go. You don't want to be late. And." She swallowed and faced him. "I don't want to be a bigger distraction in your life than I already am. Consider yourself off the hook."

He pressed his lips together so tightly they turned white.

"Say it, Connor."

"Say what?"

"So whatever it is you're dying to say."

He let out an exasperated sigh. "I'm scared. Okay?"

"Scared of what? Being a human? Having feelings? I'm the one someone tried to kill. Not you."

"That's the point. I'm scared *about you*! I'm scared *for* you, about you, about us, about everything. Do you think I've slept a wink the past few days? Come on, Katie. Be real. I'm not a robot. I'm doing everything I possibly can to help you. To keep you safe. To get your dad free. And I'm telling you it's not easy."

She turned a toe out. "It's not easy. You *literally* help people for a living."

"You're not people, Katie! That's the point. That's what I'm trying to say. You're not some random person who cut their forehead or got their cat caught in a tree. You're—" But he caught himself. Buried his face in his hands and shook his head.

"I'm what."

"You know who you are. You know why this is hard."

She dropped her chin to her chest. She knew who she was. She knew why this was hard for him, because despite every effort she made to compartmentalize the events of the last week, Connor never fit neatly into a box before and her status with him was getting increasingly confusing now.

Katie took a long breath. In for four. Hold for four. Out for four. She said, "You should go. I'm serious. I don't want you to be late. We'll work this out."

"So that's it."

"For now."

He stared at her.

"I just need to get through the day with my sanity intact. Can you appreciate that?"

He nodded then reached in and hugged her, whispering, "I do. I'm sorry."

"We both are. And ow."

"'Ow'?"

She winced. "Still sore."

"Oh, crap," he said, pulling away.

"It's okay."

And with that he left.

Her heart sank as he walked away. She wished she'd handled that differently. Much differently. And when she turned to face the house, she found five faces plastered up against the window, all grinning.

Including Whimsy.

* * *

By three o'clock, Katie was getting stir-crazy. The pain medication was wearing off and the stitches still itched. Terrified of getting hooked on the meds, she decided to tough it out for the rest of the day, or until she couldn't take it any longer.

Sitting there, binging *Only Murders in the Building* for the tenth time on Hulu and scratching Whimsy's belly, brought the full weight of what really bothered her most.

She didn't have a car.

When was the last time that happened? Then she remembered. It was college. But that wasn't so bad because everything she needed was within walking distance and for everything that wasn't, she could take an Uber.

That mental off-ramp drove her to her next thought: she should call her insurance broker and see about getting a loaner car. Maybe a Rivian. That'd be cool. She stood to retrieve her phone but her head spun so fast she was back on the couch before she knew it.

Whimsy tossed her an annoyed look that said, *You're supposed to get up slowly when you have a concussion. The doctor told you that at the hospital.*

The morning party had ended after Connor departed and the crew had gone home. Her police protection had gone from full-time to part-time because of the daylight, she assumed. If that's what you could call this gloomy day. She couldn't say she was disappointed by that. Having a cop car parked outside the house creeped her out and probably drove the neighbors crazy.

One of those neighbors knocked at her door, probably to tell her as much.

"Hey, Mr. Ramsay," she said. "What can I do for you?"

"I was wondering what I can do for you. It's been a busy few days over here. And while I don't like to pry, I am concerned. Especially seeing that wound on your head."

Mr. Ramsay was in his late sixties. Thin build. Thick gray hair. Always dressed like he was about to run a marathon. He and his wife, Nancy, had both retired to Whidbey Island five years ago from Microsoft with enough money to buy half of Cedar Bay, according to Violet. They kept to themselves, obsessed over their garden and yard, and were rarely seen out and about in town, if you didn't count their daily donations to the Cedar Bay Food Bank. Mr. Ramsay had a folder tucked under one arm, which piqued her curiosity, but then she decided it probably wasn't a good thing.

She didn't quite know where to begin with him. Surely, he'd heard about Dad, and the prospect of living next door to a murderer probably didn't sit well with him. The overnight police protection probably wasn't any better. If it were her, she'd probably assume that she was in danger from said murderer—and not just a suspect.

She could tell he was growing impatient without an answer, and the best she could come up with was, "I'm okay, but I appreciate the concern."

He frowned. "Is it something the rest of us should fret about? Mrs. Pennybaker across the street is worried sick, and the Zhangs have made noises about moving to protect their little ones." He pulled the folder out from under his arm and opened it up. She could make out a bunch of dark and grainy images. "I retrieved these from our door camera and thought they might be of interest to you."

He handed them to her.

The first one was Connor's car from the other night. The second one was a cop car from last night. The third one . . . She stopped shuffling. Her chest tightened. She checked the time stamp in the top left corner. It said 1:04 AM the morning of her accident.

"Is that helpful?" he asked with a restrained exuberance.

But she couldn't peel her eyes away. This was the car. She recognized it right away—the same vehicle she'd seen through the rain—the SUV that swerved in front of her, the one that ran her off the road. This was it.

And it had been in front of her house while she slept.

She brought the image close to her face, studying it to see if there was a dent where the car had hit her. Squinting helped a little. Bringing it so close that it practically touched her nose did the trick. A mark or a scuff near the right front headlight.

She handed the rest of the pictures back to him.

"Can I keep this?"

He shrugged. "Sure. I can print more if you'd like."

"Do you mind?"

"Not if you don't mind telling me who it is."

She sighed and raised her gaze to where the car would've been when the picture had been taken. Telling herself that she would take another pain pill as soon as she went back inside.

"I think it's the person who tried to kill me last night."

* * *

After Mr. Ramsay left, Katie found herself back on her couch, scratching Whimsy's back, with new information and no one to share it with. Lieutenant Crozier wasn't returning her calls. Connor was working, and the crew each had their own families to attend to.

The soreness in her neck had become so unbearable that she succumbed to taking another Percocet. That left her loopier than usual, but it didn't turn off her brain.

She retrieved her iPad from her bedroom, returned to the couch, and read over her notes. The suspects' list. The motivations. Dad's arrest. She was nearly positive that Ian must've done it. She had been so certain about Harold Beck's guilt initially that she had ignored her concerns about Ian. It had made her forget about the email entirely.

With Tony, Mildred, Hannah, and Ken all indisposed, there was one person she hadn't discussed the Ian situation with. Someone who should've been at the top of the list.

Her boss, Neal.

She stood. "Whoa," she said, reaching down. She turned to Whimsy. "I know. I gotta stop doing that, don't I?" Whimsy yawned.

It was nearing four o'clock. She and Neal weren't close enough for her to guess where he might be or what he might be doing. They'd only spoken on the weekend once or twice and only to discuss a work crisis, not that there were many puzzle emergencies.

She could try Marjorie, but she was even less familiar with her than she was with Neal.

There was a family picture hanging on the wall close to the dining table. Often, Katie would look at it when times were tough and pretend to ask Mom for her advice. There wasn't a tougher time than now.

"What would you do, Mom?"

She could see her mom laugh and imagined her saying, "I would've called Neal yesterday."

"That's different. You two were good friends."

"And you're my daughter. That should count."

"It's getting harder and harder to remember that. The world just keeps moving forward without you in it. Any day, I expect everyone to forget you, to stop talking about you, to stop asking me how I'm doing with the loss of you."

Mom's two-dimensional smile persisted. For an instant, Katie imagined how Elena might've designed the picture into a tiny puzzle. Or Harold Beck, rather. Ugh.

"If you're thinking about puzzles, you're on the right path. The problem is, you're focusing on one piece at a time, trying to make it fit before you know what's around it."

"What are you saying?"

"Finish the edge before you try to solve the middle. Work your way in. From the left. From the right. From the bottom. From the top. Focus on the whole puzzle. Don't try to force the piece you can see to fit. Find the piece that's missing; it'll be the one that fits. Only then will you have that magical feeling we all get when that last piece clicks into place."

Katie reached out and ran her hand over the picture of the three of them, running her thumb under Mom's chin.

"So where's Neal now?"

"Where he always is on a Saturday afternoon."

"Which is where?"

The smile in the picture appeared to widen. "At the office, silly."

A gust of wind shook the house and brought Katie back to reality.

"Whew. That was intense." She didn't believe anything that had just happened was real. The Percocet was strong. She went to the coffee table, and took out her phone and stared at it. Now the question was to text or call. His cell or his office landline. It was an easy decision. The office landline would leave no trace.

"This is stupid. He's not going to be there just because the Percocet says so."

Nonetheless, she found herself dialing.

"McMurry," he said on the second ring.

"Wow. She was telling the truth."

"Hello?"

"Um. Hey, Neal."

"Katie? Everything okay?"

She threw a glance at the picture. "Yeah. I just didn't know you worked on Saturdays."

"Is that why you called?" he said with a laugh. "You're checking up on me?"

"No. I'm sorry. I shouldn't have bothered you."

"Katie, what's going on?"

She sat on the couch, which hurt more than it should have.

"Can we talk? In person?"

"Can it wait until Monday?"

"Not really."

He paused for a beat. "Sure. I'll be here for another hour."

Chapter Sixteen

She ordered an Uber, and ten minutes later, she was standing outside Neal's office. Percocet or no Percocet. While her instinct was to have Neal help confirm that Ian murdered Elena, she wanted to keep her mom's advice in mind. Look at the whole puzzle.

She shook her head. *I'm going crazy*, she thought.

"Hey," Neal said. "Come in, come in." He jumped up from behind his desk. But when he was a few feet away from her, he stopped dead in his tracks. "What's with that?" he asked, pointing at her forehead.

She told him about the accident and Ian's threat.

"You don't actually think that one thing has something to do with the other."

"All signs point to yes."

He held her gaze for an instant, shook his head, and said, "Come with me. You want something to drink?"

She followed him into the break room. He handed her a Diet Coke from the fridge and fixed himself a coffee. *Focus on the whole puzzle*, she told herself.

"I've known Ian since I was a kid. He's a lot of things. Arrogant? Obnoxious? You bet. He's also a world-class puzzle designer and a leader in the industry. God knows he was no fan of Elena's and based on what we know now, his anger was justified. That said, I don't think he's a murderer."

"Did you see the email that someone sent complaining about Elena?"

"Of course," he said. "Marketing forwarded it to me the minute they got it. We get those from time to time. What I didn't know was that they forwarded it to you."

"I think Ian wrote it."

He shook his head. "Lieutenant Crozier was pretty sure it wasn't anyone from inside the company."

She scoffed, "And you believe him?"

"Why wouldn't I?" He leaned back against the counter and sipped his coffee. "Look, I know this is hard for you. I can't imagine what this business with your dad is like. But . . ." He sighed.

"What?"

"Nothing."

"No. Even with my concussion and my pain pills, I can spot when something isn't nothing."

He set his coffee on the counter to his left and folded his arms. "I'm going to keep an open mind and in doing that, there's one thing that I remember that may have bearing on the situation." He lifted his gaze and looked to his right. "The night Elena was murdered, I was at Cynthia's. Ian and I were supposed to have dinner together because he had something to talk with me about, but he canceled at the last minute."

Her grip tightened on the can of Diet Coke.

"Did you say anything to Marjorie?"

He shook his head. "No. And with all the chaos about the murder and Harold Beck, I forgot all about it."

"You need to tell Lieutenant Crozier."

"I will. First thing tomorrow."

"Tomorrow's Sunday. He'll be at church."

"Monday, then."

"I'll take it."

Ten minutes later, Neal dropped her off in front of her house.

He rolled down his window and said, "Are you sure you're going to be okay? You don't need anything?"

"No," she said with a wave.

"Wait," he said, raising a finger. "I do have something you'll want. Sort of a memento." He reached into his back seat and retrieved a plain box. He held it out the window.

"Take this."

"What is it?"

"Elena's last puzzle. Her real last puzzle. Not something she stole from Tacoma Toys. I watched her do it myself."

She took the box from him and opened it up. A lump formed in her throat as she studied all the pieces. The funny thing was, she could tell Elena had designed it. The cuts in the pieces were chaotically shaped—pure Elena.

Looking back at her house, she thought about the picture of her mom.

"I'll be sure to focus on the whole puzzle this time."

* * *

That night, at seven o'clock, she was alone in the house. To pass the time away, she decided to do what she did best. Work on Elena's puzzle.

She sat at her kitchen table, opened the box Neal had given her, and picked through it until she found a few edge pieces. It dawned on her that this was going to be the hardest puzzle she ever solved. Because she didn't have a picture to go by.

Her phone was on the coffee table. She was tempted to call Neal to see if he knew what it was supposed to be. But what would be the challenge in that?

No, she would solve it as is. Blind. No clue where she was going. Sort of like solving Elena's murder.

It didn't take long before she had all the edge pieces out on the table. She assumed it was supposed to be rectangle-shaped, so she arranged them as such, certain they were all in the wrong spot.

She sat back in her chair, crossed her arms, and studied the table. This was going to be even harder than she thought. So she made a few calls.

Ten minutes later, the house was full of noise, and food, and drinks. Funny how loud four people could be.

Mildred was the only one sitting at the table, pawing through the pieces in the box.

"This is how I always used to do puzzles," she announced.

Hannah leaned in, elbows on the table. "What do you mean?"

"I used to hide the cover so I wouldn't know what the picture was. It added to the challenge."

"Why'd you stop?"

Mildred looked up and shrugged. "It wasn't as fun as you might think."

Soon, the five of them surrounded the table.

Tony arranged a pile of pieces in front of him. "I guess we'll call this puzzle 'The Metaphor'?"

"How so?" Hannah asked.

"It's a metaphor for how we're going to solve Elena's murder and exonerate Jim."

Ken sat back in his forest-green V-neck sweater and patented white oxford, crossed his arms, and scrunched up his face.

"What's the matter?" Katie asked.

"I probably shouldn't say anything."

"Too late for that," Mildred teased.

"Well," he said, spreading his hands apart, "Katie, I want you to take this the right way, but I don't think exonerating your dad should be the goal."

Her mouth went dry. "Why not?"

He played around with the pieces in front of him. "I've gathered these altogether, randomly. Right? Now, I can assume they all fit together and I can lift them and place them in the middle of the puzzle, whole, and solve the puzzle quicker. The problem is, they probably won't all fit together." He picked up one of the pieces, a castle with three evenly spaced tabs. "If this piece connects to one in front of Hannah on the bottom, one in front of Tony to the top and one in front of Mildred on the right, I'm never going to solve the puzzle. I'm just going to have a bunch of disjointed parts."

Hannah nodded. "Because you're biased."

He jabbed a forceful finger in her direction. "Exactly."

"How'd she get so smart?" Mildred teased.

Katie leaned her head back and let that sink in. "So you're saying if we assume my dad's innocent—"

"We'll only look for clues to support that conclusion and possibly miss a relevant clue."

Tony nodded slowly, his thick black eyebrows knitted together. "It's not just bias. It's confirmation bias."

"Gold star for you," Ken said.

Katie sat up straight again and started arranging her pieces by color, eying the pieces in front of the others that might match. "So what do we do now?"

"Exactly what you're doing," Ken said. "We arrange the pieces by looking at the whole board. No bias. If we have the slightest suspicion—even a tiny shred—your piece may fit with Tony's, we try it. No matter what. If it doesn't fit, we move on. If it does fit, but we didn't think it should've, then we keep moving in that direction regardless of what our logic tells us to do."

She held up one of her pieces, a Gemini, which had knobs horizontally and was flat on the top and bottom. This one had ridges of green. It could've been grass, or it could've been a dress. One of the pieces in front of Tony didn't have ridges but had the same car shape. She reached over and tried her piece.

It snapped right into place.

"Now," Ken said, "let's assume your dad could've done it." He gathered everyone's pieces into the middle.

* * *

Thirty minutes later, the puzzle was half-done. More importantly, Katie had added additional details to her suspect list, as painful as some of them were. Like, "What if Jim is lying about having an affair with Elena and was jealous of Harold Beck?" Or, "What if he heard about the stolen designs and thought it would offend your late mother?"

Thankfully, that line of thinking didn't last long and those that contributed to it apologized profusely. But everyone agreed that the free flow of information also added to Ian Trembley's motivation list, which included jealousy beyond work, fear of losing his job, and being humiliated in the puzzle community.

With the puzzle taking shape, something was starting to come into focus. And it didn't have anything to do with Ian Trembley or her dad.

"Does this puzzle feel familiar to you guys?"

All of them shook their heads.

"It's a wonderful picture of the Coupeville shore," Mildred said. "I don't think I've seen a picture of it from this angle."

"It's not the picture," Katie said. "Look at the cut."

All four leaned in and studied what was already finished.

Ken got it first. "Holy cow."

"I'm not seeing it," Hannah said.

He turned Katie. "You're certain that Neal said this was Elena's design. He was positive?"

"He said he watched her do it herself. Heck, I could tell it was hers as soon as I opened the box."

Tony shook his head. "You guys are better about that part of the equation than me, but this looks a lot like the puzzles we solved last week during our meeting."

Katie tossed Tony a satisfied grin. "That's the point. This does look a lot like the puzzles we solved the other day. In fact, there's no doubt in my mind that those puzzles were designed by the same person who designed this."

Hannah sat up straight. "That means Elena didn't steal the designs."

"That's because . . ." Katie teased.

"Harold Beck did," they said in unison.

Ken shook his head. "I'm embarrassed that I didn't think of this earlier."

But it wasn't enough. If Harold Beck was stealing the designs and not the other way around, that didn't overturn Connor's assertion that Beck was nowhere near Whidbey Island the night of the murder.

She turned her attention to the top-level corner of the puzzle. It was a patch of trees overlooking the bay and several multidecked houses. It was almost perfect, but there was a piece missing. A hole in the otherwise perfect image.

"What is it?" Hannah asked.

"We're missing a piece," she said.

"We'll find it eventually," Mildred added cheerfully.

Katie shook her head. "I've studied all the remaining pieces, and none of them fit."

Tony's gaze scanned the pieces left in the middle. "She's right. It's not here."

Ken cleared his throat. "I guess I'll have to make an appointment with my eye doctor, because I didn't catch that."

Katie continued to stare at the table, but her mind was elsewhere. The words of her mother rang in her head. Or rather, the hallucination of her mother. *Only then will you have that magical feeling we all get when that last piece snaps into place.*

She said, "It's the last piece."

"We're not done yet," Mildred said, correcting her.

"No, we're not. But we will be, except for this one piece. It's not here."

Ken frowned. "You're not talking about the puzzle, are you?"

"I am, but I'm not. We've been falling into the same trap novice puzzlers fall into. We think we know how everything is going to fit before we start." She faced Ken. "That was your point about my dad. That we needed to stop assuming he was innocent."

Tony nodded. "I think that helped a lot."

"It did, as much as I hate to say it. But it's not enough. We're still looking at the pieces we can see. What if . . ." She looked down at the floor and smiled. Whimsy was spread out, looking for attention, but that wasn't all he was doing. She lifted his back paw and retrieved what he'd been hiding. She held it up.

"What if the piece we're looking for isn't on the table? What if it's somewhere strange we haven't thought of?"

Hannah shrugged. "Like the mainland?"

"Or Coupeville?" Mildred said.

"Or, what if it's someone . . ." She picked up Whimsy and rested him in her lap. "Or something that has nothing to do with puzzles."

Chapter Seventeen

Katie woke up late Sunday morning after the best sleep she'd had in days, which wasn't saying much. She was still sore. She was still tired, but the nightmares were fewer, as were the middle-of-the-night awakenings.

Still in her terry-cloth robe, she strolled into the kitchen hugging herself, wishing she hadn't forgotten to turn up the heat before going to bed. The night had ended so well, so positively, and the complete puzzle in the middle of her kitchen table was a testament to its success.

The crew, all of whom had left just before eleven, weren't meeting tonight per Ken's unofficial Seahawks rule. Since the Seahawks were playing Tony's beloved Philadelphia Eagles, the game had extra meaning. As a result, they all agreed to check in with each other before the game. Most likely that'd be by text, which given how she felt, Katie thought was for the best.

That left Katie alone with her thoughts longer than she wanted. Despite the continued soreness, it was more manageable than the day before. She eschewed the Percocet, opting for some more Aleve, which was doing the trick and would be her plan for the rest of the day. She hoped it would leave her mind clearer to focus on the to-do she'd accepted from the night before.

Check in on Dad.

She fed Whimsy, who was in a mood. He was probably still recovering from all the attention he'd received the night before and wondering why it wasn't resuming today.

She showered, got dressed, and put on her makeup. Looking longingly out the side window into her empty driveway, she desperately wished she had her car.

* * *

Fifteen minutes later, she thanked her Uber driver and ignored his unasked questions about a nice girl like her heading to a place like this: jail. It wouldn't surprise her if he already knew. It wasn't like Elena's death and her dad's subsequent arrest were proprietary knowledge.

Inside, Officer Tallon greeted her again. "Nice to see you again, Miss Chambers. I do wish it were under better circumstances."

"It's Katie and I do, too."

The officer escorted her to the room where Dad was being held. He offered her more of that awful coffee, which she refused. He understood and said, "I'll be out here if you need me."

She shook her head with a sad smile as she sat, staring at the chains holding Dad to the table. "Do they have to do that?"

"That's the least of my problems. I got a new roommate last night and he wasn't exactly a member of the Cedar Bay City Boys' Choir, if you know what I mean."

"Is there such thing as the Cedar Bay City Boys' Choir?"

"If not, there should be."

"Is the guy dangerous?"

"Nah. Not to me. I'm just Gramps. One of the few times old age has its perks." He shot her an intense look. "What happened to you?"

She bit her lower lip then proceeded to catch him up on what happened, and why she looked banged up. She assured him she was fine, but she could tell he was skeptical. After all, it was her dad. Before he could offer something she didn't want to do, like move in with Ken and his wife until this whole thing blew over, or even worse, move in with Connor, she reassured him she was fine.

"Sweetie, I'm just glad you are okay."

She switched gears to what the crew had agreed to last night.

"I want to talk about your relationship with Elena again."

His shoulders dropped. "Can we talk about anything else? Like Connor?"

She buried her face in her hands and rubbed it until her skin was hot. "Dad, why are you still bringing him up?"

"I feel bad about how things transpired between you two when you both left for college."

"Connor didn't want to make a long-distance relationship work, and I'm over it."

He took a deep breath and said, "That's not actually what happened."

Katie stood up from her chair. "What are you talking about?"

He closed his eyes and said, "I promised your mom I would never tell you, but I think under the circumstances, you need to know." He looked toward the wall. "Your mom and I had our biggest fight over this, and it took me the longest time to forgive her, but Connor wanted to make the long-distance relationship work, and asked us if we would be okay with him asking you to marry him. Your mom flipped out and told Connor that she would only support an engagement if you both stayed in town. She got him to break up with you. Your mom was the reason Connor broke it off."

Katie sat back down and didn't utter a word.

"I'm so sorry, sweetie."

She started to tear up. "Why would Mom do that?"

"She didn't want you to throw away your future. You were a kid. You were supposed to explore the world. You were supposed to be the one who escaped the confines of Cedar Bay."

"So, Connor wasn't good enough for me?"

"No. We loved Connor. He just wasn't in the picture that your mother had in mind for your future."

"So, she wouldn't be thrilled that I came home and started working at the puzzle factory."

"She would be proud of you."

"Doesn't sound like it."

"You have to trust me on that."

"Fine," she said, gripping the table. She blinked her tears away. "Can we talk about literally anything else? I think there's a small, or not small, but outside chance that possibly, maybe it was . . . Ian Trembley."

"The puzzle designer?"

She nodded. "At the moment he's the only other suspect we have."

"We?"

"The crew."

"And by other, you mean me."

She nodded.

"Hence the questions about my relationship with Elena."

"I'm sorry."

"Don't be."

And for the first time she saw in his face, something she hadn't seen from the start. Guilt.

"Dad?"

"It's nothing."

"It's not nothing. It's probably why we're here. What's Lieutenant Crozier have on you? Wait." Then it hit her. Lieutenant Crozier and her father had an entirely different relationship than she'd assumed, especially now that she knew the truth about her mom's rejection of Connor.

Her dad made fists and released them, like he was stretching his hands.

"Out with it, as you like to say."

He hemmed and hawed and finally said, "Elena and I argued that night. More than we'd ever argued. It got heated and someone overheard us."

"Who?"

He shrugged. "Dan doesn't seem to believe I deserve to be privy to that information."

"What about Mr. McQuire? Isn't that his job?"

"It'll be his job when he gets the witness list, but we haven't even had a bail hearing yet."

"Whoever it is must be the missing piece."

"What do you mean?"

She told him the story from the night before and the piece beneath Whimsy's paw.

"I guess so, but why?"

"That's what we have to figure out," she said.

"No," he said, slicing his finger through the air as far as the cuffs would allow. "No more sleuthing. No more investigating. Until this blows over, you go home. You go to work. You go home, and you stay there until you have to go to work again. And, forgive your mother."

"And no television for a week."

"I'm serious, Katie."

She rested her elbows on the table and leaned toward him. "That's not gonna happen, Dad. You know that, right?"

"And there's nothing you can do about it from here."

He glared at her, but said nothing.

Officer Tallon popped open the door. "Everything okay in here?"

"Everything's peachy," she said, standing up. "Dad, everything will be okay, and I'll see you tomorrow at the hearing."

* * *

After thanking Officer Tallon, she stepped outside into the refreshingly sunny day. She debated walking home. God knew she could use the time to clear the cobwebs from her mind. But head wounds were still prominent. Walking around with a concussion probably wasn't the smartest thing to do. Not that taking an Uber was a lot smarter, but it was a little bit smarter, she convinced herself.

She took out her phone but hadn't even opened the app when a certain Ford Explorer pulled up and the passenger window rolled down.

"Extra-Uber at your service, ma'am. We operate on brainwaves, not an app."

"Connor." She shook her head. "Do I have to ask?"

"Tallon's a friend. The Uber driver gave you up, too. So did the six people who drove by as you walked in."

"Or you've been following me since the morning."

"Or that. Get in."

She complied, not that she wanted to. Heck, who was she kidding? She definitely wanted to. Yes, they'd had an awkward end to the other night. And yes, they hadn't spoken since. And now she knew the truth about why they'd really broken up. But until the other day, they hadn't spoken in ten years, which didn't seem long enough at the time. But now? She was not ready to talk to him about what her mom made him do.

"Should I just assume you know everything that's happened since Friday night, or are you going to make me go through the charade of pretending you don't?"

He hit the gas and the vehicle jumped away from the curb. "I like a good story."

She brought him up to speed on almost everything, even the details she hadn't planned on sharing, like her conversation with her dad, except for his revelation. For all she knew he'd funnel all this back to his dad, but in reality, he wouldn't. No matter how mad he got at her, he wouldn't betray her. Not like that.

"Let me get this straight. You think Tacoma Toys was stealing CBP's designs and not the other way around?"

"You have to really know design to spot the subtleties, but yeah. We're pretty sure."

He shook his head. "Whoever killed Elena, it's still not Harold Beck."

"You're positive?"

He threw a glance her way and nodded. "I saw the videos and the phone tracking. He's definitely not the guy."

"Maybe it's someone else at Tacoma Toys. Someone who was mad at Harold, too."

He outstretched his arm toward her and held the wheel with one hand. "I thought you just said it might be someone who had nothing to do with puzzles. Wasn't that the point of the piece under Whimsy's paw?"

She slid down in her seat and pressed her knees against his glove box. "I don't want to think anymore."

Heading toward downtown in silence, Connor passed a car on the left. Traffic was heavier than she anticipated, not that she cared. Her nerves were fraying and her muscles ached. She didn't even bother to ask him why he was taking the long way to her house. She'd done such a thorough job of bottling up her feelings that she'd almost forgotten they were there. Now they were knocking on the door, dying to get out, and she wasn't sure that was such a good idea. Once those emotions started to flow, she wasn't sure she could make them stop.

"You hungry?" he asked, stopping at a red light.

"I should go home. Whimsy misses me."

"He's a cat. He'll live."

"You're just saying that because he doesn't like you."

"He just doesn't know me."

"I'm in no condition to be around people."

The light turned green and they cruised through the intersection. "I'm people and think you're doing fine."

"Seriously. I'd rather not."

"We'll get takeout."

"What happened to the man who stormed out of my house last week?"

"It was only two days ago."

She dropped her head. "Ugh. Two days. You've got to be kidding me. It feels like a hundred years ago."

"I wish. And I didn't storm out. I simply said my piece and left, quietly. If you don't believe me, ask everyone who watched. Including the cat who doesn't like me."

"I thought you said he just didn't know you."

"I was agreeing with you. I thought you'd like that." He turned onto Main Street. "I'm thinking Thai. A pair of spring rolls. Drunken noodles for me. Curry chicken for you."

She had to admit she was hungry and had no interest in cooking something at home. But this was suspiciously feeling like a date and while part of her didn't want to admit she liked that idea, the commonsense part of her thought it was a terrible idea, at least until she told him she knew the truth.

"How about we split a pizza?" He asked.

"Aren't you gonna watch the game?"

He shrugged. "I'll check the score on my phone from time to time."

"Since when?" she scoffed.

"Since . . . now." He tossed her a sad smile.

She eyed him softly, knowing that he'd never miss a Seahawks game under normal conditions and even a few abnormal conditions.

"Can we get ham and pineapple on the pizza?" she teased.

"Not on your life."

"Chicken."

"Half pepperoni and half however you ruin yours."

He pulled over in front of Pontillo's Pizza. She fished a ten out of her pocket. "Here's my half."

He took it. "You're not coming in?"

She shook her head.

He studied her and his eyes narrowed. "Do you really want me to just take you home?"

"Not unless you want Kraft macaroni and cheese, without the milk because I'm out."

"I'm serious. I know I've been trying to downplay your ordeal, but I can see that's a mistake."

"It's not a mistake. I need someone to lighten things up. Everything's so serious. The stakes are so high. I don't know what I'm doing." Tears flooded her eyes even though the absolute last thing she wanted to do was cry in front of Connor. But then she lost all control.

He reached over and hugged her, not saying a word. It took her a few minutes to regain her composure. He let go. She wiped her eyes dry with her hand. "Go get the pizza. I'll be fine."

"You'll have to forgive me for not believing you."

"I'm serious. I am hungry. And I don't want macaroni and cheese."

"Me, neither." He patted her knee and got out of the car, leaving the ten-dollar bill behind.

Then she let the rest of the tears she'd been holding back fly.

Chapter Eighteen

Monday morning came earlier than usual. She was up before the sun, and had Whimsy fed and pampered within ten minutes of getting out of bed. She replaced the bandage on her head with a simple Band-Aid. And after slipping into her stretchy jeans to compensate for last night's pizza, she donned an untucked white oxford that would've made Ken proud, with the sleeves rolled up twice. Having waited less than five minutes, she then stepped into an Uber well before her usual starting time of 8:00 AM.

It was the first time she'd ever taken an Uber to work, and she hoped it'd be her last. Had she given it more thought, she'd have asked someone to pick her up, but deep down, she secretly craved the alone time. So maybe she'd Uber to work again if the insurance company didn't come through with a rental, which reminded her.

Call the insurance company.

When she arrived at the office, she thanked her driver with a five-star review and a 20 percent tip. A few cars were already in the parking lot, including Neal's, which didn't surprise her given the text she'd sent him the previous night, as well as the fact that he was always the first to arrive.

The one car she didn't see was Ian's, thank God. Given all that had happened, she wasn't sure how to face him, but she did want to check out his car when it arrived. Or, it'd be just fine if he chose to take the day off.

Inside the office, she shook the rain from her hair, but before heading to her cubicle, she stopped at Neal's open door first and knocked.

He was on the phone but motioned for her to come in. Marjorie sat at the table in front of his desk, wearing a concerned look on her face.

"Sounds good," he said to whoever he was talking to and hung up.

"Should I come back?" she asked.

"Nope," he said, gesturing for her to sit. "You're the reason we're here. Shut the door behind you."

She complied.

Marjorie added a frown to her concerned look. "Last night, Neal forwarded me the email complaint marketing received, and I have to tell you, I'm a little embarrassed."

"Why would you be embarrassed?"

Neal raised a hand. "What she's trying to say is that we should've been more diligent in our review of our designs, and jumping to the conclusion that Elena had done anything wrong was a mistake on our part."

She shrugged. "Unless you studied the designs as closely as we do, how would you know?"

"I'm paid to know."

"No. You're paid to listen to people like me, who did miss it. Either way, and it hurts for me to say it, I'm not so sure this exonerates Elena. If she was having an affair with Harold Beck, it stands to reason that might've—"

"But she didn't," Marjorie said, holding out a piece of paper. "This is what our outside computer forensic specialist concluded."

Katie quickly scanned the document, let her jaw drop, and then looked up, "Should I even be seeing this?"

"No," Neal said. "But given the situation, I think it's warranted."

"Someone from Tacoma Toys hacked her work computer?"

The two nodded solemnly.

"It wasn't too hard," Marjorie added. "Her password was Harold123."

Katie blew out a sigh. "And I thought mine was bad." *Note, change your password when you get to your desk.*

Neal said, "I plan on sharing this with Lieutenant Crozier, but first I wanted to be sure we had our ducks in a row."

"Isn't that obstruction of justice?"

"Not according to our attorney," Neal said, checking his watch. "Who should be here any minute. We have to be careful that we're not voluntarily sharing proprietary information. Ours or Tacoma's. To do that would require a court order. This?" He gestured at the piece of paper. "Shouldn't be a problem."

She handed the document back to Marjorie and wanted to be careful with her words. If she were an attorney, she'd know if Connor's involvement in initially exonerating Harold Beck of murdering Elena was on the up and up. If she had a clearer head, she'd know if her suspicions regarding Ian were warranted. And if she were more confident, she'd know if the prospect of someone completely unrelated to the puzzles being behind Elena's murder was even something she should mention.

The more she thought about it, it was probably best not to use any words, especially—

All three turned toward the door when someone in the office made a ruckus.

Neal brought a finger to his lips.

They waited for an eternity and finally, Neal whispered, "I just want to be careful."

"My lips are sealed."

Neal got up and rounded his desk then opened his door very slowly before peeking his head out. "Okay, the coast is clear." He motioned for the two of them to leave. "We'll talk about this more later, but for now, let's keep it under our proverbial hats."

* * *

As noon approached, Katie sat at her desk, distracted and withdrawn. If she weren't wearing fake nails, she'd be biting her own.

The day had been beyond boring, which should've made her happy, but it didn't because it gave her way too much time to let her mind wander and worry. Dad's hearing had been pushed to four o'clock, for reasons that remained a mystery, leaving her to feel like a failure. She'd let him down. All this sleuthing and nothing to show for it.

Her call to her insurance company, on the other hand, went better than she'd thought it would. For some reason she'd expected them to be as suspicious as Lieutenant Crozier, to try to blame her for the accident, but they weren't, and they didn't. In fact, Jeff Adams, her agent, spent half the call falling all over himself to express his sorrow over Dad's situation. He'd laid it on so thick that by the end of the conversation she was consoling him instead of the other way around. As for the most important part of the call, what she was supposed to do about transportation, he said she was absolutely entitled to a loaner car while hers was in the shop just as soon as one came available.

Which would be tomorrow afternoon at the earliest. Friday morning at the latest.

Sigh.

Now the biggest challenge was what to do about her grumbling stomach.

Had her head been clearer in the morning, she'd have packed a lunch. Instead, she was stuck foraging through the vending machines to tide her over until the hearing. Neal had agreed to take her, which she appreciated.

As she stared at the horrible choices before her, including a sandwich she was sure had been there when she started working there six months ago, the receptionist called her name.

"Katie Chambers, you have a visitor."

She hurried to the front, fearing the worst. It shouldn't have surprised her to see Connor standing there, but it did. And if she had more strength, she'd have used that strength to refuse his offer to drive her to JJ's and avoid the town gossip that was sure to follow. But she didn't, so she didn't.

Minutes later she climbed into his Explorer, the pain in her back surging more than ever.

"You okay?" he asked as he snapped his seat belt into place.

"The bumps and bruises aren't healing as quick as I'd like."

It's been what, three days?

"Not even."

He shook his head and put the vehicle into reverse. "A normal person would be home resting after an accident like that."

"Are you calling me abnormal?"

"If the glass slipper fits, Kate."

She punched him in the arm. "Now I'm Cinderella?"

"Sorry. Low blow."

They drove to JJ's in silence, both seemingly realizing that their banter was flirting close to the edge of, well, flirting. And God knew she had enough problems without adding what to do about Connor to the list.

"Do you want to eat inside or get it to go?"

She let out a heavy sigh. "Let's just deal with it."

Speaking of flirting, inside, JJ was back at it, giving Katie the smooth talk. "And you tell your dad we'll all praying for him, okay?"

"He'll appreciate that."

She took her sandwich and her drink to a booth in the back, as far away from the front door as possible. So far, the attendance was sparse and there wasn't anyone she recognized, or more importantly, who seemed to recognize her, but that was guaranteed to change in no time.

Connor wasn't far behind and teased, "We could sit in the kitchen, if you'd like."

"I want points for even agreeing to be here."

He sat down and unwrapped his sandwich. "I offered to get takeout."

She lifted her gaze toward the door and frowned, expecting her solitary bliss to end at any minute. "I probably should've taken you up on that."

They ate in silence, which was fine with her. When she was finished, she crumpled up her wrapper, thrilled that no one had come in who could bother her.

"You inhaled that," Connor said.

"Why, Mr. Crozier. You flatter me."

"I'm just saying. The guys at the firehouse don't eat that fast."

"Are you saying I'm not ladylike?"

He chuckled. "What I'm saying is . . ." But he stopped. Appeared to study the look on her face and said, "Never mind."

As much as she wanted to continue their wordplay, her heart wasn't in it. Again. Especially knowing what she knew now.

She slumped in her seat and folded her arms. Fatigue was setting in, as was the pain. She dug around in her purse for some ibuprofen but kept scooping up the Percocet, and she didn't desire another bizarre encounter with her late mother. Finally, she wrapped her hand around the ibuprofen bottle, and popped one of the pills into her mouth. Then she lifted her drink and brought its associated straw to her mouth. She gulped down the pill and the ice-cold carbonization burned her throat. Then again, maybe it wasn't the soda so much as the line at the counter, which had grown out to the front door. All of a sudden it felt oppressively claustrophobic in there.

"Can we go?"

"Uh." He looked over at the crowd and then down at his half-eaten sandwich. "Yeah. Sure. Let's go."

He packed everything up and they said their goodbyes to JJ. She was relieved that she'd made it through lunch without so much as an awkward gaze from anyone. But they hadn't made it two steps out the door when she was accosted.

"What the hell?" she said.

In an instant, Connor had the offender pinned up against JJ's window.

"What the hell did you tell them?" Ian Trembley wheezed with Connor's forearm pressed against his throat.

"What are you talking about?" she said.

He reached over Connor's shoulder to jab a finger in her direction. "I spent the entire morning getting interrogated by *this* idiot's father for something *I* didn't do."

"You ran me off the road. I could've freakin' died."

"I didn't do jack, and you know it."

Connor reached around and put Ian into a headlock, with Ian's hair spilling all around and every head in the parking lot turning their way. He said, "Pal, you need to calm down."

Ian, knowing that his advanced years posed no threat to Connor's youth, appeared to relax a little, which Connor rewarded by letting him go.

Ian fixed his hair into a ponytail. "I didn't run you off any road. I was home all night Friday, which is exactly what I told the lieutenant."

Katie had the urge to ask him if anyone could vouch for him, but she fought against it. Anything she would've considered, Lieutenant Crozier probably asked. The biggest question on her mind was, "So is he going to arrest you?"

"You're a crazy woman. Of course he's not going to arrest me. Do you realize they impounded my car? I'm not getting it back until tomorrow morning."

"That's quicker than I'm gonna get mine."

"I told you to stay away from me. I *told* you."

"Is that another threat, Mr. Trembley?" Connor asked with an edge in his voice Katie had never heard before. "Is this something else she's gonna regret?"

Ian must've caught Connor's tone because aggressive Ian vanished, only to be replaced by supplicant Ian.

"I . . ." Ian dropped his head. "I shouldn't have said that the other day and for that, I apologize. You have to understand—" But he stopped.

"I have to understand what?"

Ian looked away, down the street, toward the theater. "It was the nomination."

Connor turned to Katie with a look that said, "Huh?"

"She knows," Ian said. "She's the one who did it."

Connor's brow furrowed. "What's he talking about?"

Katie sighed. "I nominated Elena for the National Puzzle Designer of the Year competition."

Ian stepped forward, poking his finger into his own chest. "You gave away *my* nomination. The one this company has given me for the last twenty-five years, thanks to Neal's father. That was his last promise to me before he passed away: 'Ian, don't worry. I'll make sure Neal keeps sending you until you win.' And the only reason I haven't won is because they were waiting until I was about to retire, as a going-away present." His voice started to rise and the veins in neck became strained. "Those people at Puzzle Con respect me because they know *I'm* the best puzzle designer this industry has ever seen. And you go ahead and nominate her? Elena frickin' Larsson? With her blasé cuts and her overdone color tones? Are you kidding me?"

Katie and Connor exchanged uncomfortable glances while Ian panted until he regained his composure.

"I'm sorry," Katie finally said. "I wasn't aware that Mr. McMurray had made you that promise. If I had . . ." She shrugged. "I really didn't know."

"Neal knew and he was just as enamored with Elena as you were, so . . ."

"So you did everything possible to look as guilty as you possibly could?"

"I reacted poorly and now, I guess I see things a little differently."

He seemed like he was waiting for her to ask why, but she wasn't going to give him the pleasure. She crossed her arms and waited for him to continue.

"Let's just say, I spent some time looking at Elena's designs over the weekend."

"And?"

"There's no way she stole anything from Tacoma Toys. Their stuff is so far beneath her skill set. There wasn't any need."

She wasn't about to tell him that she'd come to the same conclusion because she was still hardly convinced that he was innocent. But she was trying to keep an open mind and decided this was as good as it was going to get.

"Then what did you mean by saying I would 'rue' the day or whatever?" Katie asked.

"I don't know," he said with a shrug. "I hadn't thought that far in advance. But keep in mind, you'd been following me all over town with that ex-navy guy, Tony Foligno, who I've seen take down four angry drunks at Louie's all by himself. He's not exactly someone I'd like to mess with, no matter how many cars he sells. And on top of that, you've got Neal wrapped around your little finger."

"Excuse me?"

He raised a hand. "I mean that as a compliment. Neal always loved your mother. She could do no wrong. And while she was a great lady, that got a little annoying. It was as if all you had to do was show up and you instantly became the golden child and took the job that was rightfully mine."

Connor's demeanor changed when her mom was mentioned. As much as she wanted to argue with Ian, there was more than a shred of truth to his accusation. Neal was one of Mom's biggest fans and she had held him in equally high regard. She'd known him since he was a kid and was always impressed that despite growing with the CBP wealth, he managed to keep his head on his shoulders and turned out to become a decent human being. Which was probably why he'd given Katie her mother's job without so much as a question, let alone a formal interview.

It stood to reason that others at the company might not see giving her the job as being decent. Old-timers like Ian certainly had reason to question it, especially since he had so much experience, but Katie thought she'd overcome that. Apparently not.

A bank of clouds raced across the sky, hiding the sun, which dropped the temperature more than a few degrees. She zipped up her jacket and jammed her hands into its pockets.

"If you didn't run me off the road the other night, do you know who did?"

"How would I know that?"

"How does anyone know anything in this town?"

"Fair point, but I haven't heard anything."

"Do you know who killed Elena?"

"All I know is that it wasn't me."

She studied his eyes, hoping they'd reveal something, but they didn't. She couldn't tell if he was telling the truth or not, and there was something about his behavior that still made her suspicious.

"Am I free to go or what?"

Katie and Connor exchanged glances.

"Nothing I can do to stop you," Connor said.

After Ian had made it a block away, Connor added, "I still think there's something up with him."

"You think he ran me off the road?"

"If he didn't, I think he knows who did."

Chapter Nineteen

Midafternoon, Katie was back at her cubicle, ready to pack up for the day.

Neal had agreed to take her to Dad's dreaded bail hearing. That said, she couldn't wait to get Dad back home. His absence was leaving an incredible hole in her life, one that was being filled by Connor, which she appreciated greatly, but the longer she didn't tell him she knew the truth, the more complicated it would become. And the last thing she needed in her life was more complexity.

She powered down her computer and collected her things. It was about as useless a Monday that she'd ever had, but that was understandable given the circumstances. She decided to forgive herself and when she brought Dad home, she committed to treating them both to two scoops of Stan's mint chocolate chip ice cream.

Neal's office door was open. She knocked, but he was on the phone again. He gestured to her to sit down.

"Do they know when?" he asked the person on the phone. "This is ridiculous. It should've happened already. Now they want to push the bail hearing to tomorrow?" Pause.

"Wednesday? Oh, come on." Another pause. "Well, look. I appreciate you letting me know, but I'm going to escalate this to the mayor because I think it's crap." He slammed the phone down.

"We're not leaving, are we?" she asked.

"I'm sorry. The judge's docket is full and one of the trials went way longer than they expected."

"Can't they find someone else? How difficult should a bail hearing be? They tell us a number, we go get a bond, and they let him out. Is it any more complicated than that?"

He shrugged. "I'm not an expert on murder trials, but I am going to follow through on my threat to take it up with the mayor."

"Will that help?"

"I doubt it."

She leaned her head back and stared at the ceiling. She didn't want to cry, but it would be hard not to. She'd put so much hope in bringing Dad home today that she didn't consider it might not happen.

"Can Mr. McQuire do something? Anything?"

"That's who I was talking to. You know Carlton better than I do. If he could get your dad out, he would. Heck, if anyone in this town could, he could."

Katie sighed and stared out the door. Her memories of Saturday night had grown pretty blurry, but there was one part that remained that didn't make much sense. When Lieutenant Crozier and McQuire walked off to have their private conversation. Whatever the lieutenant had said, it changed McQuire's whole tune. Goodbye, combative attorney. Hello, Mr. Easygoing Guy. That didn't sit right with her.

"I should go see him."

"Who, your dad?"

"No," she said, standing. "Mr. McQuire. I think there's something he's not telling us."

* * *

Connor held the door open for Katie as she breezed into the law offices of one Carlton McQuire, Esquire.

If she were being honest with herself, part of her wished Connor had gone back to work and she was here alone. It was kind and chivalrous and all that sappy stuff, but this wasn't his business. It was hers. And Dad's. But she'd realized on the short ride over that Connor wasn't simply playing the role of the caring ex-boyfriend. He was replacing Dad as her emotional support animal. The thought allowed her a smile, because that was what this was. It wasn't romantic. It was supportive. At least that is what she tried to believe.

Oh, the lies she told her herself.

Inside McQuire's office, the unholy odor mixture of wood polish, leather, and cologne halted her dead in her tracks. Connor nudged her forward.

"Don't stop now. It's only going to get worse." He handed her two pieces of gum. Peppermint. Her favorite, of course. "That's the best I can do."

"Thank you," she said, popping them into her mouth.

She was about to shout hello into the cave-like dwelling when a friendly face appeared from the back. A matronly woman with fierce white hair and wearing a bright blue dress that women half her age couldn't pull off. But she could. Katie liked her instantly.

The woman extended a kind hand. "You must be Katie Chambers."

Katie took the hand and before she knew it, the woman had clamped down with both of hers, should Katie think she was going anywhere. "I'm so sorry that you're going through this terrible nightmare."

The woman turned. "And this handsome man must be Connor Crozier. A spitting image of his dad if there ever was one. Can I get you two something to drink? Some coffee?"

Katie was chewing the gum. Hard.

"How about some water? Katie, your mom, God rest her soul, was a dedicated water drinker. Does that sound good to you?"

"We'd actually just like to get fifteen minutes of Mr. McQuire's time."

The woman shook her head. "Never ask for fifteen minutes. Always fourteen or less, or he'll turn on the meter." She grinned, clearly amused with herself. "Sorry. Just a little legal humor."

Katie finally freed her hand from the woman's grasp, exercising her fingers like she was squeezing a ball to regain circulation.

She said, "Let's call it ten, then."

The woman frowned. "He's booked solid through dinner, but. . . ." She took her place behind the desk, treating her seat less like a chair and more like a throne. She lifted the reading glasses that had been clinging to a string around her neck to the end of her nose and studied the extra-large computer monitor.

"Nope," she said, swiping the screen. "Nope." Another swipe. "Nuh, uh." Another swipe. "Okay, here we go. How about Friday?" She turned a hopeful gaze toward Katie. "Does that sound good?"

Katie grimaced and pulled at her chin. "Would my odds improve if I asked for only *four* minutes?"

"Greatly," the woman said. Then she typed something on the keyboard, waited for a beat then nodded. "He's free now. I'll take you two back."

But Katie turned to Connor. "Is it okay—"

But he was already heading toward the nearest leather chair. "It's fine."

"You don't even know what I was going to say."

"You were going to ask if it was okay if you paid for dinner."

She shot him a look.

He mustered a smile. "Go back by yourself. It's none of my business. I'll be out here sampling the wine selection."

Katie thanked him and followed the woman. When she gestured for Katie to go in, Katie found Mr. McQuire sitting on his leather couch, one leg over the other, scribbling on a legal pad, his reading glasses resting comfortably on his bulbous nose.

"No need to get up," she said.

He ignored her by setting the pad down, getting up, and engulfing her in a bear hug.

"Please sit."

She took the chair to his left.

"I'm sure you're here about the hearing."

"I've been notified it's been pushed back."

"This is crap and I plan on using it in the hearing."

"Actually, I'm not here about that."

He furrowed his brow. "Is it about the accident the other night?"

"In a way." She swallowed then crossed her legs to match his. "I was wondering what you and Lieutenant Crozier spoke about while we were all there. Remember? You were pretty steamed. You and he walked away for a bit. You both came back and everything seemed to be hunky-dory."

His eyes flickered ever so slightly.

"What aren't you telling me, Mr. McQuire?"

"Please, call me Carlton."

"What aren't you telling me . . . Carlton?"

He adjusted his glasses and then scratched his chin. "I have to be careful here because of attorney-client privilege."

"Well," she said, spreading her arms. "I'm your client and I welcome the privilege."

He winced. "Actually, you're not. Your father is. And that's the tricky part. I cannot share anything with you, even though you're the most important person in the world to him, without his permission."

"Let's assume he gave it to you."

McQuire set his glasses on top of the legal pad. "That's the thing. He didn't."

"Can we call the jail and ask?"

He raised a hand. "What I'm saying is, he expressly told me not to share anything with you."

Her scalp quickly grew hot. "He said that?'

"Verbatim. Except he didn't use the word 'expressly.'"

She sat there, her mouth open and her eyes burning.

"I'm sorry, Katie. I really am."

"Wha . . ." She looked around the imperial office, praying that one of the million legal books would either fall on his head or would speak to her and teach her how to make this right. "What am I supposed to do?"

He sucked air in through his teeth. "You could, uh, stop this little amateur sleuthing you're doing? Just a thought? To make Lieutenant Crozier a little happier?"

She was incredulous. "Why? Lieutenant Crozier has already convicted him. The arraignment and the trial are just window dressing. In fact, we should import some real kangaroos so the courtroom scene can be complete."

McQuire turned his head, as if the serving tray to his left had called out to him. "Would you like some coffee? I could use some coffee." He was about to stand when Katie stopped him.

"Mr. McQuire, my five, er four minutes is almost up, and I have no idea what's going on. My dad is in trouble, and no one is trying help, including him." She stopped short of adding, *and you*.

He sighed. "I know you and the Croziers have a history. Part of that history includes the lieutenant being less than pleased with your Jessica Fletcher impersonation. But I am here to tell you, Dan Crozier is a fine, upstanding man, and *if* your father didn't do this, Dan will find the person who did."

You have no idea of my history with the Croziers. I didn't know it all until yesterday. "You leaned pretty hard into that *if*."

"Katie, please."

Her will was wilting away, as was her patience. "I know about the argument Dad had with Elena that night."

"Your father told you that?"

She nodded.

"Hmmm." The attorney seemed to be chewing on that nugget of information. "If he told you that, then you should know why this is so difficult."

"An argument doesn't make someone a murderer."

"No," he said with as much compassion as it seemed he could muster. "But it does make a suspect look guilty, especially when there isn't another viable suspect to be found."

She stood quickly, somehow managing to maintain her control. "Ian Trembley is a viable suspect. Everyone at Tacoma Toys is a viable suspect. Or maybe, just maybe, it's someone who has nothing to do with puzzles is a suspect. All's someone has to do is look."

He cocked his head. "Who would that last one be?"

"I don't know yet, but I sure as heck am going to find out."

With that, she said goodbye, marched out of the office, past Connor, past the incredibly precise receptionist, without so much as a peep, and ran out into the middle of street.

Where she literally screamed at the top of her lungs.

* * *

That night, at seven o'clock, per Ken's Seahawk rule, the South Island Jigsaw Crew formally met on a Monday at the Cedar Bay Public Library, determined this time to solve the most challenging puzzle of all: the murder of Elena Larsson.

The five of them sat around the Puget Sound Conference Room table. A very happy Ken, Katie, Hannah, and Mildred, and a very unhappy Tony. There was no puzzle, per se. No box. No pieces spread around the surface. Just Katie and her iPad and what she hoped to be a lot of clever ideas.

Amy Richardson, her hair splaying in different directions, stopped by to offer her words of encouragement.

"Please, please, please," she said, her hands brought together in prayer. "This library won't survive without Jim Chambers for much longer. I won't survive for much longer. Our favorite little furry pirate, Booker, won't survive for much longer. You have to solve this!"

Okay, maybe it was less encouragement and more begging.

Ken, his rust-red V-neck sweater revealing his white oxford, brought the meeting to order.

Then Tony, on cue, said, "I make a motion that we end the meeting here and everything that happens hereafter remains off the record."

Mildred raised a hand. "I second the motion."

"All in favor," Ken said.

"Aye," the others all said in unison.

"Great." Ken closed his notebook. "That's that. Please proceed."

Katie nodded. "The other night I think we opened our minds to the real possibility that Elena's murders had nothing to do with puzzles, which means guys like Ian Trembley and Harold Beck are off the hook. For now."

"I thought Harold Beck was already off the hook," Mildred chimed in.

"He was. I'm just saying."

At that moment, there was a knock.

"Sorry," Amy said, poking her head in through the doorway again. "But there's someone out here who's been dying to come in."

Booker strutted his stuff into the room and jumped up onto the table.

Amy tossed the group a small wave and shut the door.

"Okay," Ken said. "Now that our true leader has arrived . . ." Which garnered a few guffaws.

"I'll be honest," Tony said, which was usually followed by some absolute truth. "I have no freaking idea who it could be. I get the point. I think it's right. But we just opened the pool to everyone in Cedar Bay and maybe even a few in Redmond, Poulsbo, and Clinton."

Hannah scrunched up her face. "Why those places?"

He showed his palms. "I'm just sayin', it could be anybody."

"Not really," Mildred said.

All attention turned her way.

"We're not talking about stealing somebody's milk out of the milk box. We're talking about murder. People kill for money, love, or power. What?"

The others exchanged surprised glances.

"What?" she asked again.

"That's a great point," Katie said.

"Did Elena have money we didn't know about?" Hannah asked with a shrug. "Will somebody inherit that?"

"This is good." Katie started taking notes. "Number one. Money. Who can find that out?"

Ken raised his hand. "If there's money, there might be a will, which means probate. I can track that down."

"Perfect. Number two. Love."

It was Tony's turn. "We talked about that Harold Beck guy, but we didn't talk about his wife."

"I thought he was getting a divorce," Hannah said.

"Still," Tony said with a shrug. "You never know."

"I like it," Katie said "Number two. Love. Harold's wife." She looked up. "He could've been a serial cheater. Maybe there was another mistress."

All heads nodded.

"Who's gonna cover that?" Mildred said. "Doesn't he live on the mainland?"

"He does," Katie replied. "I have someone in mind for that task."

"I bet," Hannah said with a snicker.

"Hush, you," Katie said, pretending to be angry. "That leaves number three. Power."

That silenced the room.

"Nobody?"

Ken looked perplexed. "What power did Elena have?"

More silence.

Katie shook her head. "I could ask Neal, but I think the only people at work she had power over were the graphic designers, but that brings us back to puzzles."

"Was she a member of another group like this?" Mildred asked. "You know what they say, the smaller the stakes, the bigger the fights."

"Maybe it's one of us," Hannah added.

That brought the conversation to a standstill.

"Hey, kidding. See the smile? Just a joke, folks."

Unfortunately, nobody thought it was funny, including Katie. It put a chill over the whole room as they eyed each other.

"Seriously, I'm sorry," Hannah said. "Sometimes I just don't know when to shut up."

"It's okay," Katie said.

"Don't worry about it," Ken said.

But then Mildred cut the tension. "I thought it was funny," she said, which took some of the seriousness out of the air.

After a few uncomfortable seconds, Tony said, "I'll ask around. She and I would sometimes stop by this club after Cynthia's. Some of the folks there seemed to know her."

Katie nodded, but she had to admit, unlike Mildred, she didn't find Hannah's joke funny at all. If anything, it unnerved her. No, she didn't think one of them had murdered Elena, but it wasn't impossible, either. People did terrible things for strange reasons. Maybe there was a history between someone and Elena she knew nothing about.

History. That's what she was missing. That didn't mean Mildred was wrong. People did kill for love, money, and power. And Katie knew that murders were rarely random. The victim almost always knew their assailant, especially in a small town. It was personal history that drove those cases. That was part of Elena's life. Her friends, her enemies, her acquaintances. Those were the pieces of the puzzle that Katie couldn't find.

But she did know someone who was close to Elena. Very close. She'd tried to keep an open mind about that but had failed miserably. She'd pretended that the worst outcome of all wasn't a possibility.

She cast her mind back to the missing puzzle piece under Whimsy's paw. At the time, she'd considered that conclusion so smart, so inspired. But maybe it wasn't an inspiration as much as a revelation. Maybe it wasn't random. Maybe it was the universe trying to tell her more than she was willing to accept. Maybe, just maybe, Whimsy was trying to protect that puzzle piece, because Whimsy *knew* what that piece did. Protect her dad from being found guilty.

A hand touched her shoulder. Ken's.

"You okay?" he asked.

"Yeah. It's just that . . . every time I feel like we're getting closer to the truth, we find out that we're actually farther away from it."

"And the converse is also true."

"How so?"

"Sometimes when you think you're the farthest away from the truth, you're actually standing on top of it."

The others nodded.

"You know what we're too far from now?" Hannah asked.

"Pancakes!" Mildred shouted.

"Exactly!" Hannah said.

Tony agreed. "I make a motion that we end this meeting and continue our efforts at Cynthia's."

"No need," Ken said, standing. "I ended the meeting an hour ago."

"Yeah, but it felt good to say."

Everyone else stood, except for Katie. Her mind was miles away. Imagining the unimaginable. Thinking the unthinkable.

She turned away from the others and stared out the conference room window, in the direction of where Elena had been murdered. And wondered.

Could her dad have done it?

Chapter Twenty

Ten minutes later, Katie got out of Ken's car and thanked him for the ride. A stack of pancakes from Cynthia's was just what she needed to clear her head.

They were the first ones to arrive. She debated waiting outside for Tony, Mildred, and Hannah, but the cold, damp air and the rolling fog made that decision for her. So she went inside. She and Ken waited for Violet, who was busy taking the order for a family of four. When she noticed Katie and Ken, she simply gestured for them to take their seats.

Another server brought them water and a couple of unsweetened iced teas.

Ken folded his hands and wore a serious expression.

"You got pretty quiet there at the end."

She shrugged.

"Your dad?"

She nodded.

"I'm sure he'll be fine."

"Are you? Because I'm not. He shouldn't be in there in the first place, and now they're dragging out his bail hearing."

"I'm sure they have a reason."

"That's what scares me. A good reason gets him released." She let the second part of her conclusion hang in the air.

"Do you want me to take you home? The others will be fine without us."

"Then I'll just be alone."

"What about Connor?"

She shot him a glare.

He raised his hands in surrender. "Sorry. Not my business."

She folded her arms and rested her chin on her forearms. "Don't be sorry. It was a reasonable question. It's just that Connor is adding a level of complexity to the situation that I'm not ready to handle. What?"

"Nothing," he said with a grin that betrayed him. Then he caved. "Look. You seem happy around him, which, given the insanity of everything that's going on, is nice to see. We're all worried about Jim. We're all worried about you. Take the comfort Connor's offering. Make sure there are, what do you kids call 'em, boundaries? And take it from there."

"You act like the word 'boundaries' is from a foreign language."

"In my day, boundaries were where you could and couldn't go playing hide-and-seek. How you guys use it? I don't get it, but I am trying."

She sipped her water and agreed. The iced tea had an instant effect.

"Can you excuse me?" she said.

"Everything okay?"

She stood and dropped her napkin. "I just have to use the ladies' room."

The others had arrived. Katie waved from across the restaurant and pointed to the table, and Hannah, Tony, and

Mildred all headed in that direction. Violet was hot on their heels with glasses of water.

Katie grabbed her purse by the strap from the back of her chair and shuffled across the restaurant. Because of all the talk about Connor, the fire alarm near the bathroom door caught her attention briefly before she went inside.

Ah, Cynthia's women's bathroom. One of the great sources of respite on the island. Cynthia, a third-generation sailor herself, had infused it with a nautical theme, with shells, and cushy chairs in front of a lighted vanity where she had put little powder puffs and other girly things that Katie had seen only in Jane Austen movies. The tile was so clean it gleamed, and the mahogany stall doors were thick and had antique latches. She wouldn't be surprised one day to come in and find an attendant at the door, holding a perfume bottle and saying "madame."

Glad that day wasn't today, Katie checked herself in the mirror, pulled her hair back into ponytail, and, ugh. All that did was reveal the dark circles that had formed under her bloodshot eyes. She stifled a yawn, wishing she could sleep for a week, but she doubted that was happening anytime soon. Not until Dad was free.

Then the thought she'd been fighting forced its way to the front of her head:

If he got free.

Her bladder sent her a friendly reminder of why she was there. She took the far stall and locked it behind her. After she'd barely taken her seat, she heard the door to the bathroom open. She didn't know why that bothered her, or why she thought she should have the whole place to herself. It wasn't like—

The lights went out.

"Hey!"

It was so dark she couldn't see her hands. To make matters worse, she experienced performance anxiety. She was about to give up when the door to her stall jiggled.

The hairs on the back of her neck prickled.

The door jiggled harder.

"I'm in here."

She stood and pulled up her pants when whoever it was punched the door.

"What the—" But she stopped. Her eyes were adjusting, but she still couldn't see much. The outline of the stall. The floor beneath the door. She bent down to get a look at the shoes of whoever it was, but they weren't there. She stood on the toilet, but kept her head down, slowly raising it. She couldn't see anything, but she did hear the door close.

After waiting a few seconds, she lifted the door latch and opened the door. She poked her head out and scanned the area. Mostly, she saw outlines of things, like the sinks and the mirrors. Someone had scrawled something on the mirror in the middle.

She went to the door and flipped on the lights. And gasped.

LAST WARNING. STOP NOW OR YOU WILL REGRET IT!

Written in lipstick on the vanity mirror.

She grabbed her purse from the stall and ran out. Violet stood at the server station holding a pot of coffee in one hand and working the register with the other. Everyone else sat in their seats.

"Violet, who just came out of the bathroom?"

Her had snapped around. "What's that, honey?"

"The bathroom. Who just ran out?"

"Which bathroom, honey?"

"Uh, the women's?"

Violet set the pot down on a burner. "Is there a problem?"

Katie's nerves were fraying. "Did you see anybody run out of here?"

Violet shrugged. "I was in the kitchen."

Katie ran into the restaurant. Studied everyone. No one looked in her direction, so she ran outside, just in time to see the taillights of a car peel out of the parking lot as the car disappeared into the fog.

"Katie?"

She turned to find Ken standing at the door.

"It's nothing," she said, walking toward him, her palms sweating, her heart racing.

"It didn't look like nothing, the way you jack-rabbited out of here."

She told him about the bathroom.

"Seriously?" Without saying another word, he hurried back inside, angling toward the scene of the crime.

"Wait," she said to the wind. By the time she got inside, Ken was already back and pulling out his phone. "What are you doing?" she asked.

"What you should be doing. I'm calling the cops."

"Stop."

"Not a chance. Hey, Dan. It's Ken . . . I know . . . just listen . . ." After another pause, he raised his voice. "Would you please listen to me for one darn minute." Ken's gaze turned toward Katie. Then he told Lieutenant Crozier about the threat. "Yes, you should send someone here to check it out."

He shook his head. "Yes, I'll wait." Pause. "Yes, I'll ask her to wait, too."

Violet came over, holding the coffee pot. "What's going on?"

Ken told the story again. Without saying a word, or setting down the pot, Violet rushed into the women's room and was out just as fast.

"Who did this?" she breathed.

"That's why I was asking you who went in there before."

Violet's expression turned grave. "I didn't see anyone, I'm so sorry. I didn't understand."

By now, the other members of the crew approached. Katie didn't want to tell them what'd happened, but Ken had the story out before she could prevent it.

Tony put his fisted hands on his hips, his biceps bulging under his T-shirt, and eyed the room intensely.

"Don't bother, Tony," Katie said. "Whoever it was, they're long gone. I saw them pull out of the parking lot."

Tony shook his head. "You never know."

"I know."

Hannah put an arm around her shoulders and pulled her in tight. "You okay?"

Katie leaned her head on Hannah's shoulder. "I'm okay. I also think this means we're onto something."

They all turned to face her.

"I'm serious," she said, lifting her head. "This is a good sign, guys."

Ken looked glum. "Threats are never good, Katie. Especially after everything that's happened."

"Maybe we should stop," Mildred said, clutching Tony's arm, her voice filled with defeat.

"Why?" Katie stepped forward, her heart still racing, her adrenaline surging. "This is perfect. The police will come and do their thing. Maybe get Ian's fingerprints in the ladies' room. They release my dad, lock Ian up, and we can go back to living our normal lives."

The others didn't look convinced.

"Come on, guys. This means we're close." But she'd lost their attention. The sound of sirens filled the air. Within seconds, three cars pulled up. Two cop cars with their lights swirling.

And a Ford Explorer.

* * *

Minutes later, everyone huddled outside in the fog, which had grown so thick you couldn't even see across the street. Lieutenant Crozier conferred with two other cops behind their cars. The crew circled around Mildred, who sat on a bench.

After finishing their work inside, the forensic team gathered fingerprints from everyone, including the men for comparison, but Katie knew that was pointless. What they needed was Ian Trembley's fingerprints, but even as the thought floated through her mind, she questioned it. The missing puzzle piece. Who else could it have been?

The confidence she'd clung onto earlier was bleeding away. Maybe they weren't close at all. Maybe the message was right. She should give up. Let it go. Let nature take its course. Let the system do its work.

There was one person there who'd been hovering around the perimeter, ignoring her. Well, not ignoring her, just not approaching her. Avoiding her. His attention was elsewhere, outward. Up and down the street. The occasional glance back at the restaurant. Then it hit her how thick she was being. He wasn't avoiding her. He was guarding her.

She put her hands into her pockets, put her head down, and trudged toward him.

"See anything interesting?" she asked.

He shook his head, but didn't look at her.

"They're not coming back," she said.

"How can you be sure?"

She checked the area around her. "Because it's covered with cops?"

Connor crossed his arms. "This fog is the perfect cover." He pointed. "Someone could fire a weapon from anywhere and we wouldn't know which direction it came from."

"You think someone's gonna shoot me?"

"That's how they killed Elena. Why not you?"

That sent a shiver down her spine.

"What?" he said.

"I didn't think about that. I've been so worried about the suspects and the motives, I hadn't considered the weapon."

For the first time since this whole thing began, she was scared. Truly scared. She'd been threatened. She'd been run off the road. All this person had to do was get close enough to shoot her.

"I'm going inside," she said.

"I'm going to stay out here."

"So you can get shot?"

"Good point," he said with a nod.

As they neared the building, there was a commotion.

"What's going on?" she asked.

"Cops found something," Ken said.

She went toward Lieutenant Crozier, but one of the other officers stopped her.

"Sorry, ma'am."

"This involves me, so I have a right to know."

Meanwhile, Connor rounded the cars and went straight to his father, who looked none too pleased with his son. Katie leaned in to hear what they were saying, but didn't catch a word. Whatever it was, it was a pretty animated discussion.

Finally, Connor stepped away, turned his gaze toward her. Nodded for her to follow him.

"What is it?" she asked.

"Nothing."

"I thought they found something."

"Don't worry about it. The threat was probably just a misdirection."

"You don't believe that."

"It's a reasonable conclusion."

"It's an idiotic conclusion."

He didn't have an answer for that.

"Everybody," Lieutenant Crozier announced. "We thank you for your patience and we apologize for the inconvenience. Once we have a statement from you, you'll be free to go. We appreciate your cooperation and your candor."

The crew all exchanged glances.

Mildred summed up everyone's thoughts with one line. "I didn't see anything, can I go?"

Lieutenant Crozier's expression tightened. "We'll make this as painless as possible, ma'am."

Mildred scoffed. "Dan Crozier, I taught you and your brothers when you were kids and you were the masters at making everything as complicated as you possibly could."

Snickers abounded. The other police officers looked away to hide their smiles.

"Well, Mrs. Stanfield. We'll do our best to surprise you."

Connor arched an eyebrow.

"What?" Katie whispered.

"The only way I'd be surprised is if any of you are out of here in under an hour."

* * *

An hour and a half later, she got into the passenger side of Connor's Explorer. With the door still open, she said to Ken, "I'll be okay." Except she wouldn't be. Beyond the threat, her forehead throbbed and her back ached. If she had some ibuprofen, she'd take it, but she was certain she was done with the Percocet.

Ken gripped the open door. "You don't look okay, Katie. You look tired. You look like you're in pain. And worst of all, you like just like your mother did when she wouldn't let something go."

"I'm fine," she lied.

Ken tilted his head and looked at Connor.

"She'll be okay," Connor said. "At least for now."

Ken didn't look like he bought it, but he said his goodbyes. Connor put the SUV in gear and pulled out of Cynthia's parking lot.

"Where to?" she asked.

"It's almost midnight. I assumed you'd wanna go home."

"I do, but let's take a circuitous route."

"Let me guess. You want to drive past Ian Trembley's house and see if his car is there and try to match the taillights you saw."

"It's like you can read my mind."

He shook his head. "There's no 'like' about it."

She ignored his cocky answer, despite the fact that he was right. Maybe it was the pain talking but she did want to drive past Ian's house, despite knowing there was no way to be sure from the taillights if it was his car that had peeled out of Cynthia's parking lot. Especially with the car not running and knowing that she couldn't exactly ask him to start it so she could get a better view.

Nonetheless, ten minutes later, there they were driving down his road, which was free of working streetlights, in the fog, leaving the neighborhood almost completely invisible from the road, but not completely. Using the outlines of the houses she could see, she counted them out loud.

"Four. Five. His is number seven on the left." She pointed. "There. That one-story tucked into the pocket of Douglas firs towering over the roof."

"How can you tell?" Connor asked.

"It's called a phone." She held up the device. "You know, the thing you can search on and look at maps and about a billion other things."

Connor cleared his throat. Probably his way of avoiding what he really wanted to say, which she couldn't blame him. That wasn't exactly a nice response from her.

"I meant the firs," he said through gritted teeth. "We can barely see the curb."

"Oh," she said sheepishly. "It's just that . . . I remember it now, from when my mom brought me out here for a party once when I was a kid."

He cleared his throat. "I guess that makes sense."

"I'm sorry," she said.

"'Bout what?"

"How I'm acting. What I'm saying. If I haven't mentioned it yet, I am grateful for everything you're doing."

"Someone's gotta keep you outta trouble."

"What's that supposed to mean?"

He pulled the SUV over, against the curb, and shut it off. He threw her a look that she hadn't seen in years. "I know you, Kate. Stop," he said, raising a hand. "Yes, it's been ten years, but you haven't changed as much as you'd like to think."

"I think I've matured." She tossed him a tiny shrug. "A little."

"Yes. You've changed. Some. I'll grant you that. But I still know when you get something in your craw that you don't let go. Just like your mother. Add to that the fact that this something involves your father and jail, it's even worse than normal."

"You say that like it's a bad thing."

"I say that with . . ."

"Yes?"

"Never mind."

"No go ahead. You say that with . . . ?"

He gripped the steering wheel. "With knowing that I won't be able to change your mind, so I might as well go along for the ride to try to keep you out of as much danger as I possibly can. Besides, when things quiet down, there is something I need to tell you."

She stared at him, or rather at the silhouette of him in the darkness. She wanted to come up with some snarky reply but couldn't bring herself to do it. He was being sincere, and she knew what he wanted to talk about, and how would she have taken the news about her mother coming from him?

She would not have believed him and would have walked off in anger.

Rather than get clarification, she knew she couldn't handle that conversation now. So she opened her door and jumped out. Connor did the same.

They couldn't see much from the road. Ian's house was a wide one-story with a two-car garage on the left. The house was pitch-black, but there was a car in the driveway; that much she could make out in the fog. She started to march toward it, but Connor grabbed her arm.

"What are you doing?" he whispered.

"What do you think I'm doing?"

"Will you just slow down, please?"

"What are you waiting for?" Then she noticed what he had in his hand. "What's that?"

"That's a .22."

"You brought a gun?"

"I wanted to bring the entire police force, but Dad wasn't so keen on that. I'll be behind you every step of the way. We go up to the car. You do your thing. We back away slowly. Jump back into the Explorer and get the heck out of here as fast as we can."

"Okay," she said. She looked around, as if that mattered in the fog, and then tiptoed toward the back of the vehicle. She had her phone flashlight ready. When she was close enough to touch the car, she turned the flashlight on and shined it on the taillights. Then on the paint.

And her gut clenched.

She shut off the flashlight. "Let's go," she said.

"Will you keep it down?"

"There's nothing to keep down. It's not the car." Right then, two beams shone down the road. She pointed toward them. "But that might be."

"Get in. Now."

She complied without hesitating or complaining.

Connor started the SUV, put it into gear, and hit the gas. His head swiveled between looking at the road and looking into his rearview mirror. He didn't turn on his headlights for a full five minutes.

"Are they gone?" she asked.

"I think so."

"Did they follow us?"

He shrugged. "If they did, they turned off their headlights, too."

"Now what?" she said as he turned down her road.

"I guess I'm spending another night on your porch."

She stared straight ahead, knowing that he would not be spending the night on the porch because it was going to be too cold.

And there was nothing he could do if someone came in the back door.

She hoped he liked her couch.

Chapter Twenty-One

The next morning, Katie made the executive decision to take the day off. Neal was more than agreeable and wondered why she'd even considered working in the first place. And that was before he heard about what had happened at Cynthia's last night.

As for Connor, he was long gone. He had a shift. He looked like heck and she could tell he hadn't slept a wink.

She pulled back the curtains hoping to see a police car, but the street was empty. Apparently they didn't think she was in as much danger as Connor did.

After making a pot of coffee, she joined Whimsy on the couch. Part of her wanted to waste the day away watching trashy TV, but she knew she couldn't do that. With her mind racing about last night and the pain persisting in her back, a constant reminder of Saturday night, she'd fully accepted that she was in danger. What she hadn't fully accepted was if someone was after her, why did Lieutenant Crozier believe that Dad was still guilty?

She picked up the remote and sipped her coffee, mindlessly scrolling through her viewing options, but her initial instinct had been correct. Nothing looked appealing. After tossing the remote aside, she reached for her phone. She didn't know what she was supposed to find, but the absence of any texts or emails unnerved her. It was if the outside world had cut her off.

There was one productive thing she could do.

"Hey, Mr. Adams. It's Katie Chambers."

They exchanged the normal pleasantries and a few abnormal ones, like, "How's your dad doing in jail?"

When they got past those unpleasantries, he said, "I bet you're calling about your car."

"It's like you read my mind."

"The good news is that we have a loaner available, which your policy covers. But the better news is that I checked with Mel and he says your car is ready now, if you want to pick it up."

"Isn't that fast? I thought it'd take a week."

Adams lowered his voice. "What I hear is that he got a lot of pressure to get it done quick. The police completed their work early Sunday morning. That gave him the rest of Sunday and all day yesterday."

"Well, um. That is great news. I'll go pick it up now."

"There's some documentation you'll need to sign for your claim. After your deductible, which is pretty reasonable, your policy will be picking up the rest."

"Shouldn't the person who ran me off the road pick it up?"

Silence.

"Mr. Adams?"

"How can I put this? And don't tell them you heard it from me, but the police found no evidence that someone else was involved. I'm sorry, Katie."

She sat at her kitchen table and let out a weary sigh. *Did Carlton lie to her and the police on-site?*

"Katie?"

"I'm still here. It's just . . . never mind. I appreciate everything you've done. I'll let Mel know I'm on my way."

She ended the call and sat back. At least one good thing had happened today.

* * *

Twenty minutes later, an Uber dropped her off at Mel's, the lone body shop in town. She thanked the driver, tipped him, and gave him a five-star rating. That seemed like the least she could do for such a small fare.

The fog had lifted overnight and the air had cooled. She let the salt air massage her face and from Mel's parking lot, she took in the majesty of Puget Sound, the water white capping in the breeze.

Inside Mel's, one of his mechanics greeted her at the door.

He held out a key fob. "You're all set, Miss Chambers. Looks as good as new."

She took the fob and thanked him. The car was still in the garage, but it was on the ground. Mel, a retired navy man who, like many Cedar Bay residents, had served at WINAS, the Whidbey Island Naval Air Station, and chose to never leave, was inspecting the Outback before letting it go, she guessed. He looked up as she approached.

"Well, hello there," he said with a warm grin.

He grabbed a nearby rag and stood. After drying his hands, he tossed the towel and extended his hand, the nautical star tattoo on his forearm staring up at her as he did. He'd explained once that the tattoo was a symbol of a sailor always being able to find his way home. And despite having grown up in western Massachusetts, he considered Cedar Bay his home.

After shaking her hand, he asked, "Did Hector give you your key?"

She held it up. "I appreciate you moving so fast on this. I thought I'd be without her for a week."

"So did I," he said. "But Lieutenant Crozier can be pretty darn persuasive."

She froze. "*He* was persuasive? Why?"

Mel shrugged. "Don't know. He was here with the forensic team first thing Sunday morning, keeping them moving."

"He skipped church?"

"I know. That was the first thing I asked, but he said this was a priority."

"Hmmm." That didn't sound like Lieutenant Dan Crozier.

She studied the car and had to admit, it looked as good as new. Her attention moved to the front-left corner, where she was certain the other car had clipped her. She rubbed her hand over it, almost caressing the headlight.

"That's all brand-new. A dealer in Bothell was the only one around who had a headlight in stock. Got it to me by noon yesterday. It was almost like he flew it here." Mel looked up and shrugged. "Maybe he used a drone."

She ran a hand over the new headlight again. "Are you positive that another car didn't hit me?"

"Hard to say."

Her head spun. "That wasn't a no."

"Of course it wasn't a no. The whole thing was covered in mud and smashed to bits. Even if someone had hit you, there'd be no way of knowing. Unless some of their paint got lodged into some of the plastic. Or maybe the fiberglass."

"Didn't you check for that?"

"Me? No. Not my department. You'd have to ask Lieutenant Crozier. His gang has it all."

"What do you mean, they have it all?"

Mel looked surprised. "What would you expect? They're the experts. They have the tools and the processes to figure out that stuff. I'm all about the future, about making it look as good as new. It's his job to put together the past. But . . ." He lowered his voice to a whisper. "The guys here were pretty sure no one hit you. That should be a relief. It'd be terrible to think that someone did this on purpose."

She knew someone did this on purpose. And what was terrible was to think that no one believed her about that.

* * *

It felt good to have her own car back. She'd spent enough on Uber the last few days to buy a year's worth of sandwiches from JJ's.

For a fleeting moment, she considered going into work, but Neal was right. She should take some time off. Heck, she should've taken yesterday off.

It wasn't the pain so much, at least not at the moment. It was manageable today. It was everything else. She needed to clear her head. She needed to focus. Her mind drifted to the prospect of a nice, hot bath. Maybe even some bubbles. But that fantasy was short-lived when a call came in.

She hit the answer button on her steering wheel. "Good morning, Mr. McQuire."

"Please, Katie. Call me Carlton."

She wasn't about to do that. She turned down her road and braced herself for some good news for a change.

"Has Lieutenant Crozier come to his senses about Dad?"

"Not exactly. But he would like to speak to you."

"About what?"

"He wouldn't say."

"Why isn't he calling me, then?"

McQuire didn't answer.

"Carlton?"

He chuckled. "I deserve that. Honestly, Katie. I don't know what he wants, but I suspect it has something to do with what happened at Cynthia's last night."

"That's great," she said, turning her car around. "Their forensic team must've gotten a hit on something."

"Uh, you could say that."

She stopped at a stop sign and then turned right toward downtown.

"I can be at the station in five minutes."

"Perfect," he said. "I'll meet you there."

* * *

In four minutes, she parked her car in the police station parking lot, pulling up the hood on her rain jacket as a soft rain began to fall.

When she got inside, clutching her purse under her arm, Officer Tallon was off to her right, watering the philodendron under the front window. He tossed her a sad smile. Mr. McQuire was already there, waiting for her. His patented happy-go-lucky expression was nowhere to be found.

"The lieutenant will be a minute," he said.

"Sounds serious."

"I think it is."

"Miss Chambers?"

She turned to see Lieutenant Crozier standing to her right. If McQuire's expression was sour, Crozier's was a mouthful of sour balls.

"Follow me," he said in a formal tone.

The next thing she knew, she was standing in an interrogation room.

"Is this really necessary?" McQuire said.

Crozier nodded glumly. "Please take a seat." He shut the door and glanced over Katie's shoulder. She turned and saw the glass, wondering who was on the other side.

"What's this all about?" she asked with a shaper edge than she'd intended.

He pulled out an evidence bag. Inside was lipstick.

"Is that what the person used to write the threat?"

Crozier nodded glumly again.

She straightened. "That's great. Did you get a fingerprint?"

Again with the glum nod.

"Whose is it?"

Lieutenant Crozier's gaze moved to Mr. McQuire, who looked not so pleased.

"What is this, Dan?"

Lieutenant Crozier opened a notebook and pulled out a lone piece of paper. "We matched this lipstick to the writing on the bathroom mirror. We also found a fingerprint, and we found some DNA. Both from only one person, the same person."

Katie leaned in. "Do you really think Ian Trembley uses lipstick?" she asked.

The lieutenant let out an uncomfortable laugh. "It's not Mr. Trembley's, Katie." He then stared her straight in the eye.

"It's yours."

* * *

After sitting silent for what seemed like forever, she finally managed to ask, "What do you mean, it's mine?"

He sighed. "We found your fingerprint on the case. We found your DNA in the wax."

"That can't be." Frantically, she picked up her purse and opened it. "Mine's right here." She dug around the bag, finding everything but her lipstick. "It's here." She shrugged. "It's gotta be." She was about to turn it upside down and drop the contents on the table when Mr. McQuire stopped her.

"What are you implying, Dan?" he asked.

The lieutenant spread his hands. "I've already discussed this with the district attorney, and we've agreed not to press charges."

Katie's head was spinning. "You've agreed not to press charges against who?"

When neither man replied, the weight of what was happening fell on her like an avalanche.

"You think I did it. That I . . . threatened myself?" Her face grew hot. Her breathing became shallow. It took all her strength not to flip the table over and storm out of the room. "And the car, you think I made that up. You think I've made all of this up."

"Katie, as your attorney—"

"Stay out of this, Carlton."

But he grabbed her hand. Tightly. And glared at her. "Stop talking. Now."

She met his gaze with the white-hot intensity of a thousand suns. But in the midst of her anger, she realized he was probably right.

"Katie," Lieutenant Crozier said. "We all understand the stress you must be under, with your mom passing so suddenly and your dad being . . . um . . . in a tough situation. Saturday we can explain away. Maybe you were confused after you lost control, but last night?" He shrugged. "You filed a false police report, not to mention how many department resources you've exhausted."

Her mouth opened but words wouldn't come. She pinched the back of her hand. Then her cheeks. Then her forearm. "Come on, Katie. Wake up. Wake up." She had to be dreaming. That was the only explanation for this insanity.

McQuire said, "It's not a dream. It's a mistake."

"I agree. They must've made a mistake."

"I don't mean them, Katie."

She scoffed and shook her head. "You think I made it up, too."

Now that the seriousness of what Lieutenant Crozier was saying had hit her, she agreed. It was time to shut up. Anything she said could be used against her. Heck, it would be used against her. She was sure of that.

"Can I go now?"

Crozier nodded, but said, "You have to promise me something, though. Promise me that you'll stop interfering with this case. That goes for you and your crew."

She stood up. "Which case? Mine or my dad's?"

Neither man laughed. Her attorney looked up at her with hopeful eyes.

"Fine," she breathed, raising her hands. "I promise. That it?"

Lieutenant Crozier agreed that it was.

She marched out of the station without saying a word, McQuire behind her, and spilled out onto the sidewalk without putting up her rain hood. She balled her hands into fists and wanted to scream at someone.

"Can you believe that?" she asked McQuire, the rain dripping in her eyes.

He put a hand on her back. "Let's take this conversation elsewhere. How about pancakes? You want some pancakes? My treat."

Chapter Twenty-Two

Katie didn't want pancakes. She didn't want anything to do with Cedar Bay at the moment. And it took twenty minutes to decipher if McQuire's treat meant he was paying the bill but still on the clock or if "My treat" was really "My treat."

At this point, she didn't really care, because they decided not to eat close-by and that was good enough for her.

With her car still at the police station, McQuire pulled into a greasy spoon along the road, about fifteen minutes out of town. The rain had cleared up, for now, but more dark clouds hung in the sky off in the distance.

They walked into the restaurant, simply called the Roadway Lodge, and seated themselves. It was glorious, Katie thought, to look around and not recognize a soul.

A server with less interest than Violet had ever shown the crew approached with two glasses. "I'll be back for your order in a few minutes."

Katie wondered what could take so long since the place was practically empty.

After downing half of his water, the attorney said, "I think you handled the situation back at the police station well."

"You think I handled the lieutenant accusing me of being a liar well?"

"That," he said with a shrug. "Among other things."

Maybe it was the pain. Maybe it was the stress. But for the first time since Lieutenant Crozier had entered her house last week, she was completely convinced that Dad was going to jail for the rest of his life.

The server returned for their orders.

"Ice cream," Katie said. "Chocolate. Three scoops."

The server froze. "For breakfast?"

"It's five o'clock somewhere. Make it four scoops."

The server turned to McQuire as if to ask, "Is she kidding?"

"I'm not kidding."

The server shrugged, took McQuire's order, and then slinked away.

McQuire lowered his head, and his voice, in a conspiratorial manner. "Tell me the truth. Did you write that threat on the bathroom mirror?"

She leaned back and threw her napkin on the table. "You've got to be kidding me."

"I have to ask, and keep in mind, we have attorney-client privilege. Anything you say to me, I take to the grave."

She shook her head. "Someone ran me off the road. Someone turned off the lights in the bathroom and wrote on the mirror. I don't know how they ran me off the road without leaving any evidence. I don't know how they got a hold of my lipstick to write on the mirror."

"I believe you," he said in a manner that implied no such thing. "But for your dad and his case, I think you need to dial back your efforts. And by dial back, I mean stop. For real, this time. No vigilante stuff. No accusing people or following people or anything else that could ruffle Lieutenant Crozier's feathers."

"You mean just let my dad go to jail now that I'm absolutely positive he's innocent because proving his innocence will somehow inconvenience Lieutenant Crozier? Is that what you're saying?"

Before he could answer, their food arrived. Katie dug into her ice cream so fast her brain froze, but in a really, really good way.

McQuire dug into his chicken-fried steak and with his mouth still full, he said, "Look, I get it. If it were my dad, I'd do the same thing. Try everything possible to create some reasonable doubt. But I'm telling you, the way you're going about it—"

"You don't believe me."

His eyes widened as wide as her ice cream bowl. "I gotta tell you, it looks bad. I'm not one to judge, but—"

Her voice rose. "But you are judging. Because you think I made all of this up."

"Do you have any evidence?"

She folded her arms and looked away.

"That's what I thought."

"Since when was it the victim's responsibility to provide the evidence?"

"Since . . . I don't know."

The next few minutes passed in silence.

McQuire finished his meal and wiped his mouth. "You know what? I think I like this place better than Cynthia's."

She didn't agree, despite everything that'd happened the night before. She liked the food at Cynthia's. Violet always took great care of the crew. And they didn't have to drive fifteen minutes to get there.

That said, she'd have a hard time going back. It'd be hard to put last night behind her, especially since no one believed her, including her own attorney, apparently.

It was just so darn depressing.

She shoved another spoonful of ice cream into her mouth.

Despite having a ton of questions for McQuire, she didn't have the strength to ask them. He'd lost her trust, and she didn't know how she was going to recover from that, either. What she needed now to was regroup with the crew. She still wasn't convinced of Ian Trembley's innocence and continued to hold out hope that either he or someone who had nothing to do with puzzles killed Elena.

Unfortunately, she was running out of time to prove it, and now had even less people who believed in her and her efforts.

* * *

That afternoon, she picked up her Outback from the police station parking lot, shooting daggers at the building as she pulled away, thinking that her sick day was actually making her sick.

It was tempting to go back to work and let the busyness blow away her frustration, but she didn't want to run into Ian Trembley after everything and she wasn't sure she wanted to tell Neal what was going on, and he was sure to ask.

The fire station was only a block away. Odds were that Connor was working a shift, but while he would certainly be a source of comfort, one that left her more unsure of herself, she didn't want to face the embarrassment of the confrontation with his father or the conversation she and Connor needed to finish.

She decided to go somewhere else close that didn't involve driving far, either, barely a block away, visiting the one person she actually felt like talking to today.

"Thank you, Officer Tallon," she said after he escorted her to the visitation room. The officer shut the door behind him. Katie sat down at the table and said to her dad, "How are you?"

"I think the bigger question is how are you?"

It wasn't the easiest question to answer. It was an impossible question to answer with any positivity, and the last thing she wanted to do was dump all her negativity on him.

She looked around. "Do you think they record these conversations?"

Dad shrugged. "Don't know. I suppose so. Are you afraid of saying something you shouldn't say?"

She hardened her gaze and told him about Cynthia's, leaving out the part about no one believing her. Something in his eyes flickered. "What is it?" she said.

"Tell me that again. Start from the top."

She did, telling it extra fast to get to the end. His quizzical look remained. "Do you know something?" she asked when she finished.

He looked around the claustrophobic room. "It's just a strange story, that's all."

"And you're a terrible liar."

He raised his handcuffed hands as far as they would go. "Guilty as charged."

"That's not funny."

"Maybe not, but that's how it's starting to feel."

"What do you mean?"

"I had a long conversation with Dan Crozier yesterday."

"Without your attorney?"

He scowled. "Do you think I'm crazy?"

"Why didn't Mr. McQuire tell me about that?"

"Why would he tell you anything? He's not allowed to do that. It's called—"

"I know what it's called. He told me."

Dad straightened. "You met with Carlton. When?"

She didn't respond.

"Katie?"

"I just had breakfast with him. Is that a problem?"

Dad's jaw clenched. "He's not supposed to do that."

"Don't worry, he didn't tell me anything about you, including your interview with Lieutenant Crozier."

"Oh," he said, almost disappointed.

Katie continued. "Mr. McQuire heard about what happened last night." She sank a little lower in her chair. "I left out an important part of last night. Or this morning, rather."

"Which is?"

"Which is the part where Lieutenant Crozier didn't believe me. He thought I'd made it up, along with the accident on Saturday. There's no proof someone ran me off the road, so he assumes I made that up, too."

"You met with Lieutenant Crozier?" he asked, clearly shaken.

All of a sudden, the lights in the room felt hotter. She gave him a slow, guilty nod.

Dad's expression turned serious. "Are you in trouble?"

She squirmed in her seat. "Not really?"

"Not really? Katherine, what aren't you telling me?"

Katherine. Dad's code for "You're in big trouble." She took in the room around her and realized what it was really for. It was for interrogation. And in this scenario, she was the interrogator. Not the other way around.

She put on a formal air. "Mr. Chambers, where were you last Monday at nine PM?"

"This isn't funny."

"I'm not trying to be funny. I'm trying to solve a murder."

"That's not your job."

"It's Lieutenant Crozier's job, and he's not doing it. Just play along, maybe I'll learn something."

He relaxed. A little. "Fine, but you need to be careful. You know where I was. I was at work. I met with Elena earlier in the evening. Then I went outside to get a book from my car. I took some time to read it. I came back inside. That's it. There's nothing more to tell."

"Did you see anyone else when you were outside? In the parking lot? In their car? Off to the side?"

He shook his head. But again, there was something about his reaction that bothered her.

"What aren't you telling me, Dad?"

"I can't be sure."

"I can be, because I saw someone on the front camera across the street. Then they rounded the corner down Vienna. *Toward you.*"

Dad leaned back and took a deep breath.

"Tell me, Dad."

He looked up and to his left. "I did see someone, and at the time I figured it was Elena, but now I'm thinking it might not have been her."

She leaned toward him. "Why?"

He shrugged. "How do I say it? The person wasn't . . . shaped like her?" He closed his eyes, shook his head and let out a sigh. "I don't know anymore."

"Shouldn't you tell Lieutenant Crozier?"

"You know he's made up his mind. He has it in his head that we were an item, it was a relationship gone bad that ended in violence."

"He really believes that?"

"He really believes that, just like he says he doesn't believe you. He says he has proof."

"Has he shared that with you? Or Mr. McQuire?"

"I don't think they have to until the trial."

He glanced over her head. She turned. The clock had caught his attention. Because they were out of time.

Without warning, he reached for her hand but she was too far way. She leaned in closer and took his. He lowered his voice to barely above a whisper. "Forget what I said before. Don't stop, honey. Dig and dig and dig. Something smells about this, and I *can't* figure it out in here. I didn't do this, but I have a suspicion who did."

"Do you want to tell me?"

He shook his head. "If I'm wrong, I'll regret it. If you come to the conclusion on your own, I'll know I'm right."

"Is it someone you know?"

He nodded.

"Is it someone I know?"

He nodded.

There was a knock on the door.

She stood and said, "Consider it done."

* * *

"Consider what done?" she asked herself when she got home. "Finding a killer? For some reason the request sounded harder coming from Dad."

Whimsy corralled her to his food bowl and she obliged.

She hated that Dad hadn't told her who he thought did it. She wasn't even sure she understood his reasoning. What she did understand was his fragility, which she couldn't blame him for, given his situation.

It was close to five o'clock. The workday had ended for most people. By now, much of her pain was gone both in her back and her head. She'd even ditched the Band-Aid on the drive back from visiting Dad, before she picked up takeout from Hangzhou Palace: Kung Pao chicken, egg drop soup, and a spring roll.

Once she got home, she dumped the pieces of a small 300-piece puzzle onto the table, away from her plate. Multitasking, they called it at work. Doing a bunch of things at the same time. Solve a puzzle. Eat Chinese. Scratch the cat. She would do it all. Get those neurons in her head firing.

With her chopsticks at the ready, she prepared for a puzzle and a nice, quiet, satisfying meal. Because, for once, since this ordeal had begun, she wanted to be alone. If there was ever a time to get away from people, clear her head, focus on the problem at hand, it was—

Ding dong!

The temptation to pretend she wasn't home was great. She'd just pinched a large chunk of chicken between her chopsticks, lifted the chicken to her mouth, and—

Knock knock!

"Coming," she said, dropping the sticks onto her plate.

It was Connor.

She opened the door but blocked any entrance he might've been conceiving.

"Hey," she said.

"Hey," he said.

"Hopefully we're not getting paid by the word," she said.

He stood on the porch, in the cold. The temperature must've dropped about ten degrees since she'd come home. Another night, she'd have invited him in, but she just couldn't bring herself to do it.

"So, uh. Anything new?" he asked.

She leaned against the doorjamb. "It's been a long day. I just got some dinner. I feel a nap coming on."

He put his hands in his pockets and stiffened when a breeze blew through.

"I've got some news," he said.

"Anything I wanna hear?"

"Probably not," he said with a head shake.

"Let me have it."

He turned his head and looked down the road before returning his attention to her. "Harold Beck is a no-go."

"We knew that."

He shrugged. "I was holding out hope. That's not all."

She braced herself.

"Ian Trembley's off the board, too. I overheard my dad talking to someone on the phone. Apparently, ten people vouched for seeing Ian at some bar just outside town. The place's security cameras confirmed it."

"Your dad just let you listen to his conversation?"

He tried to use his boyish charm. "I may have tricked him a little bit." The charm didn't work. He glanced over her shoulder, toward the kitchen. "Am I interrupting dinner?"

She nodded.

He leaned to his left. "And a puzzle by the looks of it. Three hundred pieces?"

She chuckled. "Who taught you that?"

"Ken. He made a cheat sheet for me anytime I wanted to impress you with puzzle talk."

The temperature continued to drop and the wind continued to blow. Her conviction was starting to weaken. But then it hit her that he'd spent time with his father.

"Did your dad tell you anything else? Anything about me?"

"Not exactly."

"Wow," she said with a snort. "You're a worse liar than my dad."

"Perhaps, but for the record, I believe you. And I told my dad so."

"So your influence over him is quite dazzling." She definitely wasn't ready to talk about the breakup. It wasn't the time.

He pulled his hands from his pockets and blew into them. "How'd someone get ahold of your lipstick?"

She dropped her head. "You don't think I've been asking myself that all day? I used it yesterday. Multiple times. I just don't remember the last time I used it."

"Was it at the restaurant?"

"I don't think so."

He shivered and jumped up and down.

"Problem?" She asked.

"Is it hypothermia or hyperthermia when you get too cold?"

"They didn't teach you that at fireman's school?"

"I'm testing your knowledge." He turned his attention to the porch chair.

"You don't need to do that."

"Is there any other way to prove to you that I believe you than try to protect you?"

"You don't need to prove anything to me."

He gazed into her eyes. "I think I do."

She sighed. "Connor—"

"Let's do this. Put your food away. You can heat it up tomorrow. Let's go out and, I don't know. Get a pizza. A good old-fashioned pizza."

"Your father thinks I'm a bloody liar," she blurted out.

He took a step back. "I don't. I know you."

"I'm sorry," she said. "But I can't get over your father not believing me. Someone *threatened* me. And that was after someone tried to run me off the road and your *father* thinks I'm lying."

He opened his mouth to talk.

"Connor, it's okay. I don't blame you. But I've tried everything this past week. I've worked with you. I've worked with the crew. We've had parties. We've done puzzles. And all I have to show for it is . . . my father's in jail." Her eyes welled with tears. "And I haven't been able to help him. I think it's all over. My dad's going to jail. For good."

He reached out to hug her, but she pulled back.

"Not tonight. The one thing I haven't done is spend some time alone. Just me. With my thoughts." She threw a glance over her shoulder. "My Kung Pao is getting cold."

"Extra hot?"

"With no peanuts."

"You know they're what make it Kung Pao. Otherwise, it's just Szechuan chicken."

She allowed herself a grin. "I appreciate it, but I'll be okay." Now she eyed the chair. "And no, you don't need to sleep out here."

He raised his hands. "If you say so."

"I say so. I also say . . . I'll call you tomorrow. Let you know I made it through the night."

He nodded solemnly. "I'm sorry about my dad. When this is all over, I think I can clarify things."

She smiled. They said goodbye. She shut the door and leaned against it.

"That was pretty stupid, wasn't it, Whimsy?"

The cat nodded.

Chapter Twenty-Three

The next morning, Katie was back at work, having what was as close as she could get to a normal day. Her phone was filled with texts and calls from the crew wanting to know how she was. She responded to each of them.

Her phone was free of messages from one person. Connor. But she couldn't blame him. She'd made it clear that she'd call him when she was ready.

After catching up on her email from the day before, she went to Neal's office for a meeting and nearly gasped when she saw Ian in the room. Partly because he was there in the first place. But mostly because of his appearance. His hair was pulled back in a bun. He'd ditched the black concert T-shirt for a light-blue oxford. He even wore slacks instead of jeans. But it was his sour expression and how he glared out of Neal's window, presumably at the cedars, paying no attention to her whatsoever. That unnerved her.

The others all looked her way, including Neal, seeming as uncomfortable as she felt.

She took her seat next to Marjorie, which was as far away from Ian as possible. Neal started the meeting, making no reference to anything that had occurred over the last week. He ticked through his agenda items like he was in a hurry, and when he reached the end, he'd somehow managed not to even mention Elena's name when he spoke about her puzzles.

He held up a blank box. "This is going to be our next release. Thanks to Katie and her crew, they've given it their seal of approval. Thanks to the design team and the production team. I think this one's going to be a winner."

Marjorie raised her hand. "I've had some distributors ask if this could be available before Thanksgiving."

Neal raised his eyebrows and looked around the room, nodding as he went, and was met with a room filled with murmurs of agreement. "That's great. It only gives us a few weeks, but I think we can do it. Does anyone not believe we can do it?"

Katie was tempted to say something and Neal must've noticed.

"Concerns, Katie?"

"The long pole in the tent will be the box cover design, which as you can see, is far from complete."

"Actually," a woman said, holding up her laptop. "It's done. Sorry, Katie. We reviewed that yesterday. The request for approval should be in your inbox."

Katie tried to swallow her embarrassment. She'd thought she caught up on her email, but obviously she'd missed one. Something she never did. Neal quickly covered for her.

"Problem solved. Katie will get the cover design approved ASAP and we'll be on our way. Anything else?"

Everyone's heads shook.

"Great," he said with a clap. "Let's go out there and make some great puzzles."

Everyone stood and headed for the door, including Ian, who absolutely would not look in Katie's direction. She was nearly out the door when—

"Katie, can you hang back for a bit?" It was Neal.

She waited for the others to leave. "What's up?" she asked.

"I just wanted to check in. See how you're doing. We missed you yesterday." He nodded toward the door. "As you can see."

"I'm fine," she said.

He folded his arms and shot her an I-don't-believe-you look.

She sat back down. "Yesterday was hard."

"Ian tells me he's been cleared of any wrongdoing."

"No thanks to me, I bet."

A smile crossed Neal's face. "His report may have included some editorializing like that."

"If he really didn't do it, then I apologize for any disruption I caused."

Neal waved her comment away and sat back down. "Ian lives for the drama. In fact, I think you made his day in his own weird sort of way. But to be honest . . ." He adjusted his glasses. "I thought you could've been right."

"How so?"

"I saw him at Cynthia's that night. He walked in, looked around, and walked out before I could say something. He didn't order anything. He didn't talk to anybody. Just in and out."

"Did you ask Violet? If anyone would know what was going on, it'd be her. She's like the town-gossip switchboard."

"I would have, but she wasn't there."

Katie cocked her head. "On a Monday night? That seems odd. I thought she worked every night, except Fridays and Saturdays."

"Who's the town gossip now?"

"I can't help it if I pay attention to people."

"Well, my server didn't pay attention that night. I think she was new because she got my order wrong about five times."

"Whew," she said. "I hope Cynthia didn't find out. That stuff drives her crazy."

"It drove me crazy, but I didn't say anything. She just needed some training. Anyhow, how's your dad?"

She ran a finger across the table. She'd done a pretty good of shifting thoughts about Dad aside during the day, but now it was all coming back.

"He's in a tough spot. The police seem to be done. They've asked me to give up. Or rather, told me to give up."

"That doesn't sound like you."

"It's not, except for the fact that I have nothing to go on. Like you said, Ian was cleared. Harold Beck and anyone associated with him seems to be clean."

"For murder," Neal said, correcting her. "Beck has a whole lot of other trouble when it comes to corporate espionage. I wouldn't want to be in his shoes when those charges are read."

She ignored the comment. "That leaves my dad and whoever really did it, and I gotta be honest, I don't have a single person in mind."

Neal leaned back in his chair and stared up at the ceiling. That was what he did when he was trying to solve a tough problem.

"You don't have to do that, Neal."

"Do what?" he said, returning his gaze toward her.

"Try to solve it yourself."

"I'm not trying to solve it. I'm trying to interpret something Ian said."

She scooted up to the edge of her chair.

"After launching his tirade about you, he said he felt badly for your father."

"That's a surprise. The feeling sorry for my dad. Not the tirade."

"He said he'd hate to see Jim go to prison for this."

"Does he even know my dad?"

"Come on, Katie. He worked side by side with your mother for years. Between the company picnics and the occasional extended family dinners, everybody got to know your dad. Mostly because people wanted to get to know the lucky guy married to your mom."

A lump formed in her throat. *Focus on the whole puzzle. Don't try to force the piece you can see to fit. Find the piece that's missing; it'll be the one that fits.*

"She's the missing piece of the puzzle," she said. "That's it." She jumped to her feet. "You just said it. She's the missing piece of the puzzle. Ian knew it; that's why he was there. He was looking for her. *But she wasn't there.*"

"Who wasn't there?" he asked, standing up.

"Someone I should've suspected from the start."

* * *

She ran to her desk and pulled her iPad out of her bag. Quickly studied her notes. She'd never mentioned Violet once, even though she'd been there the whole time. She was in love with Dad. She was angry at Elena. It was her car. *She* had Katie's lipstick. The person who drove away from the restaurant the other night was just that. A person driving away from the restaurant.

Violet had been at the server station, which was about three feet from the bathroom, holding the coffee pot, which she could've just picked up.

She ran back to Neal's office. "I need to do something."

"What was all that about?"

"Don't worry about it. I'll fill you in later. Can I go?"

"Will you tell me what's going on?"

"No."

She left his office. But then ran back.

"Yes. Of all people, Ian Trembley just helped me with the case. But don't tell him. Not until I have proof."

He didn't look convinced. "What are you thinking?"

"I can't say for sure," she lied, because she was absolutely positive. "Nothing to Ian, remember?"

"Go get 'em, Columbo. Get the truth."

"You promise?"

He pretended to lock his lips.

Then she flew out of the building, running past the receptionist, forgetting to say goodbye to her. Feeling guilty. She ran back inside. Apologized for not saying goodbye. Said goodbye. Left again, for her car, fumbling her phone on the way. She picked it up then unlocked it and scrolled through her contacts.

"It's Violet," she said into the phone.

"What's Violet?" Connor said.

"The last color in Roy G. Biv."

"Roses are red. Violets are blue."

"And if you don't step messing around, I'm gonna hang up on you." She opened the Outback's door with her phone against her ear. "What I'm trying to say is . . . Violet killed Elena."

"For real?"

She jumped in, pressed the engine start button, and was pulling out of Cedar Bay Puzzles before she responded.

"I'm serious. Are you at work?"

"I can be. I was just out getting some coffee."

"Do you ever work, or is it like being part of *The Flintstones* Bedrock Fire Department for you?"

"What?" he said with a laugh.

"I'll meet you in front of the station in five minutes."

* * *

In four minutes, she pulled up in front of the Cedar Bay Fire Station, fully expecting Connor to meet her, but he was nowhere to be found. She put the car into park and ran inside.

"Where's Connor?" she asked.

"Getting coffee," one of the firefighters said.

"Of course. Thank you."

He wasn't still getting coffee.

She ran back out of the station, headed toward Cynthia's. Hurried into the building and nearly crashed into Connor on the way out. Nearly covering him with coffee.

"She's not here," he said, nonplussed.

"I told you I'd meet you at the station."

"And I'm telling you, Violet's not here."

"Because she works at night."

"Oh. Well, that explains it. Cynthia said she expected her tonight because Violet never calls in sick, and she didn't expect her to call in sick for the second time in a couple of weeks. Any guess when the first time was?"

"Last Monday night."

"Bingo." He held up a thumb drive. "I also have the video surveillance from this Monday."

"I thought it didn't show the bathroom."

"It doesn't. But I'm hoping it'll show Violet grabbing your purse when you weren't looking."

"No! Cynthia gave that to you?"

"Yes and yes. Come on. We need to talk to my dad."

She grabbed him by the arm and he stopped.

"We can't."

"What are you talking about? It's Violet. You said so yourself. You have the proof."

"I have the suspicion. I have circumstantial evidence at best. She's the missing piece of the puzzle. I know that now, but I still can't make it fit. If we go to your dad too soon, he'll never believe us, and if we show our hand to Violet too soon, she'll either leave town or find some other way to get out of it."

"Okay," he said. "What are you thinking?"

She turned and looked down the street "I'm thinking I need to pull the crew together at the library and solve this puzzle for good."

"It's a Wednesday morning. Do you think you can get them all here?"

She nodded. "Ken and Mildred are retired. Tony can step away from the dealership for an hour. The hard part will be getting Hannah a hall pass."

"Truancy. The key to crime fighting."

"Let's go," she said. "I feel like walking."

"Well, it's only three blocks. I think you can make it there safely by yourself."

She flung her head around. "Where are you going?"

"Work. I'm not retired, and my chief won't accept a high school hall pass."

If she were being honest with herself, she was crushed, and it surprised the heck out of her. He was right, of course. He had to get back to work. But he'd become such a security blanket over these past few days. She'd managed without him last night but didn't know how she'd get through the rest of the day.

"How about," he said, "you go to the library. Work your magic. I get off at five. We'll gather tonight."

"At Cynthia's."

"Exactly." He handed her the thumb drive.

"Your dad's going to kill you," she said.

Connor shook his head. "He'll get upset, but he's not a killer. And neither's your dad."

This time, she accepted the hug.

Chapter Twenty-Four

The crew met in their normal spot, the Puget Sound Conference Room at the Cedar Bay Public Library. And while they usually just sat around the conference table to work their puzzles, today, no one was seated. Everyone stood, buzzing with energy. Except Ken. He was studying the security tape from Cynthia's. And Mildred, of course. Okay, it was just Tony and Hannah. The excitement was getting the better of Katie.

She stood at the whiteboard, which Amy Richardson had generously supplied. The lunch order had been placed at JJ's, which was due any minute.

"This is so cool," Hannah said, her hands gathered in prayer.

Tony looked perplexed. "How did you get out of class?"

"Parent emergency. My mom sent a note. She just didn't say whose parent." She waggled her eyebrows.

Tony shook his head. "I wish I had parents like that when I was in school."

"Okay," Katie said, weapon in hand, i.e., the blue marker. "Here is what we know." She pointed to each line she'd written supporting her thesis that Violet was the killer. "The problem is, we don't know how to prove it."

"So she had the hots for your dad, huh?" Mildred tossed out there. "That's awkward."

"And it's pretty hard to prove, unless you have some spicy texts or emails you can find," Hannah said.

Katie shivered. "Let's move on."

Tony said, "We have the figure in the library video who we think is the same one who followed *you* outside the library."

Katie crossed her arms and put a toe out. "I remember, but I can't definitively say that either one is Violet."

"What about her car?" Hannah said, standing on the other side of the whiteboard with the same posture as Katie.

"Has anyone seen her car?" Mildred asked.

"Probably," Tony said.

"I agree," Hannah said. "But I can't tell you what it is."

"We've probably seen it every week but didn't pay much attention to it," Katie added. "Maybe someone can find out. I'm a little concerned, because I didn't get a good look at it Saturday night. All I remember is gray, but even then, I could be wrong."

Ken buried his head into his hands and shook it.

"What's the matter?" Katie asked.

He spun his laptop around. "It's almost conclusive. Look here." He pointed to an image of Katie at Cynthia's sitting at the table. "You can't see your purse, but you can see Violet approach, do something when you're looking the other way, and leave. Then she comes back, directs your attention down the table, and does something again."

"By something, you mean take my purse to get at the lipstick."

"That's exactly what I mean. The problem is that the purse is hidden from the shot."

"As if she knew the camera was watching," Mildred tossed in.

Ken nodded glumly.

"That's not enough," Katie said.

"Not even close," Ken said.

Hannah tapped her finger on her chin. "She doesn't know that, though."

All eyes turned in her direction.

"We know what we have isn't enough, but she doesn't. What if we find a way to use what we do have and trick her into confessing?"

They all exchanged glances. Mildred was the skeptical one of the bunch.

"You don't think so, Mildred?" Katie said.

"What if she doesn't get the hint?"

Ken shook his head. "We can do better than hint." He held up the thumb drive. "This is the video recording. That's a fact. Cynthia gave it to Connor. That's a fact. Unless she's studied the video herself, she doesn't know what we can see."

"That's a start," Katie said.

Tony raised a hand. "I can check out the car. You just tell me the make, model, and color."

"I think it was gray. I think it was an SUV. That's as good as I can do."

"Again," Hannah said, raising her finger. "She doesn't know what we know. We could bluff on that, too."

Mildred grinned broadly. "I always loved the devious kids in my classes. I just could never tell anyone."

"Devious it is," Katie said. "But I'd still like Tony to get a good view of her car."

Tony agreed. "I'll swing by her house. It's possible she'll drive a different one to work now that you've told everyone about the accident."

"Good point."

Ken still looked skeptical.

"Problem?"

"We've been avoiding the most important piece of evidence from the start. The smoking gun."

Hannah looked confused. "What smoking gun?"

He spread his hands wide. "I mean the actual gun she used to murder Elena. Frankly, I don't know how they've charged Jim without it."

"Or maybe they have it and they haven't told us," Tony said.

Ken turned to Katie wearing a serous expression. "Does your Dad own a gun?"

She was stumped. "I don't know. He's never mentioned one, but that doesn't mean . . . Maybe after Mom died? What are you thinking?"

He sat back and interlaced his fingers behind his head. "What if the evidence Dan has on Jim is the gun? They were able to match the bullet to it."

Katie's pulse spiked. "Are you saying my dad did it?"

Ken shook his head. "I'm asking—what if Violet somehow got ahold of Jim's gun and used it to frame him? Everything about this looks like a frame-up. I don't think Violet did it to get revenge on Elena." He stared directly at Katie. "I think she did it to get revenge on your dad."

Her heart jumped into her throat. How could anybody do that to her dad? He was this great big teddy bear everybody loved. Apparently, Violet loved him too much.

"So where is the gun?" Tony asked.

Ken ran his fingers through what was left of his hair. "Either the police have it, or . . ."

"She's hidden it," Katie said.

"Yep," Ken said. "Now we have to figure out where she'd hide it."

"Easy," Tony said. "It's either someplace where Jim will get blamed or someplace it'll never be found."

Katie said, "Or . . ."

"Or," Hannah said. "She keeps it with her."

That took the air out of the room.

"Wouldn't the police have checked for that?" Mildred asked.

Ken shook his head. "She's not the suspect. Jim is."

"But they didn't search my house," Katie said.

The five of them stayed silent for a beat.

Finally, Ken said, "Write it on the board with a big question mark?"

Katie did.

"Speaking of question marks," Tony said. But there was a knock on the door before he could complete his thought.

Amy Richardson came in with one of her assistants, both pairs of arms filled with bags of food. They handed everyone their respective lunch until one bag remained. Amy opened it up, gazed in, and then looked up quizzically.

"Who ordered chocolate ice cream for lunch?"

Katie snatched the bag from her. "Don't judge."

* * *

Forty-five minutes later, the crew walked out the back door of the library, except for Mildred. Tony was pushing her in her chair. There was a chill in the air, but the sky was clear. The sunshine warmed Katie's face while the saltwater air was a balm to her mind.

Ken stopped at the curb, put his hands into his jacket pockets, and faced the others.

"Last chance. Are we all agreed about this?"

They all nodded.

He tilted his head. "Our plan has some holes in it, including one very big hole."

"I'm not worried about the gun," Katie lied. "Everything Violet's done has literally been in the dark. As long as we're in the light, she won't do anything, including pull out a gun."

The others eyed her with suspicion.

"I'm pretty sure," she said with a shrug.

It was Tony's turn to express concern. "This is all on you, Katie. It's your dad. It's your personal risk. I don't need to remind you that Crozier's laid out the consequences if you keep interfering with this case. Even your own attorney thinks you're nuts."

Mildred cocked her head, looking up at him. "That had to be the worst pep talk ever."

"I'm just sayin'," Tony said, showing his palms. "No one could blame her if she wanted to back out now."

"He's right," Hannah added. "We'll understand if you change your mind." Then she smiled wide. "But I really hope you don't."

"I'm not changing my mind. We'll meet at Cynthia's at seven. We'll follow the script exactly as we've written it. We'll expose Violet as the killer, and my Dad should be home by the evening news."

The others said nothing.

"This isn't crazy, is it?" she said.

They all shook their heads.

"Good," she said. "That makes me feel better."

* * *

"They lied," she told Whimsy. "This is crazy. I mean totally crazy. As in, I am out of my freaking mind crazy."

The cat agreed with her completely, provided that she filled his food bowl again.

It was dinnertime, so Whimsy had a good point. Katie was holding off eating until Cynthia's, but maybe that wasn't such a good idea since the whole point of going there was to confront Violet and expose her as Elena's killer.

Whimsy's interest in her problems faded the minute he buried his head into his bowl.

She went out to her back porch, bringing a blanket with her and a cup of tea. She sat on the chair and wrapped herself in the blanket, staring above the trees, enjoying her view of Puget Sound. Wondering what the folks in Rose Point and Kingston were up to, not that she really knew anybody over there. It was just nice to wonder.

A car came down her street toward her house. It drove on past, the driver tossing her a kind wave. For all the negativity that had come her way lately, she was probably being too hard on Cedar Bay. She really did love the place, Violet and Lieutenant Crozier notwithstanding.

Yes, she missed Denver. The Rockies were beautiful. Trading three hundred days of sunshine for half that here was tough. And the skiing? Wow, she loved that, even if she spent most of her time either falling down the hills or curled up around a nice cup of hot chocolate in the ski lodge.

She sipped her tea. This was home, maybe now more than ever. The last week had surrounded her with reminders, both good and bad, and if she were being honest with herself, the bad was outweighed by the good.

Where else would she find a crew so dedicated to helping her and her father through this impossible situation? They didn't have to do that. That was loyalty. That was dedication.

Another car came down the street, but she recognized this one. It belonged to Mr. and Mrs. Ramsay. They pulled into their driveway next door. Mr. Ramsay tossed her a wave before going in the house. It didn't convey the judgement she'd expect from a person who lived next door to a man charged with murder. If the shoe were ever on the other foot, she hoped she'd be as open-minded.

She blew the steam from her tea as the sun dipped deeper in the western sky. The folks near the Swantown Marina were about to be treated to an amazing sunset.

Which brought her to Connor. Especially Connor. He was playing an important role in the drama, one she'd never have expected. One she wouldn't even have hoped for. It was confusing, though. It was going to take some time for her to sort out her feelings now that she knew the truth about their breakup. She loved her mother, but it was going to take some time before she got over that it was her mom who really broke her heart. Not Connor. Now she wasn't sure whether she was enjoying Connor's presence because she really missed him or she missed her dad, and he was temporarily filling that role. Could she have her conflicting emotions surgically removed?

She tightened the blanket around her and sipped her tea. Time would tell her all the answers she needed.

She shivered when a frigid wind blew through. She set her tea on the floor and tossed the blanket over her shoulder. She was about to stand when another car came down the road.

Speak of the devil, she thought.

"It's hypothermia," Connor said, pulling up to the curb with his window rolled down.

"What's hypothermia?"

"What you're doing now. Sitting outside in the freezing cold."

She stood and collected her cup. "If you think this is freezing, you should spend a day in Vail when the temperature drops below zero."

He opened the Explorer's door and got out. "I keep hearing that it's a dry cold."

"Cold is cold."

He stopped at the stairs to the porch. "Permission to come aboard?"

"Do you really want to sail on this sinking ship?"

"I'll take my chances."

They went inside. He immediately picked up Whimsy, scratched the cat's neck.

"If you feed him," she teased, "he'll be yours for life." She couldn't believe it when Whimsy starting purring.

Connor set the cat back down. "The last thing I need is another hungry mouth to feed."

"Another?"

He shrugged. "Two others. Two dogs."

"You?" she said with a laugh. "Have two dogs?"

"And a rabbit, if you count the one tearing up my backyard."

The surprises kept on coming. She didn't know Connor had become an animal person. In fact, she didn't know much about him, other than their history. They'd been so wrapped up in the drama around Elena's death, they hadn't had a single, actual conversation about ordinary life. They'd have that conversation about the past soon.

Connor crossed his arms. "I assume you and the crew have come up with some God-awful plan."

"The worst."

"Let me guess. It's dangerous as heck, and if you had any brains at all you'd call it off and go straight to my dad."

"That's exactly what I'd do if I even had one brain cell in my head."

"To make matters worse, you have no intention of telling me what it is."

"Not even the slightest."

He sighed. "That's fair."

She recoiled. "Really."

"Really." He dug into his coat pocket and pulled out something. Lipstick. He handed it to her.

"Where'd you get this?"

"Drug store."

She shook her head. It was the right brand and even the right color.

"So your dad told you?"

"About what?"

She held up the lipstick and frowned.

"Oh, no. He'd never tell me something like that."

"Then how did you know?"

He shrugged.

She furrowed her brow. "Do you know everything that happens in this town?"

"And the mainland, too."

She grabbed her purse from the counter and put the lipstick inside. "Thank you," she said.

"My pleasure." He paused. "And I'm sorry he doesn't believe you."

"Do you believe me?"

He nodded.

"Really?"

"Really."

"Why?"

He wrung his hands. "My dad doesn't know you like I do."

"Do you know me? We haven't spoken in ten years. I've changed. You've changed. I mean, we're not teenagers anymore."

He cast her a puzzling expression. "How about we save that knock-down, drag-out for another day, when we can focus and be honest with each other. Like, when after all this craziness passes. Speaking of craziness . . ." Then he frowned. "When do you plan on launching this crazy plan of yours?"

"That's confidential."

"You're meeting the crew at Cynthia's at seven o'clock," he said as smugly as he could. "I was asking to be nice."

"How'd you—" But his grin gave him away. "I just told you when, didn't I?" She pulled a chair out from under the kitchen table and took a seat. "I'm not the scheming mastermind I thought I was, am I?"

He took the seat opposite her.

"Not really. And that's a good thing. Besides, it's not like I can blame you. If my dad were in trouble, I'd do everything I could, too." He brought his hands together in prayer, rested his elbows on his thighs and his chin on his fingertips. "Do you want me to come?"

She shook her head.

"Do you think in a million years that I'm just going to let you go in there without being as close to the action as possible?"

"That's not necessary."

"But it is."

She nodded. "Thank you."

Right then, her watch vibrated. A new group text from Ken.

Showtime.

Chapter Twenty-Five

Katie huddled with the others in the chilly Cedar Bay Library parking lot. It felt like high school and they were all sneaking out of their parents' houses in the dark. Except it was six thirty in the evening and they were all grown adults. Except for Hannah, of course.

"Scene of the crime," Ken said, his hands in his jacket pockets. "Seems appropriate."

"Is everybody certain that they want to do this?" Katie asked.

"It's either this or study for my calc test tomorrow," Hannah said. "So yeah, I'm in."

The others nodded.

"Okay. We're going to drive over like it's any other crew meeting night."

"Except it's not Sunday!" Mildred tossed in for amusement. "And it's not nine o'clock."

"Except it's not Sunday. And it's not nine o'clock. And the Seahawks aren't playing. Do we know each of our roles?"

They nodded.

"Remember the first rule of warfare, *mi compadres*," Tony cautioned. "After the first shot is fired, the plan goes out the window."

"Though," Ken said, "it would be best if no shots are fired tonight."

"Agreed," Katie said. "But I hardly think she's going to shoot me in front of everyone in the restaurant."

Ken held his gaze on her.

"She's not. Okay?"

"If she does," Mildred said, "she'll be easy to catch!"

With that, they each got into their respective cars. Mildred with Tony, as usual. Hannah with Ken, and Katie alone in her Outback. It was a short drive but it lasted forever, it seemed. Katie hit both streetlights. Got caught behind a Nissan Rogue with its flashers on.

She was the last to arrive, which was actually per the plan. When she stepped inside the restaurant, the other four were waiting to be seated.

After a minute or two, Violet approached, as cheerful as ever. Coffee pot in hand.

"This is a treat," she said. "The puzzle factory must be working you guys overtime."

"Except we don't get paid," Mildred announced from her walker. She shrugged at the glares. "Well, we don't."

Violet turned to face the rest of the restaurant. "There's no one at your tables, but they have to be bussed."

"That's fine," Katie said, her heart pounding in her chest. "We can sit now."

What she really wanted to do was turn around and run out of there as fast as she could, but she successfully fought that urge.

She followed the others across the room, her mind buzzing with anticipation, doing her best to ignore the muffled argument in the kitchen and the '80s music pumped in from above. Then three things happened that she hadn't anticipated. First was Neal waving ferociously from where he and his wife sat at a table along the far side of the room. She lifted her arm to wave but it was as heavy as Thor's hammer; still, she managed a few strokes. But that wasn't enough. Because the second thing she didn't expect—or want—was him wanting her to come over to his table.

And if that wasn't bad enough, the third thing that happened made her question everything she was doing.

Because Ian Trembley was sitting at another table, kitty-corner from Neal and his wife. Ian saw her but didn't so much as acknowledge her beyond a withering stare.

Ken must've noticed as he stepped aside as the rest of their crew reached their seats.

"I think this is what Tony meant by the first shot fired."

"What should I do?"

"He's your boss. You have to go say hi. As for Ian, ignore him."

He was right. She couldn't ignore Neal without calling more attention to herself. She weaved her way through the maze of empty tables, the clinking of forks, knives, and glasses now overpowering the pumped-in music, as she clutched her bag for the trek. Based on the angle she took, Ian must've misinterpreted that she was heading his way, as he jumped out of his seat, his chair falling to the ground. He practically ran the long way toward the bathroom.

Neal greeted her with a hopeful face and an angelic smile.

"This is a surprise," he said. "Are you here why I think you're here?"

"Uh." She didn't know what to say. She hadn't considered that Neal might actually remember their conversation from earlier let alone show up at the restaurant for a front row seat. "I can't really say?"

He threw her a conspiratorial nod.

"Oh," he added. "You remember Kristy?"

"Of course," she said, reaching out her hand. "Nice to see you."

"You, too." Kristy let her gaze roam around the room. "This is so exciting," she whispered.

Katie shook her head. "There's nothing exciting going on. We're just hungry. Nothing to see here."

"There's always something to see here," a new voice said.

Katie jumped when she turned to find Violet nearly attached to her hip.

"You okay, hon? You look like you just saw a ghost."

Katie swallowed. Glanced toward the crew. They were all staring at her. "Stop it," she mouthed, waving them away.

"Not a ghost. Just a nice surprise. Neal. Kristy. You." She swallowed. "Ian. The gang is all here."

"Oh, honey," Violet said, reaching past her to refill Neal's coffee. "You don't have to include Ian. There's nothing nice about that man, if you know what I mean."

Katie furrowed her brow. "No, I actually don't."

Violet paused and arched an eyebrow, and while she may have intended it to be cute, Katie saw through it. There was a threat in that gaze, as if Violet already knew what the crew had planned, the probability of which wasn't exactly zero, given how she seemed to know everything that went on around her.

Katie jerked a thumb over her shoulder. "I should really get back. It was nice to see you again, Kristy, and bye, Neal."

She hurried back to her seat, leaving the aroma of Seattle's Best fresh roast behind her, sat down, and tried to breathe.

"You okay?" Hannah asked, putting her arm around Katie. "You look like you just saw a ghost," she added with a mischievous grin.

Katie's head snapped up. "You heard Violet from all the way over here?"

Hannah shook her head as if to imply that was preposterous. She raised her finger. "But I do read lips, and I think you handled yourself very well."

Ken, who was seated against the wall with his jacket off, and wearing a loud red sweater and his usual white oxford underneath, leaned forward. "What'd you learn over there?"

Katie pushed two dirty plates and a half-finished cup of coffee out of her way. "I learned . . . A. That while my boss isn't good at keeping secrets of his own, he can easily figure out mine. B. You're dressed like a fire hydrant, which is really distracting. C. I learned that Violet allegedly believes that Ian Trembley isn't a nice man. And, worst of all, D. She's acting like she knows what we're going to do."

The other four exchanged uncomfortable glances.

"Don't look at me," Mildred said. "I was asleep all day."

"I'm not accusing anyone," Katie said. "That was just the vibe I felt."

Tony scoffed, "She's bluffing. The only thing she knows, or suspects, is that you might be on to her and she's trying to throw you off your game."

"Well, then she's doing a pretty good job because it felt like she'd thrown me all the way to the sound."

"Shhh," Ken said. "Here she comes."

Violet strolled up, coffee pot still in hand. "You guys keep coming here this often, we're going to have to give you aprons and put you to work."

Nothing.

"Wow," she said. "Tough crowd. Will it be your usual orders, or do you plan to make tonight a little more interesting?"

"I'll have the same," Ken said.

"Same."

"Same."

"Same."

"What was the question?" Mildred asked.

"What do you want to eat?" Tony told her.

She scowled "What I always want. Why would you ask that?"

Tony rolled his eyes and leaned back in his chair.

"I'll get you some water, kick Alex over here to bus this stuff, and let you kids get back to your plotting and scheming."

Violet strolled away with a slight twinkle in her eye.

"See," Katie said.

Ken's gaze followed Violet to the kitchen. "I think you're right."

"I think she's playing us," Tony said.

"I think we need to change our plan," Hannah said.

"I think I'm hungry," Mildred said.

The others chuckled, but Katie's head was a million miles away. She was tempted to dump their plan and call Lieutenant Crozier, but he wouldn't be convinced without irrefutable proof and the only way to do that was to trick Violet into confessing. The funny thing was, it was almost as if Violet was dying to do it.

Katie got Hannah's attention after their meals were delivered. "Do you have the you-know-what handy?"

"My phone? Yep. Recorder app open, and phone hidden under the table. Thumb hovering over the button. You just say the word."

Katie gulped her water down and held up the empty glass. Violet spotted it right away and headed for the server station. Seconds later, she was back with a pitcher.

"Say when," she said.

"Top it off," Katie replied.

"How's that?'

"Perfect. Before you go . . ."

Violet paused.

"I wanted to ask you a few questions about my dad."

"Why me?"

"He told me something the other day that I didn't know."

"Which was?"

"He said . . ." She cleared her throat. "He said you two were close."

"Oh, yeah," Violet said as her face became that of a teenage girl with a crush. "Me and your dad were buds. *Are* buds," she said, raising the water pitcher to make her point. "But this whole thing with him and Elena." She mournfully shook her head. "I don't know. Sorta takes the wind outta ya. Don't ya think?"

The other crew members pretended to be eating their meals and let's just say, no Academy Awards would be doled out tonight.

"I don't think," Katie said. She threw a sideways glance at Hannah, who returned a slight nod. "I think it was you and Dad."

Violet flushed. "Me? What would he want with an old hag like me when he could have that young thing?"

"The heart wants what the heart wants."

Violet's red face remained but her attitude briskly chilled. She gripped the water pitcher so tightly that it looked like it might break. She said, "That heart didn't want this heart."

"And that really bothered you, didn't it?"

Violet glowered at Katie.

Come on, Violet. You're so close.

"It did . . . not." She shrugged. "I've been around the block, honey. Men come and go. Anything else I can get you folks?"

They all mumbled no. After Violet walked away, Katie dropped her head in defeat.

"Strike one," Tony said.

"More like a red card," Hannah added. She held up her hand and pretended to blow a whistle. "You just got tossed out of the game." She paused. "It's from soccer? You know, that sport everyone in the world plays? FIFA? Premier League? The World Cup?" No one replied. "Wow, tough crowd."

"What do I do now?" Katie asked, the aroma of Mildred's ever-present coffee keeping her alert.

Ken brought a cool head to conversation. "Tony's right. It's strike one. You had her going, but she's definitely on to you. The question is which will win out, her desire to gossip about what's been done or her desire for self-preservation?"

"Weren't you guys supposed to say something? Wasn't that part of the plan?"

Mildred looked around. "I thought we were supposed to get her to the table, but you did that all by yourself. There wasn't any time for us to do anything."

"You're right." Katie poked at her food. It didn't look appealing. Besides, she'd drank too much water, which meant. *Uh oh.*

She turned her gaze to the bathroom. Could she even go in there again?

Thankfully, Violet was still near the kitchen window. And besides, the others would be on the lookout.

"I'll be right back," she said.

"Plan B?" Ken said.

"No. Plan P."

She got to her feet, handed Hannah her bag, and returned to the scene of that crime. On her way, she looked back at least a hundred times to make sure Violet didn't see her. Inside, her reflection in the mirror caught her attention. She looked exhausted. Hannah had her bag and the lipstick. So she didn't have to worry about that.

Still, she threw a nervous glance at the door. Then knelt down to peek under the stalls to make sure they were empty. Satisfied she was alone, she ran the tap and splashed cold water on her face. After a few calming breaths, she was starting to relax. Maybe she wasn't going to trick Violet into confessing. At the moment, she was okay with that. She grabbed one of the neatly folded towels from the vanity when a clicking noise behind her captured her attention.

"Violet?" she said without turning.

"You don't sound surprised."

She refolded the towel and set it back down. "Oh, I wouldn't say that."

Katie made a mental note to tell the crew they'd assumed wrong.

"I thought we should finish our conversation," Violet said. "If now isn't too inconvenient for you."

Katie slowly turned to find Violet sitting on one of the cushy chairs in the far corner, near the door, her hands folded on her apron.

She also noticed that the door was locked.

"To answer your question," the waitress began with a coolness that more than disconcerted Katie, "you're right. I was mad. Probably madder than I'd ever been in my life."

Violet slowly stood and pulled out the gun she'd been hiding under her apron. Without thinking, Katie raised her hands.

"So," Violet said, taking a small step forward, her voice rising slightly. "I had two choices. Take my anger out on Jim, the man I've loved for years. Or, I could take it out on young Miss Larsson, who had no business being associated with him in the first place." She flashed a malicious grin. "It was an easy decision."

Violet took another step, her voice becoming shrill. "Do you know how long I've waited for your father? High school. College. Work. And then . . . your mom. So much time. And then, God smiles on me. He takes your mom and leaves Jim for me. But what does he do? He goes for a child. That girl was almost your age, for heaven's sake."

By now, Katie had accepted that her plan was, well, in the toilet. Had she brought her bag, she'd have her phone and she'd be recording this. Now she'd have to solve this puzzle a different way.

"Elena was just dad's friend, Vi. Nothing more."

"Oh, come on. You're not that naïve."

"But I do know my dad that well. I asked him point-blank. He said no."

Violet let out a sardonic snicker. "You're as dumb as that girl," she said.

"It's true, Vi. They were just friends. And I think if you look into your heart, you'll find it's true, too."

A fluorescent light flickered overhead. The gun started to tremble in Violet's hand and her lower lip started to quiver. If it weren't for the weapon aimed at her, Katie would have tried to give the older woman a hug.

"How about setting the weapon down and turning yourself in, Vi? If you ever really loved my dad, you know this is wrong. He doesn't deserve to go to prison, and he certainly wouldn't want me dead."

"No, honey. This is as right as it gets. It's only a matter of time before you and your strange little crew screw this up for me. So how about I count to three and end this once and for all? Deal?"

Katie said nothing.

"Deal," Violet said. "Here we go. One. Two." The gun shook harder. "Two and a half." Violet grabbed the weapon with both hands to still it. It didn't work. "Two and three quarters."

Ring!

The fire alarm blared so loud it hurt Katie's ears.

"What the—?" Violet cried.

In that moment of confusion, the door burst open. When Violet turned her head, Katie reached out and grabbed the gun, and aimed it back at the waitress.

"Three," said a new, deep voice.

Connor's voice.

"How much did you hear?" Katie asked without turning her head toward the door.

"I heard enough. So did he."

"He?"

Lieutenant Crozier stepped forward, wearing a stone-cold expression and with his gun drawn. "You can put down the weapon, Miss Chambers."

She turned, dumbstruck to see Lieutenant Crozier standing by his son. She set Violet's gun on the vanity.

"He loved me, Katie," Violet said in defiance. "I know he did . . ." Then she slowly put her hands behind her head, and knelt down on the floor. "Tell him I'm sorry."

"I'm sorry, too," Katie said, shaking her head. Because Mildred was right. Violet had been easy to catch, once the last unexpected piece fell into place. Connor.

Epilogue

Katie and the other crew members huddled in silence outside Cynthia's, with their rain hoods up as the cold, persistent mist coated the ground around them. Red and blue flashes shot out from the two cop cars blocking Main Street, showering the crowd like a rock concert light show.

Katie hugged herself and bounced on her toes to keep warm as Lieutenant Crozier loaded Violet into the back of his cruiser, hands cuffed behind her back, defiance upon her face.

"Incredible," Ken said.

"Unbelievable," Tony said.

"I never would've dreamed Violet could've done this," Hannah said.

"She was a terror as a child," Mildred said, holding the handles of her walker. "I'm not surprised one bit."

Even though everything had turned out fine in the end, Katie wished she felt better about it. Violet was their friend, or so she thought. All those conversations with the crew. All those meals. And in the end, Violet was more troubled than she could've ever imagined. And apparently, Dad was a bigger catch than she ever thought.

Cynthia, the restaurant's proprietor, had spent the last twenty minutes apologizing to Katie for Violet's behavior as if it were her fault. In turn, Katie thanked Cynthia for giving Connor the thumb drive of the surveillance video.

Cynthia smiled and said, "What are you talking about, dear?"

Katie let out a soft laugh. "Nothing," she said, putting her hand on the older woman's shoulder. "Nothing."

Cynthia's eyes flickered with suspicion, but then she excused herself to go back in and mind the shop. "The other customers can't feed themselves," she said.

As if complying with a stage director's cue, Connor approached from the shadows, still in his fireman's uniform, rain hood down, hair soaking wet. "Well," he said. "I'm glad to see that my distraction worked."

"Isn't it a crime to pull a fire alarm if there isn't fire?" Katie said.

He looked both ways and lowered his voice. "I won't tell if you won't."

"And your dad?" she said. "He just *happened* to be at Cynthia's when I needed him?"

He tossed her an exaggerated shrug. "I *may* have implied that you and the crew were planning on doing something that he'd consider stupid and that he should hover nearby just in case one of his less-than-smart constituents found herself in danger."

"Are you calling me less than smart?"

He leveled his gaze on her. "You baited a killer into pulling a gun on you. That's not exactly Mensa material."

"Touché, but that wasn't really the plan. Nonetheless . . . Thank you."

An uncomfortable silence passed between them until his father walked up, wearing a sheepish look.

"I guess I owe you an apology," he said. "I should have believed you. And after what Connor told me, I will admit I was a little biased toward you."

Connor gave his dad a look that said, "Would you please stop?"

She said to Lieutenant Crozier, "I'm just glad you heard the truth."

He held up his phone. "So will the jury."

She turned to Connor. "Your idea."

He raised his hands. "I plead the fifth."

Just a terrible liar. Something she'd always loved about him.

Two other police officers canvassed the rest of the crowd for their statements. The crew had all given theirs right away. Including the not-so-smart parts, not that she regretted it one bit. Results were results. Puzzle solved. Now to the next part.

"What about my father, Lieutenant Crozier?"

"We're all adults now, Miss Chambers. You can call me Dan. I mean, Katie."

That wasn't happening, she told herself.

"As for your dad, I've already made the call. Unfortunately, it'll take some time to get the paperwork squared away, but all charges will be dropped, and he'll be free to go. Jim will be sleeping in his own bed tonight."

That warmed her inside, but it also raised a question.

"Speaking of free to go. Why wasn't he free to go before? I mean, he should have had his bail hearing last week, and I'm sure we could've come up with the bond. Why the delay?"

"You'll have to ask him about that."

"What do you mean?"

"I mean, you have to ask your father. He swore me to secrecy." He threw a glance back at his cruiser, at Violet in the back seat. "If you'll excuse me, I have some additional business to attend to."

Hannah crossed her arms and glowered at the police car. "I guess our original plan didn't work. First shots fired and a plan and all that."

The others nodded.

"I don't know," Katie said. "The way I look at it, we were almost done with the puzzle. A cat knocked it onto the floor. We picked up the pieces and finished it anyway, just not in the order we intended."

* * *

The next morning, Katie took yet another day off. Boss's orders. And it wouldn't go against her vacation days. In fact, "I'll fire you if I see your face," Neal had said.

"Really?"

"No, but . . . you know. Spend some time with your dad. Okay? It couldn't have been easy for him."

The day was unseasonably warm. The sun was out. An aroma of pine and earth filled the air, a never-ending reminder that she was home. She was almost tempted to have breakfast out on the back porch, but it wasn't *that* unseasonably warm. Instead she decided to simply enjoy her coffee out there.

It was close to nine. The trees behind her house rustled in the wind while the water in the sound rippled serenely behind them. A chorus of birds entertained the neighborhood, at least those who hadn't left for work yet.

Last night when they'd gotten home, Dad looked more haggard than ever. Maybe even more than after Mom's funeral, as if the experience had sucked some of his soul out of him. Like Neal, she'd left him no option about work. He had to stay home. Though, unlike Neal, she caved when Dad said, "Amy and the library need me."

"You need rest more," she'd wanted to say, but he already knew that. He didn't need a reminder.

Usually, she drank her coffee while sitting on the front porch, when she had time to drink it. It was her way of watching the world begin, as people shuffled off to wherever they were going for the day. Work. Play. Breakfast with friends. A hopeful beginning. For some reason, she liked it better on the back porch today.

Today, she was looking back. It'd been a terrible week. Easily the worse since Mom had died. She didn't know how she'd endured it. Then again, without the friendships from the crew, she probably wouldn't have. Just another reason to be glad she was back in Cedar Bay.

And then there was Connor.

Still standing, facing the lush tree line, she smiled, thinking she could stand there all day. Except . . .

Scratch, scratch, scratch.

She turned to find Whimsy at the door. Pawing at the glass, pretending that he wanted to come out and join her. But it was a ploy.

"I already fed you."

Scratch, scratch, scratch.

"You're not fooling me."

Scratch, scratch, scratch.

She reached out and pushed open the door.

"Come on. It's nice out here."

But the cat ran back inside, ever so hopeful that she'd follow him to his food bowl.

Which she did. And then realized there was somewhere she needed to be.

* * *

Minutes later, she found herself at the library, showered in fluorescent light in Dad's office.

"Hey," Dad called out, jumping up from behind his desk. "What are you doing here so early?"

"I decided this was where I needed to be."

"Doesn't Neal need you at work?"

"Snow day."

He chuckled.

"How's Booker treating you?"

"Same as Whimsy last night. He's giving me the cold paw."

"Can't be as bad as Whimsy when I came back from Colorado." She took the seat in front of his desk. "How are you?"

Dad lifted his head, like he was considering the question deeply. "To be honest, I'm three things. Relieved. Glad. Proud."

"Proud?"

"Of you."

That choked her up. It took her a minute to regain her composure.

"You had me pretty scared," she said, her voice cracking.

"I had me pretty scared, too." He bit down on a protein bar.

"It's all over now. That's the most important part." She leaned back in her chair and crossed her arms. "Except for one thing. When I asked Lieutenant Crozier why you weren't given a bail hearing, he said I should ask you."

Dad hurriedly picked up his coffee mug, pointed to it, and pretended he couldn't talk.

"Oh, that's mature."

He shrugged.

"Come on. Out with it."

He set the mug on the desk. "You promise you won't get mad?"

"I promise."

"You sure?"

"I'm sure."

"I don't believe you."

"Oh, come on."

"Okay." He swallowed before he said, "I asked them to delay the bail hearing."

"You what?" she cried.

"You promised."

"That was before . . . that was . . . you what?"

Booker jumped up on the desk. Even he was incredulous. Or he just wanted pats.

Dad shrugged. "I was embarrassed."

"By what?"

"This whole thing with Elena. So many people thought something was going on, I thought you might be one of them. Heck, I was starting to believe it. I guess . . . I just couldn't face you, kid."

She tapped her lips.

"What?" he said.

"It was your idea?"

"Yep."

"You stayed in jail rather than face me?"

"Yep."

"You stayed locked up with murderers and rapists rather than let your only daughter comfort you?"

"Yep. Well, more like with two drunks and one guy who hadn't paid his parking tickets."

She nodded. "That's just swell, Dad. There's just one problem."

"What's that?"

"I don't believe you."

He feigned indignation. "*Moi?*"

"Stop it. Tell me why you really refused your bail hearing."

"Okay," he said showing his palms. "It is partly true that I didn't want to face you. But . . ."

"But . . ."

He shrugged. "I knew I didn't do it. I also knew Dan had given up on finding who really did. But mostly, I knew you wouldn't stop trying to find out who did it if I was still locked up. So . . ." Another shrug. "I stayed."

"You really don't think I would've tried everything possible to find out who did it if they'd let you out?"

"Honestly? No. Not everything. I think you would've been too distracted taking care of me. Just like you did after Mom died. If you recall, I had to pretend I had a business trip in Spokane just to get you to focus on yourself for a few days."

Her eyes widened. "You lied about that?"

He scoffed. "Do you really think librarians get business trips except to ALA?"

She was about to let him really have it when she realized that he was right, because that was exactly what happened. She'd become so overwhelmed with worry that she cared for him by putting everything else in her life on hold. And she would've done it again.

"You had that much faith in me?"

"Yeah, kid. I did. And Ken and the others. Keep in mind, they started coming to the library every Sunday years ago."

"Because of Mom."

"Because of Mom. And now you."

She thought of Whimsy with the puzzle piece under his paw. And the picture of Mom on the wall. "I had a lot of help," she said. She got up, rounded the desk, and hugged him from behind. "Thank you," she said.

"And please go easy on Lieutenant Crozier. You obviously remember what I told you about your mom and Connor. Well, Dan always thought you initiated the breakup and broke Connor's heart. That's why he has been treating you harshly."

"That explains a lot. I need to have that conversation with Connor, and soon."

"Today looks like a good day." He smiled and with tears in his eyes said, "Thank you," hooking his arm around hers.

When he let go, she gently slapped him on the back of the head. "But never do that again."

* * *

After getting takeout from JJ's with Dad at the library, their usual order, of course, Katie knew there was one more thing she needed to do to get this whole episode behind her. One more person she had to face before she could move forward. She was going to take her dad's advice.

"Do you have a fire to report, ma'am?" Connor asked, leaning against the front of the firehouse with his arms crossed. "Or is Whimsy stuck in a tree?"

"Whimsy would have to see a tree before he could get stuck in one."

They stayed silent for a few beats, until she said, "Were you expecting me?"

"Nope. It's just a lovely day and I thought I'd enjoy the fresh air."

"And Amy told you I'd just left the library," she said.

"And Amy told me you'd just left the library."

"What made you so sure I'd come here?"

He narrowed his eyes and flattened his tone. "I've known you for years, Kate. I can still read your mind." He gestured down Main Street. "How about we walk and talk?"

"Did you read that in my mind, too?"

He shook his head. "I just want the exercise."

They walked several blocks in the sunshine without saying a word, past the Palace, past the police station, even past the Cedar Bay Public Library and Vienna Street, where Elena had been murdered. They both waved to the four cars that passed them and each driver waved in return. The smell of salt water let her know they were close to the Cedar Bay Marina when Connor finally broke the silence.

"You did good last night."

"I got lucky."

"That's for sure. I'd say it was a fifty-fifty chance that Violet would've shot you if my dad hadn't intervened."

"More like ninety-ten."

They stopped just outside the marina entrance. She let her gaze roam over the small armada of sailboats inching their way across the bay.

"You really think so?" he said.

She nodded. "Violet was losing control. Her voice was shaky. Maybe I'm wrong. Hopefully I'm wrong. But I was pretty sure I was a goner." She smiled. "But thanks to you, I wasn't."

"Aw shucks, ma'am," he said, looking down and kicking at the gravel. "Just doin' my job."

She briefly looked behind her. "Speaking of your job. Shouldn't you be working?"

"I'll hear the siren if it goes off."

"What if it's someone falsely pulling the fire alarm again?"

"No one would be that stupid," he said with a grin.

They rounded the marina, toward the water until they reached the docks, where the sunlight sparkled off the ripples of the sound.

"We haven't snuck down here in a long time," she said.

"It's not sneaking in the daylight. And when you know the owner." He grinned. "Being a fireman has its privileges."

She looked out across the sound and like a damn burst in her head, a flood of memories overwhelmed her. She held out her hand but snatched it back before he noticed. It'd been pure instinct. A mental muscle memory formed years ago.

A seagull screeched overhead, swooping down to the water, collecting its takeout.

She glanced over at Connor, whose attention was laser-locked onto the bird. Together, they'd seen hundreds of seagulls do that. Or maybe it was the same seagull who'd done it hundreds of times. Either way, she didn't need ESP to know his mind was tracking very close to hers. Asking himself, where'd they been, where they were. And where they were going.

"We need to talk—"

"We need to talk—"

They giggled like they were kids.

"You first," she said.

"Ladies before gentlemen," he said.

"Age before beauty."

"Oh, come on. By two months."

"And four days."

He didn't say anything. If anything his face was full of compassion.

"Dad told me about Mom," she said.

He looked toward the seagull again. "That was one of the worst days of my life, when I broke up with you. I didn't want to do it."

"It was the worst day of my life."

They reached for each other's hands and smiled.

"I'm still not over my mom. I need to forgive her for breaking us up, and I won't be over all this . . ." She waved back at downtown. "For a long time. I'm still not over being back, which hasn't been easy. Besides, I've got my job. I've got the crew."

"You've got everything but . . ."

"Everything but . . . me. I need to fix me."

He drew her in for a hug and she buried her head into the crook of his shoulder.

He said, "I can wait."

When she pulled away, she thanked him, leaving her to wonder if she'd just solved one tricky puzzle only to start another.

Acknowledgments

The journey a novel takes is rarely straight and never predictable. *Picking Up the Pieces* was no exception. But like putting together a challenging jigsaw puzzle, snapping those final pieces into place was what made the entire process so worthwhile.

To our editor, Tara Gavin, whose enthusiasm and support for the novel helped us to turn it into a reality. To the rest of the Crooked Lane team, including publisher Matt Martz, marketing and publicity gurus Dulce Botello and Mikaela Bendery, production and editorial phenom Thaisheemarie Fantauzzi Pérez, sub-rights specialists Stephanie Manova and Megan Matti, art and design star Rebecca Nelson, illustrator extraordinaire Katie Thomas, and operations expert Doug White. Thank you all.

* * *

To Terry. You are my world.

To Greg and Samantha. Thank you for making me a proud dad every day.

Acknowledgments

To my agent, John Talbot. Since I was a kid, it has been a dream of mine to be a published writer. Thanks to your support, guidance and friendship, I'm now living the dream. Thanks for being on the journey with me.

To International Thriller Writers. Thank you for the education and lifelong friendships.

—Jeff

* * *

First and foremost, I'd like to thank my wonderful wife, Joy, for all her love, patience and encouragement throughout my writing journey.

To Kelly and Robbie. The strength and courage you display every day inspires me.

To my agent, Terrie Wolf (from AKA Literary Management). Thank you for believing in me and in the story—and for your dogged persistence in finding Picking Up the Pieces a wonderful home. Yay, wolfpack!

To everyone at the DFW Writers' Workshop, especially Leslie Lutz, Brooke Fossey, John Bartell, A. Lee Martinez, Melissa Lenhardt, Katie Bernet, Helen Dent, J.B. Sanders, Lauren Danhoff, Colin Holmes, and many, many others. You've all made me a better writer.

Special thanks to Steve Berry, Karen Dionne, David Morrell, and JT Ellison for showing me the way.

And lastly, to Linus, our late, great tabby cat—the cat with the puzzle piece beneath his paw that solved the mystery!

—Brian